TAMING

Sea Island Wolves 2

Jenny Penn

Ménage Amour Romance

Siren Publishing, Inc.
www.SirenPublishing.com

A SIREN PUBLISHING BOOK
IMPRINT: Ménage Amour Romance

TAMING SAMANTHA
Copyright © 2008 by Jenny Penn

ISBN-10: 1-60601-197-9
ISBN-13: 978-1-60601-197-3

First Publication: December 2008
Cover design by Jenny Penn
All cover art and logo copyright © 2008 by Siren Publishing, Inc.

Printed in the U.S.A.

PUBLISHER
Siren Publishing, Inc.
www.SirenPublishing.com

TAMING SAMANTHA
Sea Island Wolves 2

JENNY PENN
Copyright © 2008

Chapter 1

Saturday

Sheriff JD McBane paused outside the large paint booth. A scrawny kid was inside giving a hot rod a custom paint job. Through the viewing glass, JD watched the boy work with fast, quick strokes of the paint gun.

The paint suit was one size too big, and the facemask enveloped his whole head, but there was a human under all the gear, the first JD had seen in the hundred-plus-acre race park.

Not that he had searched the entire park, just the main area around the entrance. His plan to put off coming up to the park until the weekend had backfired. The idea had been to introduce himself to the staff and have a word or two with the manager on a day they were sure to be around.

He'd searched the large hotel, the small rental cabins, through all six garages, and the several other log cabins serving as offices and staff housing. Besides an amazing collection of motorcycles, go-carts, cars, emergency equipment, and assorted mechanic's tools, he had not seen a single person.

Not until he found the kid painting the hot rod. When he banged on the glass to get the boy's attention, his head popped up. He hesitated before giving JD a little wave and turning back toward his work.

JD felt his muscles tense at the brat's dismissal. He was the sheriff and alpha. Everybody showed him respect. Those who didn't quickly learned the error of their ways, just like this kid was about to.

JD banged harder on the Plexiglas. Pointing to the door, he mouthed "now." The boy hesitated before putting down the paint gun and stomping to the door in obvious annoyance. That was fine with JD. He was just as irritated by the kid's attitude.

"Whada' you want?" The words were muffled by the face mask, but there was no hiding the demand in his tone. "I got work to do."

"I want to talk to you for a moment." JD's expression darkened. He was used to dealing with snotty adolescents. They were easy enough to intimidate.

"About?" The kid's hand went to his hips, obnoxiously mimicking JD's stance.

"I can't understand you."

"Sounds like a personal problem."

"Take off the mask."

"Is that an order?"

"Do it!"

This snot was getting on his last nerve. JD could hear the brat muttering to himself. The mask muffled the words, which was probably for the best. He didn't want to do all the paperwork required to haul the kid down to the station just to scare some respect into the delinquent.

A second later JD forgot how annoyed he was. She had the face of an angel. Her hair was dark with rich, deep reddish streaks mixed through. It contrasted with the pale perfection of her soft-looking skin. Her large green eyes bewitched him, the glint of anger making them more captivating.

Her lips had every muscle in his body tightening. Those full lips would drive a saint to dirty thoughts. JD was no saint, and his mind quickly produced a myriad of visions, all having those sweet pink lips wrapped around his cock, his hand buried in her silken tresses as he set the pace. His twin would be behind her, riding her to orgasm, or perhaps Caleb would have his head buried between those lush thighs and…

"Well?" The girl's sharp tone clawed through his fantasy. "What do you want?"

* * * *

Sam put the mask on the crate next to the door, intentionally ignoring the enormous deputy. Boy was he annoying, the arrogance to demand her to stop working. Who the hell did he think he was?

Sam did not respond well to authority, especially male authority, and definitely not when the man was handsome. The deputy fit all her prejudices.

The clarity of his vivid blue eyes stuck out against the rich darkness of his hair. It was a little long and fell forward, highlighting his angled features. That rugged chin looked like a master sculptor had carved him from stone.

The dark colors of his uniform were anything but slimming. His navy blue jacket emphasized the broad width of his shoulders, while his enormous thighs thinned out the crease in his matching slacks.

The thick black gun belt slouched slightly, defining the narrowness of his hips and assuring a woman that it was hard muscle filling out the rest of his clothes and not flab. The solid perfection of his physique would have made a quarterback jealous.

"So what do you want?" she repeated while ripping at the zipper of the paint suit.

The interest she felt stirring in her body drove her agitation up a notch. Her wayward hormones annoyed her as much as the oversized deputy in front of her. It didn't matter what her body thought of him.

Sam had to remember that things were different now.

With her pleasantly plump body and dirt brown hair, few men looked at her long enough to realize she had pretty eyes. Bruce had looked, and she had been naïve enough to think that he wanted her and not her money. Well, she would not make that mistake again.

Sam scowled with the direction of her thoughts and turned her attention back to the deputy. He was staring strangely at her. What the hell was wrong with him? Were his eyes actually going gray? Too weird.

* * * *

"What do you want?"

"I…uh…" For a moment JD felt as if he were sixteen again. The girl stepped completely out of the paint suit. The large T-shirt she was wearing fell to mid-thigh, giving the illusion that was all she was wearing. That did not help his problem.

Distantly JD realized who the girl had to be. Never in his life had he so strongly responded to a single woman. JD felt a moment of light-headedness as he realized the day had finally come.

Finding a mate was hard, serious business, and most of his pack traveled the world just to locate theirs. As alphas, neither Caleb nor him had that luxury. It was not unheard of for alphas to pass through their reign without ever meeting their mate.

Though he had never said it, JD had been worried, borderline depressed, by the prospect of never having a family. The feeling had gotten worse when his fathers had been killed. Their family had been left decimated, quiet and too small.

That would become their past. With their mate, Caleb and he would begin to rebuild their family. It would not be a year before their home was filled with babies. Two to start, but soon many more would come. It would be no chore to get their mate pregnant.

What a little beauty she was, all curvy and rounded. She was physically perfect. Her disposition, on the other hand, needed some fine-tuning. That was all right. He would be glad to instruct her on the proper way a woman should behave.

Those instructions would begin now. The little slip of a woman in front of him was going to learn that he meant business. When he issued an order, he was not to be defied.

"I'm looking for the manager?" JD kept his tone testy lest the girl realized how happy he really was.

"Do I *look* like one?"

"You look like somebody who is asking for a spanking," JD snapped.

"A what? Is that a traditional punishment for you backward hicks?"

"Backward? Hick?" JD did not have to fake his anger this time.

"A spanking." The girl seemed oblivious to JD's rising anger. "And what great sin did I commit to earn one of those? Did I fail to bow down to the almighty authority of a deputy sheriff who *happens* to be *trespassing* on private property?"

"For being one lippy little brat."

"That wouldn't be your problem if you left. Perhaps you need to go back to cop school and freshen up on the notion of an individual's rights. I'm allowed to be as bratty as I want on private property."

Her eyes were flashing now as she whipped her hair back over her shoulder with a shake of her head. The motion was meant to be defiant, but it drew his attention to her long neck, which led his eyes to the well-developed chest and the gently rounded stomach.

God, she was soft-looking. All JD wanted to do was to put her beneath him and rub against her, feel all that silky skin against his own. Then he would devour her. He would taste and stroke every inch of her body until she had no mind left to issue sharp comments.

Her fingers snapping in front of her chest drew his attention away from his fantasies.

"Do you mind?"

Perhaps he was taking the wrong track with her. Direct demands were getting him nowhere. Maybe some smart-ass comments would penetrate her thick skull.

"You know, you're kind of cute when you're mad."

* * * *

"Excuse me?" Sam blinked.

Her mind could not devise a suitable comeback to that. Normally, she would have ripped into a man for such a condescending comment. The deputy's grin threw her off. Damn the man. He had a dimple. It was almost too irresistible to ignore.

"All flushed and sweaty." His eyes traveled down her body with an undeniable heat. "Like you just got done having a really good time. I always enjoy a good time with a sexy woman. What's your name, sweet cheeks?"

"A good…sexy…well it sure as hell isn't sweet cheeks!"

"You have anger management issues, don't you?" The deputy's eyes strayed back to her breasts.

"And you must need glasses because my face is up here, buddy."

Sam crossed her arms over her chest. She told herself her nipples were puckering from the cold winter day. It had nothing to do with the heat in his gaze.

"I thought that was the idea of you standing there wearing next to nothing. You can't flaunt your body and then get mad at a guy for admiring it."

"Can I blame him for having the manners of a pig?"

Sam knew that her comebacks lacked in wit or bite. It was hard to think when her body was already responding to the look in his eyes. That embarrassing fact fueled her anger.

"What's got your panties in a twist? Perhaps you enjoy the attention?"

"Screw this. I'm going back to my painting."

It was a perfect exit line. She matched her action to her words and slammed the booth's door behind her. It took her all of a second to remember that she was not dressed to paint. It took another second for her to gag on the fumes in the booth.

"Damn it!" she bellowed and threw the door open.

The arrogant jerk was still there. The bastard had two dimples. He had been hiding the other one. Sam snarled and tried to storm past him, muttering to herself about overgrown jerks. Her mistake was walking too close to him.

* * * *

JD grabbed her by the arm, bringing her to a dead stop. The minute he touched her, JD knew he was not going to let go. Her sweet scent was mixed with the strong odor of the paint fumes. Still the hint of her natural smell teased him, driving the blood from his brain to his cock.

He wanted to drown himself in that scent. First, he was going to have to strip his mate to get rid of the stronger odor of paint. Hell, he may even have to bathe her. JD grinned at that idea. Images flooded his brain of what he could do with her naked and wet in his arms. His cock thumped, straining against his slacks in agreement with his thoughts.

"I asked you a question." JD used his stern cop voice, though there was no heat behind the tone. As fun as teasing the girl was, it was time to use the ground gained to get some answers.

"No, I'm not the manager."

"What's your name?" JD sighed. He felt as if he were going in a circle.

"What's it to you?"

"Just answer the damn question!"

"Or what? You really going to spank me?"

"Don't tempt me."

"Wow!" Her eyes widened in feigned fear. "You got me quivering in my boots, big boy."

"Your name."

"Tell me yours!"

"Can't you read?" JD pointed to the nametag sewn on to his uniform.

"Lawsuits require a first name too," she informed him curtly. "Everybody knows that."

"What lawsuit?"

"The one I'm going to file against you for harassment."

"Harassment?"

"I'm going to add trespassing too. And if you don't let go, I'll throw in police brutality as well."

"I haven't begun to brutalize you."

"You're hurting me right now." Her whisper was just as soft. "Just look at your hand, at the size of that paw. It is as overgrown as the rest of you. Now look at me. Do you think a jury will have a hard time at seeing me as a weak, innocent girl who was intimidated and abused by an overgrown jackass, drunk on the power of his position?"

Her eyes grew wide as a look of fear filled them. In a little girl voice constricted by fear and pain, she began to recite what she would say.

"I was all alone, working in the paint booth, when a large man surprised me. He was a cop, so I felt like I had to obey his commands. I did everything he asked…"

"Like hell," JD muttered, torn between annoyance and amazement. He was transfixed by the change that came over her as she continued to tell her story.

"He started to yell at me and go into a rage." Her voice was wavering now as her lips began to quiver.

"A rage?" JD watched in astonishment as a single tear slid down her cheek. Her other hand came up to pathetically wipe it away.

"He started making lewd comments while he stared at my breasts.

I was so scared." Her voice broke into a sob, and she buried her face pathetically into her free hand.

"Then he grabbed me, and I wasn't sure what he intended to do. He's so big, and I was completely defenseless." She blubbered.

"That's it! That's enough!" JD bellowed over the racket she was making. Jesus. The girl probably could convince a jury. If he had not been privileged to see her true attitude, he would have believed her.

"Don't mess with me, muscle head." Her head snapped back. Her cheeks were wet, but her smile was pure devil. "I'll have that jury eating out of the palm of my hand."

The mischievous chuckle sealed her fate. His mate was a brat. Obviously, she had been getting away with murder. With that body and those acting talents, it was little wonder why. That was about to change.

The last thing JD was going to allow was for his mate to run roughshod over him. No way was he going to tolerate that. She would be obedient, sweet, and accommodating at all times. If she did not know the meaning of those words, he would teach them to her.

Chapter 2

"What the hell are you doing?" Sam struggled to get away. It was futile. In seconds, he had her arms twisted behind her. The cold link of the handcuffs answered her question.

"I'm placing you under arrest," the deputy stated calmly as he began to drag her back to his patrol car.

"Y-you c-can't do…that," Sam sputtered. As dirt turned to asphalt beneath her feet, so did shock morph into rage. "I haven't done anything!"

"You are impeding a police investigation."

"What investigation? Goddamn it! Let me go!" She pulled hard, using all her weight to try to break free. Even with only one hand latched on to the cuffs, she didn't break the deputy's stride.

"Who would I be letting go?"

"Samantha. All right? I'm Samantha!"

"Samantha…"

"Jeanne."

Sam was angry enough with his high-handed tactics to lie. She was not going to tell him the truth. Let him discover whom he had pissed off when her lawyers walked into his office and slapped him in the face with a lawsuit.

"Now let me go!"

"Can't do that."

"Why the hell not? This is crap! When my lawyer is done with you, I'll have not only your badge but every other sorry thing you own!"

"I'm quaking in my boots." He brought her to a stop by his patrol car.

"Arg," Sam growled.

Before she could consider the stupidity of her actions, she kicked him as hard as she could in the shin. It was supposed to help vent her anger. It didn't work. Her canvas sneakers provided little protection for her toes when they collided with his hard flesh.

"Damn!" Sam hollered, jumping on her good foot. "What the hell are you made of? Titanium?"

"That would be assaulting an officer," the deputy informed her happily, all but laughing at her. With a shake of his head over her imprudent actions, he shoved her against the side of the car.

"What the hell are you doing now?" Sam demanded, alarmed as he used his massive thigh to spread her legs.

"I've got to frisk you. I wouldn't want you to hurt yourself on the ride to the station."

"Don't you touch me!"

Sam thrashed against the hood, trying to break free of his hold. Her struggles got her nowhere. All it did was make her look weaker. She panted as she tried to figure a way out of this humiliating situation.

Nothing came to mind. At least the crew was out working on the track for the dirt bikes. So there was nobody to see her in this embarrassing situation. Of course, if her brother Mike had been around, things probably wouldn't have gotten this out of hand.

Even knowing what he was about to do, she still flinched when his large warm palms smoothed up her confined arms. Sam sucked in a deep breath and immediately felt light-headed. There was a scent in the air now.

A strong, musky, masculine odor hit her senses like a shot of aged bourbon. Hot, burning, potent lust roared through her. It made her muscles tremble and go pliant beneath his hands.

She wanted more. She needed to feel him touching her, skin to skin. She ached for the feel of his mouth on her body, tasting her, pleasing her, pleasuring her. Oh God, she needed more than that. She needed him buried deep inside, driving her toward oblivion.

Sam did not have the mind left to know where these thoughts were coming from. All she knew is, with every breath, the desire eating through her became unbearable.

* * * *

The soft sound of his mate's moan was almost drowned out by the thump of her head hitting the hood. She went limp beneath him, and JD smiled. The mating musk was working on the little spitfire. The musk was used to seduce and stimulate mates. It was a Covenanter specialty.

While the musk did not work on him, the smell of her desire was just as potent. It drove the need already filling his balls. The sweet scent made his cock swell and strain against his slacks. All JD wanted to do was strip her naked and fuck her right against the patrol car.

He was going to do just that, but first he was going to hear his sharp-tongued mate beg for it. Only when she swore to the heavens above that she was his and would never again deny him anything would he give her what she needed.

With that goal in mind, he kept his touch light and gentle as he explored her body.

* * * *

Sam groaned and bit back a plea for him to press harder. His hands traced over her curves with teasing caresses that had her grinding her teeth in frustration. The incessant aching of her pussy fed a need so carnal Sam was sure she was going to expire if it were not soon satiated.

When his hands brushed against the sides of her breasts, they swelled. Her nipples hardened in preparation for more. His thumbs flicked over the straining nubs. The quick caress sent a lightning bolt of pure heat straight from her breasts to her cunt, making her internal muscles quiver with tiny explosions.

It felt so good. She wanted more, much more. Arching her back, she thrust her breasts deeper into his hands. He ignored her silent demand. His hands slid down her sides and away from her chest. Sam's growled complaint ended in a groan as his hands settled on her hips. He was just inches from where she wanted his touch the most.

Those strong fingers tightened as if he were sizing her up. Just as quickly, they released her and slid down the outsides of her legs. The feel of the warm, callus-roughened hands on her legs made the hairs on her neck stand up.

Goose bumps followed in their wake as they traveled back up the inside of her legs, over her shorts, stopping just short of her crotch. Sam's breath caught as one hand moved to cup her mound.

She jerked, her hips jutting backward and bumping into the hard evidence of his arousal. Unable to control her body's reaction, she rubbed her backside against him. Silently she tempted him to take more liberties. She heard the deputy chuckle, his hands moving to her hips to control her motions.

"Do you like that?" he asked huskily as she ground her back into him.

Sam was incapable of answering. The hard, thick feel of his cock pressing into her ass sent flickers of heat to her clit. Between the swollen folds of her sex, her sensitive nub came alive with the need to rub against his hard shaft.

She wanted him to turn her around, spread her legs, and press his magnificent erection into her weeping core. The need to be filled, to have him drive ruthlessly into her came over her, and she whimpered.

"Please."

Sam was beyond caring that she was now begging the arrogant deputy who, just a moment ago, she had kicked. How things had changed so rapidly was a mystery her lust-fogged mind could not recognize. With every breath, the musk filled her body. It drove the desire and need for him higher until Sam was sure she would expire if he did not fuck her soon.

"Please what, Samantha?" he asked as one hand slid up under her shirt. The soft cotton bunched over his arms until he was gently cupping one breast.

"Oh God." Sam moaned from the painful lash of tension that tightened her nipples to hard little points. "Please."

"Tell me what you want, Samantha." His smooth, deep voice warmed her blood, making her twist beneath him to press her swollen flesh more firmly into his palm.

"Tell me."

"Touch me." Sam was helpless to deny the harsh demand racking her body. "Please, touch me."

"Touch you? Where?" His thumb slid under her bra, and he raked a callused finger over her nipple. "Here?"

The sound of delight that escaped her lips was all the confirmation he appeared to need. His thumb began to roll her nipple. Her clit twisted with the echo of the sharp sensation. Desire burned deep inside her other breast, making it ache with the need to be touched in the same manner.

"Please, more." Sam sobbed. "Both breasts, please."

"I've got a better idea."

He pinched her nipple hard. The sudden assault made her cry out and distracted her from the hand sliding under the waistband of her shorts. Sam's shriek turned to a gasp when her clit was suddenly trapped between two fingers. He rolled the sensitive nub in rhythm with his thumb as it swirled over her nipple.

Pleasure shot violently from her clit, to her nipple, and back again. The onslaught of ecstatic pleasure made her hips buck and her thighs widen in bold invitation for a deeper, more intimate caress. He took her offer.

His hand abandoned her breast to join its mate buried in her panties. With one hand, he tormented her clit while the other slid toward her wet, hungry pussy. Sam moaned as he began to tease her swollen flesh.

It was good, so good. It was not enough. He was playing with her, teasing her and driving up her need. He kept her on the edge of insanity without a single second of mercy.

Sam tried to force the matter. She rose to her tiptoes and arched her hips frantically toward his touch. She tried to impale herself on his finger, but it was pointless. He moved with her, denying her.

She was so empty that she hurt. The desperate need to be filled by him was a painful ache. All she needed was one thick finger. It would be enough, more than enough. Seconds stretched into eternity as she fought him, straining her hips and trying to capture his meandering finger.

It was a useless fight, and Sam growled with her growing anguish. Her growl turned into a groan as he finally slid into her. The walls of her passage tried to clamp down on his finger and pull it deeper.

Finally, the deputy heeded the calls of her body. His thumb began to rub her clit harder, faster as he thrust his finger deep into her body. Electric shocks of pleasure shot from her pussy, up her spine, and out of her body. Sam panted as her hips bucked in time with his penetrating strokes.

The coil of tension holding her on the edge began to snap as small tremors of ecstasy rippled through her body. Just when she was sure that her orgasm was going to explode over her and give her the release she desperately needed, he stopped.

* * * *

JD ground his teeth as his mate whimpered and writhed beneath him. Her body's silent demands for completion tempted his control. His cock was rock hard and ready to give in.

The wolf within him seconded the demand. The beast wanted to feel his mate's tight, wet sheath wrapped around him as he pumped them into oblivion. JD leashed the beast with the promise that soon its desires would be fulfilled.

First, though, his mate had to be punished for her earlier attitude. The musk had helped him bring her under control, but only when she willingly accepted her punishment and his dominance would he know that he had her complete submission.

Leaning back from her, he ignored her cries as he made quick work of removing her shorts and panties. He tossed her garments onto the hood and admired the sight of her bent over and open for his possession. She had a beautiful, lush, pale ass that ended in dark curls giving him a teasing glimpse of the pink, wet folds of her pussy.

The hair would have to go. As much as JD loved the sweet taste of a woman's cunt, Caleb was more addicted to eating pussy. His twin liked to devour his cunts bare. Later tonight, Caleb would shave her.

It wouldn't matter if Samantha agreed. It would be done. Samantha was theirs. They would pleasure, protect, and love her, and for their devotion, the brothers would demand complete compliance to their desires.

It was apparent Samantha needed training in the concept of complete compliance. That thought did not trouble JD. Just the opposite, he anticipated the pleasures they would all take in those lessons just as he intended to take his pleasure in this one.

* * * *

Sam held her breath, waiting for the return of his fingers, anticipating that she might get his cock instead. Oh God, how she wanted that. Her pussy wept for the feel of his thick dick pounding into her.

When she felt the glide of his fingers over the curves of her bottom and into the folds of her pussy, she shivered and widened her stance to allow him better access. His fingers dipped into her clenching opening to twist and swirl. They hit that magic spot, and she jumped, groaning with pleasure. Instantly his hand withdrew, denying her again.

"Please."

"Please, what? What do you want, Samantha?"

"Don't stop. Please, I need more."

"More? More what?" He teased her slit again, letting his fingers brush against her clit. "More of my fingers or do you want something else? My tongue? My cock?"

"Yes. Oh God, yes."

"Yes to what?"

"All! I want it all. Please."

"You want to come, don't you, Samantha?"

"Yes."

"Say it."

"I want to come." Sam was beyond caring that she was not just begging him, but obeying his commands. Her body was a twisted mass of painful needs that only he had the cure for. She would do whatever he wanted, say whatever he wanted, if only he would give her release.

"You want me to let you come."

"Yes. Please let me come. I need it."

"I might." He teased her with another gentle stroke against her clit. "You weren't very nice earlier, though."

"I know. I'm sorry."

"You want my forgiveness. What if it doesn't come so easily? Will you do whatever I ask?"

"Whatever you ask, whatever you want, just please let me come!"

"Fine, but first your punishment."

Punishment? The word echoed through the daze in Sam's mind. A small voice warned her that something was not right. She was not being herself. She sucked in a deep breath in an attempt to clear her head. The fog of lust thickened with the spicy musk that flooded her senses and overrode any warning.

His hands felt rough and hot against the smooth flesh of her ass as he caressed her generous globes. Sam had just begun to relax when a sharp smack made her cry out in shock. The unexpected pain radiated outward, turning into sparkles of pleasure that had her pussy tingling.

He did not pause as he struck her repeatedly. Each blow felt stronger than the last. Each sent a powerful shower of pleasure through her until she could feel her juices spilling down her thighs. Sam would have been shocked at how excited she was if wasn't for the overwhelming rapture beginning to peak in her.

He punished her right to the edge of orgasm. Every smack landed on a new stretch of skin until her whole ass felt on fire and her pussy ached with the savage need for release. When he finally stopped, she cried out begging for more. She was so close now. One or two more smacks would send her over the edge.

"No." The deputy's breath sounded labored. "You'll come when I let you. Understand, Sam?"

"Please, I need to come."

"In a moment, sweetheart." He soothed her, gently rubbing his hands over her burning ass cheeks and sliding them down toward her dripping core.

"Widen your legs." He pushed against her thighs. "I want to see your pretty little pussy."

Sam groaned. His words turned her on. The erotic idea of him seeing her, naked and vulnerable before him, fed the forbidden thrill his spanking had ignited. She was in the grips of a passion so beyond anything she had ever experienced. It left her incapable of denying him.

His heated breath tickled her sensitive folds and sent shivers of anticipation through her. Without instruction, her back arched, her hips flex in an unspoken invitation that offered her pussy up for his tasting.

A single finger parted her folds. His velvety tongue instantly followed it. He licked his way straight up her slit to her clit, adding heat to the inferno of desire decimating her insides.

She lifted her pussy to his talented tongue as he began to work over her clit. His amazing tongue swirled over her tender nub. He toyed with it in the same manner his fingers had done earlier. *Oh, dear God.* She was coming apart at the seams as every cell in her body detonated with ecstatic explosions.

Distantly she heard herself demanding, "Yes, just like that. Oh God. More, please more!"

The waves of her orgasm had barely begun to recede when a second set rose to take their place. The deputy did not stop his ministrations. He forced more pleasure on her already ravaged body and stretched her climax out. Each release was stronger and more powerful than the last one.

A scream ripped from her throat as he thrust two thick fingers into her tightening sheath. He stretched her muscles wide and caused lightning bolts to rip from her head, to her fingers, to her toes and singe every nerve ending in between.

Still he fucked his fingers into her as she bucked against his hand and mouth. Her need could no longer be satisfied with his mouth or fingers. She needed to be truly filled. Her body demanded the hard thickness of his cock penetrating her.

"Please." She arched away from him. "I need more."

Chapter 3

JD groaned, unable to deny her request. The alluring scent of her desire mixed with the sweet taste of her cream fired the needs of the beast inside him. The wolf was no longer willing to wait.

He ripped at his pants, not bothering to lower them before he pulled his cock free. His hands went to her hips, and he tilted them upward so he could line up his cock with her wet opening. Without waiting another second, he rammed his full length all the way into her dripping cunt.

He heard her cry and felt her inner muscles tighten around him in welcome. It was sweet heaven to finally be buried balls deep inside his mate. Her moans of pleasure fed his desire.

Not giving her a moment to adjust, he began to pound into her with all the savage need boiling in his blood. He gripped her hips and held her still for his fucking as he picked up speed and strength.

* * * *

Everything that he had done to her before magnified the tension clamping down on her muscles, warning her that this time her climax just might kill her. He was fucking her with incredibly hard, pounding thrusts. Each stroke drove his thickened cock deeper than any had ever gone.

She struggled to keep from screaming, but could not take any more. He was driving her further than she had ever been. The tide burst, and wave after wave drowned her in a sea of ecstasy.

He continued to slam into her, and she could here him grunting "mine" with every thrust. A moment later, he bent over her, and she felt a sharp pain as he bit into her shoulder. The small discomfort was quickly lost as his body jerked against hers and his hot seed flooded her body.

Sam collapsed onto the hood of the patrol car, unable to move or see beyond the black dots swirling in her vision. A strange form of elation warmed her body, and, for some weird reason, she felt safe, loved, cherished.

* * * *

JD had never felt so good and pained all at once. He had just experienced the most devastating climax of his life. Still, he wanted, needed more. Not here, out in the open where anybody could ruin the moment, JD didn't want anything to interrupt him once he got started on her again.

He needed to get her back to their home. There he could spend the night drowning in ecstasy. With that single objective, he pulled out of her. It took him less than a second to right his slacks.

There was no need for her to re-dress. He liked having her almost naked. The only thing that could be better was having her completely naked. Soon, he promised himself. It would only take fifteen minutes to get home.

He did pause long enough to remove the cuffs. It turned him on to see her restrained, but he didn't want her to be uncomfortable. There were rings on the bed and velvet ties in the wardrobe at home that would work better. No metal, not for his mate. He did not want her to hurt or chafe herself while she was writhing and bucking beneath Caleb or him.

Samantha offered him no resistance as he pushed her into the front seat. He didn't offer her the shorts or panties back. He did snatch them off the hood. Somebody might notice them and get concerned when they found her missing.

The last thing he wanted was a call from the station house telling him a woman had gone missing under suspicious circumstances. This way the station would tell anybody who called to report her missing that they had to wait twenty-four hours to fill out a report. Twenty-four hours was probably not enough time to convince her to stay.

The mating scent would keep her pliable to his desires, but it would wear off once he left her side. The solution was obvious. He'd have to keep her close, keep her hot, wet, and ready for him until he found some other way to bind her to him.

* * * *

Sam's mind began to clear as they drove. Thoughts and worries tried to assail her. Her reaction to him, her instant arousal confused her. How much his dominance had excited her, shamed her.

There was no denying what had happened. She'd never experienced a single orgasm like any of the multiple ones the deputy had given her. It was also obvious that he was not done with her. Sam might not have known where he was taking her, but she knew what he planned to do when they got there.

His arm shot out, and he grabbed her by the hair. Before she could respond, he shoved her face-first into his lap.

He's either really anxious to get a blowjob or he's hiding me. Oh God, he's not married, is he?

It was a little late to be worried about that. If he were married, his wife would have to get into line. Sam was going to be the first to kick his ass. That thought slid slowly away from her and with it the emotions it inspired.

The intoxicating scent was back, thickening in the air once again. That was not the only thing that was thickening. The deputy's cock was quickly hardening beneath his slacks. Unable to resist, she slid his zipper down.

As the rounded head appeared, she could see it was already

leaking desire. There was no constraining her compulsion to taste it. Her tongue snaked out to lick around the sensitive head. It jerked, and she had to hold him still to continue her explorations.

He was so hard and smooth, like silk-encased iron that was still warm from the fire. She could not help but rub her cheek along his length. He growled in response. A hand twisted in her hair, forcing her head up.

"Suck it, Samantha."

Darting a quick look up at him, she watched his features darken as she teasingly licked around his head again. The hand in her hair tightened painfully as his face twisted into a mask of agonized pleasure.

"Now."

Opening her lips wide, she lowered her mouth over his cock. Never letting her lips touch his inflamed flesh, she let her tongue continue to tickle him as she slid down his shaft.

"Don't tease." It was supposed to be an order, but it sounded like a plea. That was all Sam wanted, recognition of her power over his body. Latching her lips tightly around his shaft, she sucked as hard as she could.

* * * *

JD clenched his teeth and bit back a groan as he fought to keep from coming down her throat. No way was he going to let this little minx have the upper hand. God, what she did to him made his balls feel like they were on fire from the need to explode.

He screeched through a turn and took off at full speed down the road. Their house was the last on the long, winding street. Most of the higher-ranking members of the pack had big houses on Mossy Oak Lane, but the McBane brothers' was by far the biggest.

It was the party spot for small, sleepy Holly Town. Caleb instigated almost all of the events. They were loud, free-for-all, adult-only events with half-naked women running free like deer on the range.

That was about to change, and JD could not be happier about it. Not that he had objected to Caleb's more adventurous get-togethers, but he was more than ready to settle down. After all, they had built the house with the concept of a family in mind.

Their family, the one they would make with their mate. Now that he had found Samantha, that fantasy was about to become a reality. It was a welcome relief from the past years of cold and silence that had filled their small family get-togethers since his fathers had passed.

Sure, they had the pack to fill in the gaps on holidays and special occasions, but they weren't always there for Sunday dinners and Wednesday game nights. Those had been traditionally private family affairs that had fallen away without his fathers to hold them together.

They would come back now. This time it would be JD and Caleb who were the fathers. JD looked forward to them. All Samantha had to do was bear him some sons and a few daughters.

That was just why JD was not about to waste a single sperm down his mate's throat. He wanted her fat and pregnant as soon as possible. With that thought in mind, he braced himself and dragged her off his cock. It was the hardest thing he had ever done. JD hit the button to send the garage door up before he rammed his patrol car through the damn thing.

Thirty seconds later he was dragging her across the seat and then hustling her through the kitchen door. There was no making it to the bedroom. Her oral explorations had made an angry dictator of his cock, and he needed to be inside her now.

As he propelled her into the living room, he pushed her down to the floor. He did not bother to lower his pants before he was again pushing his cock into her wet little cunt. She groaned beneath him, her arms giving out and her chest falling to the floor.

His lips curled into a grin of feral triumph at her submissive position. There was no doubt who was slave and who was master in this relationship. She was his, and that knowledge drove him past his control.

He kept hold of her hips, making sure that she did not escape him as he slid deep into her welcoming heat. God, nothing had ever felt as good as the feel of her small channel gripping his cock, making him force his sensitive flesh past constricting muscles. Every inch was pure torture and agonizing pleasure.

* * * *

Sam bit back a whimper as he began to thrust into her. His cock was much bigger, thicker than anything she had ever taken. It stretched her tender muscles wide, adding a pinch of burn to the pleasure as he glided in and out of her.

Quickly he picked up speed and power. Within minutes, he was banging savagely into her. In the distance, she heard the slam of a door, but the noise meant nothing to her. The hard cock violently pounding into her defined Sam's world. It felt so good, so thick and filling. Nothing else mattered.

Of their own volition her hips began to flex, pressing back and meeting him stroke for stroke. He growled his pleasure, reaching around with one hand to cup her mound. He trapped her clit between two roughened fingers.

The intense friction on her sensitive nub as she bucked against him sent her over the edge. Sam screamed as her body exploded with ecstasy. Her world ripped apart around her, and she collapsed beneath him.

He followed her after three more powerful strokes. His roar echoed in her ear as she felt his hot seed flood into her body. He fell forward, molding his front to her back as his ragged breath caressed her ears. She was sweaty, sticky, and tired. All she wanted now was a soft bed to take a nap in. Apparently, she was not going to get that.

Sam groaned in protest when he forced her up. The movement

made her legs, weakened with pleasure, hold her weight as she leaned back on his hard thighs. He was still buried deep inside her, his cock not softening in the slightest. She felt skewered on his thick length.

Drowsily she opened her eyes as she felt the deputy lift her shirt. He tugged it from her body and made short work of her bra, leaving her naked and on display for the stranger standing in the archway between the kitchen and living room.

They were nearly a perfect reflection of each other and it took her brain several moments to focus on the fact that his man was not the deputy. Dressed in black slacks and t-shirt, he wore the same air of authority, of danger, of heated desire as his green eyes raked over her bared body.

Instinct tried to kick in, whispering through her mind to cover herself, to feel embarrassed that one man watched when another man's cock already filled her body. Her muscles refused to respond, to strengthen and aid in saving her own decency.

Even her mind gave over the battle when the deputy's hands came around to torment her. One hand cupped her breast, immediately pulling and rolling her nipple as the other slid down between her spread legs.

The deputy forced her thighs even farther apart simply by spreading his own. The new position not only gave the stranger a perfect view of her pussy, but gave the deputy better access to her sensitive folds.

* * * *

Caleb watched as the lush beauty trapped in his brother's arms moaned, her head tilting back and her eyes closing in pleasure. The dark-haired woman was gorgeous with her full breasts and softly rounded stomach. She looked soft and inviting.

This was their mate. JD did not have to say a word for Caleb to recognize that fact. The bite mark on her shoulder said it all. He wished he could smell her so he could know the truth for himself. The combined scents of sex and JD's mating musk were too thick for him to distinguish her scent.

Soon enough, Caleb promised himself. Once JD was done pleasuring their woman, Caleb would take her up for a shower. Then he would know the sweet smell of her as well. As he watched his brother's thick, tanned fingers part the soft pink folds of her sex, he knew what else he would do once he got her into the shower.

He was going to shave that pussy bare and then devour her. His cock, already hard from the erotic sight before him, nearly doubled in size with that thought. It was all he could do not to go and rip their mate out of his brother's arms and take her just as JD had, on all fours on the floor.

The brothers had shared many women in their time. Caleb had always enjoyed watching his brother pleasure them. This time was different. Despite the erotic thrill of watching the lovers before him, he felt a sharp pang of jealousy that it was JD and not him pleasuring their mate.

He couldn't take any more. Caleb strode forward and lifted her off JD's lap. Like a pirate making off with stolen bounty, he slung her over his shoulder and rushed up the stairs. He carried her straight into the master suite that JD had built and stocked for this day.

It had never been used. This was her room, and they wouldn't have disrespected her by carrying on with irrelevant liaisons here. Caleb took her directly into the large bathroom and set her down in the oversized shower stall.

Blinking her glassy green eyes rapidly, she tried to focus on him. He smiled down at her, wondering if she knew he was not his brother. Identical in appearance, the only way to tell JD and him apart was the fact that JD had blue eyes and he had green.

"What's your name?"

"Sam…Samantha."

The breathy, hesitant sound of her voice was like a stroke to his cock. Nothing turned him on like a shy and submissive woman. The Fates had blessed him with a mate who was both.

"Relax, Samantha." Caleb leaned down to feather kisses over her cheeks. "I'm going to make you feel very good."

* * * *

Sam jolted when the cold water suddenly hit her skin. Her brain was jump-started by the refreshing water and the sudden absence of any man.

What the hell was she doing?

She was in a strange shower, having just fucked a strange man and apparently about to be fucked by his brother. That was so not her. This was not the way she behaved. She needed to get out of here.

She turned and slammed straight into a hard wall of naked man. The brother had returned and with him that intoxicating odor. This time the scent was even stronger, more potent as it congealed in the now-steaming shower stall.

The water was hot now, but not nearly as searing as the hands that began running up and down her body. He shifted, and for a moment his hands left her. Sam heard herself whimper, protesting the loss of his touch.

A moment later his callused hands were back, slippery with soap. She felt cherished, almost treasured as he gently washed away the evidence of her early passionate encounters with his brother.

As much as she enjoyed his gentle cleansing, her body began to heat with the desire for a more intimate touch. She could not stop from squirming in his arms, enjoying the friction of his hard, hairy body against her softer, smoother one.

"Be still."

Despite his tender touch and earlier assurances, there was no denying the hard demand in that statement. Sam ignored him as she continued to rub back into him. Already hard, his cock was growing even bigger against her bottom. She wiggled her hips enticingly against his length.

"I said be still." This time the order was followed by a sharp slap to her pussy. Her clit took most of the impact, and shock waves sent shivers racing through her.

"Again."

"Be still, or I'll take you to the edge of orgasm and leave you there," he growled in her ear.

Sam whimpered in protest, but fell still, believing he would do just as he said. It was difficult, though, as he finished bathing her and leisurely washed her hair. All she wanted to do was turn around and pin him to the wall.

Then she would take her pleasure despite his threat. The problem with that plan was he was bigger, stronger, and her muscles were already limp from pleasure overload.

"Yes." She sighed her encouragement when finally his hands slid around to cup her breasts.

"Do you like that?" he asked as he began to roll and pinch her nipples.

"Mm-hmm." Sam moaned. "More."

"You're a demanding little thing." He chuckled as he moved around to her front.

"Please," Sam begged. Her hands came up to cover his and make his fingers tighten and work her breasts with a harder grip.

"I shouldn't let you get away with that," he growled as his hands turned and caught hers. Sam struggled futilely as he forced her arms behind her back. He used his hold to bend her backward, arching her back and offering her breast up to his mouth.

The fight went out of her when his sensual lips closed over one of her nipples and began to suck. He spared nothing in his assault on her tender nubs, using his lips, his tongue, and his teeth to bring her pleasure.

He let go of her breast at the same time he let go of her hands.

Lost without him as an anchor, Sam stumbled backward. She hit the hard wall of the deputy's chest behind her and let out a breathy sigh.

The deputy would ease her aches. He was a man of action.

Chapter 4

Thick arms came around to cup her breasts. The deputy began where his brother had left off. Slowly his thumbs tormented her nipples, rubbing the already sensitized nubs back and forth.

His brother was licking and nibbling his way down her body. He followed the path left by his mouth with his fingers. They traced the curves of her softly rounded stomach and hips and stopped at the edge of her mound. He pulled slightly on her folds, revealing the swollen pink lips hidden in her dark curls.

"Such a pretty little pussy," the man growled. "I will enjoy tasting, teasing, fucking this pussy for hours."

As he spoke, he worked two thick fingers into her wet passage. Sam groaned, her head falling back on the deputy's shoulder. The inferno of lust was building inside her again, and Sam was beginning to realize it could never truly be extinguished.

Sam offered no protest when the deputy's arm slid down and hooked her leg. The deputy lifted her limb out of the way so his brother could have better access to her tender folds. His brother leaned in, accepting the offering as he licked his way up her slit. He paused only to tease her clit with a little sucking kiss before pulling back.

"More."

"You like that, do you, little one?" The man chuckled, his heated breath tickling her moist curls.

"Yes." Sam's hands tangled in his hair, and she tried to force his mouth back on her aching flesh.

"Would you like us to spend hours eating your delectable little cunt, Samantha?" The mixture of the deputy's husky voice and blunt question made Sam shiver with need.

"Please."

"We enjoy tasting the sweet cream of a woman's desire," his brother assured her with another lick. "But we like it bare and smooth."

"Will you let us shave you, Samantha?"

"Yes." Sam was beyond understanding what she was agreeing to.

"And you will keep it smooth and naked for us always?" The deputy's solemn tone made the question sound like she was taking an oath.

"Whatever you want. Please, I need more."

"You will be punished if you break this promise."

There was that word again. *Punishment.* It should have broken through her desire and snapped her back to reality. Instead, it made her shiver with erotic anticipation, her body warming with the memory of her last punishment.

His brother made quick work of shaving off the hair covering her mound. Sam barely paid him any attention. She was too distracted by what the deputy was saying. With dirty, forbidden words, he painted one erotic image after another in her head. She wanted to try them all.

She shrieked when a sudden, powerful burst of water hit her pussy and tickled her clit. Her eyes snapped open, and she looked down. The man kneeling in front of her was using the detachable showerhead to clean her, and the sensation was amazing.

* * * *

Caleb angled the showerhead so a steady pulse of water pummeled her clit. As beautiful as she was, she was gorgeous as her skin flushed with her rising excitement. She convulsed and screamed as her orgasm took control of her body.

Her back arched, thrusting her pussy forward toward him. Caleb could not resist the invitation to taste the smooth flesh he had revealed. Without giving her a chance to recover, he buried his face between her shuddering thighs and latched on to her clit.

She was so responsive, so passionate, and tasted so sweet. He wanted to drink from the climax he brought her to.

* * * *

It was too much, too intense. She just needed a moment to catch her breath. Sam tried to wiggle away from the mouth driving her insane, but found herself trapped between the two men.

She was managing to hold on, riding the edge of the wave of ecstasy trying to overtake her body, until the brothers began to work in unison. Whether planned or by accident, the deputy pulled and rolled her nipples in beat with the sucking mouth and flickering tongue tormenting her clit.

It was not until two thick fingers worked their way deep into her sheath that Sam gave over. Screaming and bucking as wave after wave of rapture crashed through her, she drowned in the bliss. Still they did not stop.

The feel of the deputy's hands stroking down her spine was almost lost to Sam amid the pleasure of his brother's mouth tormenting her. When his fingers trailed between the cheeks of her bottom, spreading them, she gave a startled yelp and jerked away. The movement shoved the fingers stroking into her deeper and earned her a quick, hard smack from the deputy.

"You've never been fucked here, have you, Samantha?"

"No." Samantha gasped as he pushed one finger deep into her virgin entrance.

For a moment, blinding pressure and pain clogged her ability to feel anything else. Then the pain blended with the pleasure radiating from her pussy. The mixture bloomed through her body, making every nerve ending fire. The sensation confused her, making her body shiver with anticipation and fear.

She sucked in a breath full of spicy, lust-inducing musk and felt all her reservations disappear. Sam relaxed. Her eyes rolled shut as she was swept away by the sensual rhythm of the mouth on her pussy and the fingers stroking into her ass. It felt good, filling, but not nearly enough.

Too soon, she was back on the precipice, needing another release to ease the tension boiling through her body. As if understanding the changes in her sounds of desire, the deputy's fingers slid out of her and were almost instantly replaced by the smooth, cool, rounded head of a foreign object.

"What—"

"Shh. Relax. You're going to enjoy this."

Before she could respond to that, he pushed the plug deep into her, making her scream at the sudden penetration. Almost instantly, the pain popped into a magnificent shower of ecstasy.

Her muscles tightened down around the toy, intensifying the sensation as she writhed on its hard, unforgiving length. Neither man gave her any space or time to recover. The deputy began to smoothly guide the toy in and out of her. Each stroke made her buck toward the mouth and fingers still tormenting her pussy.

Sam could not breathe, could barely see. One climax fed into another until her heart threatened to give out and her muscles began to cave inward. She was no longer able to hold up her body.

* * * *

Caleb caught Samantha as she began to slide downward. He could wait no longer to be buried deep inside her. He did not bother to dry her or himself off before he placed her on the king-sized bed.

She was a beautiful feast for his hungry eyes. All pink and flushed, her generous breasts bounced as she panted for breath. Her freshly revealed pink folds were swollen and wet with need.

Caleb pushed her thighs wide and settled between her curvy legs. She murmured beneath him, but he ignored her weak protests. With one hard thrust, he slammed his cock all the way into her clenched, clinging heat.

Heaven, being fully buried inside his mate's pussy was a heaven he had never experienced before. Nothing had ever felt this good. No other woman ever would. Caleb felt a warm and strange emotion mix flow over him. This was what waited for him the rest of his life. Perfection, and it always would be there. She would always be his.

Caleb hooked her knees over his shoulders, forcing her legs up and wide, and then grasped her wrist in his hands, holding them up over her head. The sight of her completely vulnerable and open to him broke his control.

Faster, harder he pistoned into her, racing the white fire of need streaking through his body. Beneath him, Samantha thrashed and cried out as her hips fought to keep up with his ever-increasing pace. He transferred her wrists to one hand and used the other to press against her clit, rubbing against the sensitive nub with the speed of this thrust.

Samantha screamed as her tight channel fisted around him and she gave over to her orgasm. Caleb could not stop. His breaths were coming out in pants as a pleasure so intense ripped through him and his hot seed spilled into his mate's body.

His cock did not soften. Nor did the desire abate. He wanted to do it again, wanted to stay captured in the bliss of Samantha's body. Being locked deep inside her felt better than anything ever had, and he did not want it to end.

* * * *

JD held his cock as he watched his brother fuck Samantha. Nothing had ever been so erotic as watching the pink flesh of her pussy lips stretch and swallow Caleb's cock. His cock jerked, leaking with the desire to watch his cock being eaten up by her wet little cunt.

When Caleb restrained her so artfully and Samantha had allowed it, JD's control had been tested. He had wanted to be the one pounding into her, making her thrash and scream as she came.

JD could tell from the way Caleb's muscles were twitching that his brother was not done yet. He was not about to get off their mate and share. JD was not about to stand around and watch until he shot his load all over himself.

He smacked Caleb in the back of the head and gave a jerk of his head. Caleb understood exactly what JD wanted, but he could see Caleb's reluctance to withdraw even for a moment. Slowly Caleb moved, turning her onto her stomach.

"Hands and knees, Samantha."

"That's it." Caleb grunted as he helped her into position. "Arch that back, and show me your pussy. Yeah, just like that."

JD moved in front of her as Caleb leaned down and gave her a rewarding kiss on her clit. Samantha shot forward with a shriek and banged her head into JD's stomach. He grunted under the impact. A second later a sharp smack echoed in the large room as Caleb punished her for moving.

"Be still!"

JD grabbed her by the hair, tilting her face up so her glazed green eyes met his. Her lips were swollen and trembling. It was an invitation JD was looking forward to accepting.

"You're a noisy little thing, you know that?" JD commented as he traced her soft lips with the tip of one finger. "I got a cure for that."

Caleb had lined himself up, and, with one powerful thrust, he impaled himself inside Samantha, making her eyes widen and her mouth gape open as she moaned. JD did not hesitate, but slid his aching cock between her cherry red lips.

Good God above. There was nothing like the feel of her lips stretched tight over his hardened flesh. Nothing but the feel of her tight sheath clamping down on him as she climaxed and milked his orgasm from his balls, JD corrected himself.

He matched his thrust with his brother's, pushing his hardened cock all the way to the back of her throat and groaning as it slid past her powerfully sucking lips. Slurping sounds mixed with the slap of flesh against flesh filled the room with an erotic music that drove JD closer to the edge.

Every muscle in his body tensed as he felt his orgasm building. He did not want to let go, to waste his seed down her throat when it would be better spent inside her body, but he could not bring himself to stop her either.

As if sensing his internal struggle, her head bobbed faster. Then, sweet mercy, she swallowed. Agonized groans were ripped from his throat as he fought the extreme sensations riding through his body.

He tugged on her hair, trying to pull free of her mouth, but she sucked hard, fighting him. JD ground his teeth together and yanked free. The air felt cold around his cock and it shrank slightly in distaste.

Sam let out an ear-piercing scream that was immediately followed by Caleb's shout of satisfaction. The pair collapsed on the bed at his knees. JD watched as Samantha's eyes closed and smiled to himself.

If she thought they were done, she was sadly mistaken. His little mate was about to pay for that stunt she just pulled.

* * * *

Sam groaned as she felt the weight of the man behind her disappear. She was exhausted and more than ready to melt into the soft mattress beneath. It was too much sex. Her body was ready to give out.

"No," she mumbled in protest when she felt herself being turned back over. "Tired."

"That's too bad, sweetheart, because we're not done with you yet."

The deputy's smooth, smug voice had her eyes opening. He was crawling up the bed between her spread thighs. One hand was wrapped around his erection. From the carnal look tightening his features, she knew what he was about to do.

Her body told her to protest, but she was transfixed by the look in his eyes. They were completely gray with need. It was a need for her that went beyond simple desire, into feral lust. Sam felt shaken to the core by that look. Nobody had ever looked at her like that.

"Tell me you want me."

"I want you." She was helpless to deny him.

That was all he needed to hear, apparently. In the next breath, he leaned down and buried himself to the hilt inside her. Sam bucked and cried out from the impact. She was still tender from his brother's possession.

At least he was giving her a moment to adjust, staying still as he wrapped his arms around her and rolled. Sam found herself looking down at him and wondered if he expected her to have enough energy to ride him.

That was not what he intended. She flinched and gasped as he reached behind her to pull on the plug. The feel of it sliding out was both a relief and stimulation. A thick rounded head pressed back into her bottom, and, for a moment, she thought it was the toy. This was not the smooth, cool feel of plastic. It was the hot, thicker feel of a flesh-and-blood dick.

Sam tipped back her head, moaning as the head popped past the restrictive ring of muscles at her entrance. Ragged claws of pleasure raked through her as her body reveled in having two large, thick cocks lodged inside her at the same time.

This was a dark fantasy of pure eroticism that she had never indulged in. To be taken by two sexy men at once, to share the intimacy of her body with total strangers, it was too much for her mind to handle, and it shut completely down.

An animalistic urge rose up and claimed control of her body. It took over as the men began to thrust and counterthrust. Their slow and unhurried movements drove her insane. Being stretched by one cock as the other was leaving her was both filling and frustrating.

Lust burned through her veins, igniting every cell in her body into motion. She began to fuck them back. Bucking into their incoming cocks, she growled out orders for them to go faster, pump harder.

They gave in to her demands, and in moments the room filled with masculine groans and feminine cries of pleasure. Hips jerked, flesh pressed and rubbed desperately against flesh until there was only savage thrusting, rapid retreating, as her two lovers claimed not only her body, but her soul as well.

Sam threw her head back and screamed as wave after wave of her climax traveled over her. It would not stop, not with both men continuing to slam into her. Every sensation was heightened as her muscles clamped down on their cocks with the power of her orgasm.

Still they kept going, fucking her until the world went black and her body caved under the pleasure, escaping into oblivion.

* * * *

"Do you think we killed her?" Caleb asked when he finally found his voice.

He had pulled out of their mate and rolled onto his side. JD was still lodged underneath the girl, holding her and trailing his fingers through her damp hair in an unusual display of tenderness.

He had been worried they'd hurt her when she had screamed loud enough to wake the dead and then immediately passed out. Their intention was to pleasure their mate, but he had been so lost in his own release he had forgotten to be concerned.

That had never happened to him before. He had never been so blinded by lust or need that he forgot his partner's pleasure. It seemed unfair to him that it should happen with his mate. Of all his partners, she deserved the most pleasure he could bestow on a woman.

"I think she just needs to rest." JD yawned.

"She is beautiful, isn't she?" Caleb could not stop himself from touching her.

"Beautiful doesn't do her justice. She's perfect."

Caleb smiled at JD's words. That was as close to poetry as JD had ever gotten. Normally when Caleb commented on a woman, JD just grunted. Because they were twins, Caleb could normally tell whether the grunt was in agreement or disagreement.

"So sweet and shy. Just the way a mate should be."

"Don't bank on it." JD snorted. "When the mating musk wears off, we'll have a she-devil on our hands."

"What are you talking about?"

Caleb's scowl deepened as JD told him about how he met Samantha and just how unwelcoming she had been. That simply would not do. From what JD was describing, her adjustment to her new life was going to be difficult.

Caleb knew his brother well. He knew JD was used to issuing a command and having it obeyed immediately. That tendency had certainly led to enough fights between the brothers and now it sounded like it had created a battle with their mate.

Caleb sighed, wishing it had been him who had found their mate. While he could be just as demanding and expected total submission in the bedroom, Caleb also understood the fine art of seducing a woman into submission.

He was sure things would go a lot easier if JD would just follow his advice, just as he knew that was not going to happen. It was pointless to even suggest it. Instead, he suggested that JD go find food as he stood and reached for their mate.

JD glared at him, his arms contracting for a moment as if he would not let Samantha go.

"Why do I have to get food? I'm not hungry."

"Not for you, for Samantha." Caleb rolled his eyes and lifted her off JD. There was a loud pop as his brother's hard cock slid free of their mate's body.

"I was comfortable."

"I can tell."

He was hard too, but they were going to have to wait until Samantha woke back up. Then, if JD was to be believed, they were going to have to keep her drugged on musk to keep her pliant and soft in their arms. Caleb wondered what they would do Monday, when they were away at work.

Chain her to the bed?

Chapter 5

Monday

Sam grimaced as the bright sun intruded on her sleep. Scrunching her eyes tight, she rolled deeper into the pillow in an attempt to block the offending light. It was no use. The fragile web of dreams had been burned away and reality flooded in.

Her mind roused itself, taking inventory of aches and pains. Her lower body was sore. Her thigh muscles burned from excessive use. That was not the only thing burning from use.

Oh God.

Sam buried her head deeper into the pillow as memories from the past two days assailed her. The images taunted and teased her. Her mind wanted to reject everything, but there was no denying all she had done and what had been done to her.

Okay, deep breath. It's all going to be all right.

A hysterical laugh escaped Sam. The second the sound rang in her ears, she clamped her lips shut. She did not know if the dyno-duo were close by. If they were, she did not want to alert them to her condition.

Lord knew that if those two realized she was awake, they would be joining her in bed to pick up where they left off. They certainly had for the past two days. Every time she had rolled, sighed, or shown the least signs of life, they had their hands and mouths all over her, their cocks buried deep inside her, driving her insane.

It had been good. Better than good, a fantasy come true with two of the sexiest men she had ever met spending hours dedicated to her pleasure. Sam rolled over slowly, cautiously, biting back a groan as a new soreness made itself aware.

Okay, so maybe it was a little too much of a good thing.

Man, did her pussy ache. Never before had it been so thoroughly used. Like a child who was willing to eat ice cream until she threw up, her cunt was willing to dismiss the pain if it had another chance to be filled by one of the sex gods.

I don't even know their names.

Sam felt her face blush at that thought. Part of her wanted to bury her head under the pillow, but there was no use hiding from it. What was done was done. There was little point in beating herself up over the matter. She needed to focus on getting herself out of the situation and back to the reality of her life.

With that in mind, Sam opened her eyes to face the new day.

Damn, this is a big bedroom.

It was the first time that Sam had bothered to look at her surroundings. The room was filled with oversized furniture. The bed itself had to be bigger than a king. It looked like a giant must live here.

Make that two giants, Sam corrected herself, remembering the large, well-muscled sex demons that had ravished her through the night. With her five-foot-five frame, Sam considered herself average height. In this room, though, she felt like a dwarf.

It was time to leave. Sam started to roll off the bed, but found herself yanked backward as her wrist caught on a metal bracelet. Scowling, she pulled back the pillow to find herself handcuffed to a metal ring built into the bedpost.

Goddamn those sons of bitches! They chained me to the fucking bed!

* * * *

JD stretched his arms behind him as he leaned back in his chair and checked the clock. Eleven fifteen. In ten more minutes, he would break for lunch. It would be a long lunch, starting early and ending late.

Hell, if he did not have an afternoon meeting with Derek Jacob, the police chief of the neighboring Wilsonville, he would expand lunch right into dinner and keep going all night long. JD grinned at the idea, wondering if his mate could keep up.

JD felt something inside him warm at the thought of Samantha. She had looked so adorable all curled up in the middle of the bed that morning. Her full lips parted as she breathed deeply, her fragile little hand clenching at a pillow.

Despite the image, her contrary attitude made itself apparent. Even in her sleep, she had muttered an obscenity when he had brushed a kiss across her cheek. He had been tempted to wake her fully for another round, but he had been running late.

Besides, Caleb and he had already worn her out an hour before when Caleb had gotten up for work. She probably needed her rest after the long night. She was certainly going to need it for the long night coming.

JD sighed. This was the way life was supposed to be. After so many years of pain and grief, things were finally going to get better. Soon, they'd have Samantha fully mated. Then she would grow fat and round with their kids. If he were lucky, she'd give them several sets of twins.

As much as JD loved Caleb, he'd always wanted more siblings. It had been too risky for their mother, though. She'd almost died giving birth to them. JD scowled as that thought slithered through his mind.

What if Samantha had the same problems? What if they lost her? That wiped away his good feeling. He never again wanted to experience the feelings of helplessness he had endured when his fathers had passed.

Against his will, JD's mind drifted back to the police photos of that horrible night. The dark images of night, blood, and bodies were forever etched into him. In all his years, he'd never seen such horrifying images.

Even if it hadn't been his own fathers, JD would have been chilled by the overwhelming rage depicted in the pictures. Part of him had thought that no human could be capable of such brutality. When they had finally caught the men, he'd been surprised at how scrawny and weak they actually were.

How they had managed to wreck such damage was a mystery that plagued JD. He often thought that if he had been there he could have saved his fathers, but he hadn't. Caleb and he had both been out of the country, serving in the Marines, looking for their mate.

The death of their fathers had put an end to that dream, but somehow fate had been merciful enough to deliver her to them anyway. JD was not about to take a chance at losing her now.

They were taking Samantha to the doctor first and having her completely checked out before they seeded her womb. Soon enough the full moon would rise and the official matting ritual would commence. The moon would fade, but the promise of a future life would grow round and strong beneath Samantha's heart.

Soon enough she would give them a set of sons to raise and train. The dream dancing in his head filled him with an emotion he'd not felt since childhood. Contentment, warmed him in ways he'd never thought he'd be.

Soon, very soon he'd see that dream come to life.

The vibrating of his cell phone interrupted his thoughts. Unclipping it, he scowled at the code that was flashing on the screen. He knew the number, but had never seen it before on his phone. It was the home security system alerting him that one of the exterior entrances had been opened.

Fear flashed through him. Immediately it was followed by rage. It could not be Samantha. He had left her cuffed to the bed. It had to be an intruder. If the man found Samantha, chained naked to the bed, JD had little doubt what would happen.

He made the twenty-minute drive to their country home in fewer than ten minutes. Crashing through the open front door, he did not pause as he raced up the stairs and down the hall to Samantha's bedroom. Slamming open the door, he skidded to a halt when he saw the empty bed, the handcuffs dangling from the post.

Not there? Where the hell was she?

* * * *

Sam was beginning to feel normal after getting a shower and dressing in clean clothes, clothes that fit, her clothes. Reality was beginning to reorder itself to the logical, rational life she led. The only thing reality couldn't fix was her sister, Vicky.

Sam had confessed, not to the specifics, but generally what she had spent the weekend doing. She had little choice after calling her sister to her rescue and then running out of the house wearing a T-shirt that came down to her knees and a pair of sweatpants that she had to hold up.

Vicky had been delighted, and Sam had looked sunburned when she had finally managed to escape her little sister. She'd spent the last thirty minutes hiding in the small apartment she now called home. The crew would be back from working out on the tracks soon, and it would not be long before she had to endure their ribbing.

Sam did not delude herself into believing that they would not hear about her romantic evening. Vicky was not one to keep secrets. She could only hope that Vicky would keep the number of men Sam had passed the night with to herself.

The screech of tires followed by the sound of gravel being spun off in several directions turned Sam's attention to the window.

Shit! What the hell was he doing here?

The deputy was back, and he looked pissed. Actually, he looked hot in his uniform, especially with that big brimmed hat on that cast a sharp shadow over his rugged features. It hid most of his face, highlighting his hard jawline and his lips compressed in displeasure.

Despite the apprehension tightening her muscles, there was no way Sam could deny the warming of her blood as her body began to reawaken with desire. As much as she wanted to be annoyed that he was here, a part of her was secretly thrilled.

Sam was not one to lie to herself. She knew her appearance was at best pretty for an average girl. Men like the deputy never noticed her, much less pursued her. As annoying as he was, she could not deny the sense of excitement that filled her knowing that this man was so intent on her.

Don't think that way.

Sam warned herself. She was not so shallow to be turned by a hard-bodied bad boy. She'd made that mistake with Bruce. As sexy as the deputy and his twin were, as fantastic as they were in bed, Sam was not about to repeat her past errors.

Best thing she could do was hide. That option disappeared before Sam's eyes as Vicky strode across the parking lot, obviously intending on intercepting the deputy. Things were about to go from bad to critical, and fast.

* * * *

"Samantha, come here!"

The deputy barked that order before she was halfway across the parking lot. She had been too far to hear what Vicky was saying when the man interrupted her, but Sam heard Vicky's response to the deputy's command perfectly.

"She's not a dog, officer. She doesn't come when you call or stay just because you handcuff her to the bed!"

Oh God.

Things were going worse than she thought. If the deputy's feral snarl was any indication, they could get even worse. The last thing Sam wanted was to have Vicky land in jail. Then she'd have to explain to Mike how her one-night stand had blown completely up in her sister's face.

Mike, their brother, would completely lose it then. When the dust finally settled, Sam would have to bail out not one sibling, but two. If the deputy knew anything about women, he'd know they didn't like it when their family was arrested.

"Your assistance is no longer needed."

He doesn't know.

The deputy made to push past Vicky, but she sidestepped and blocked his path. Sam could swear the deputy's growl echoed through the complex. It was an inhuman sound, and the image of the two bite marks came to her mind. They did not exactly look human either.

"Woman!"

"Oh, you did not just call me that." Vicky's head swirled backward as if she had been slapped.

"Samantha, I told you to come here!"

"Listen here, buddy." It was almost comical the way the deputy looked down at the finger Vicky had poked into his chest. "She is not going to obey your commands. Nobody here is. Now, get the hell off our property or you're going to get slapped with a lawsuit for harassment."

"Does everybody here think that the answer to their problem is to sue?" It was unclear whom the deputy was asking that question of. He was still staring in disbelief at the finger lodged against his chest.

"Leave! Now!"

"Woman, you'd better get that finger out of my chest and step back."

"Or what?" Vicky pulled her finger back only to shove it harder into his chest. "You going to hit me? Take your best shot, big guy."

"That's it. Samantha, you had better put this woman back on the leash or I'm going to put her into cuffs and take her down to the station house."

"Vicky—"

"On what charge?"

"Assaulting an officer."

"Assaulting? What? Does this hurt? How about this?"

Sam caught Vicky's hand before she could slap the deputy. The action finally brought Vicky's attention away from the deputy.

"That is enough. I'll take it from here, Vicky. Thank you."

As she spoke, Sam forcibly turned her sister and began to walk her back toward the main house. Sam outweighed Vicky by at least twenty pounds, and, despite Vicky's resistance, she easily managed to get her sister several feet away from the deputy and danger.

"I'm not going to do anything rash." Vicky whispered her complaint.

"You almost did."

"The asshole deserves to be slapped."

"I agree, but just imagine what will happen when Mike gets back to find you playing a harmonica down at the county prison." Sam let Vicky go now that she was moving in the desired direction on her own.

"He never misses a chance to play the man of the house, does he?"

"No, he doesn't, but I am the oldest, and this is my problem. So let me handle it, okay?"

"I don't think that is wise, Sam." Vicky cast a dirty look at the deputy. "You shouldn't be alone with him."

"I'll be all right."

"If you say so," Vicky agreed reluctantly. With another dirty look at the deputy, she turned to give Sam one final bit of advice. "Just yell rape if you need me."

Vicky said it loud enough to make sure that the deputy heard her. Not bothering to see how the man reacted to her taunt, Vicky sauntered back into the main house.

"You two are obviously related."

"I think you should just leave now, Deputy."

"It's sheriff. If I leave, you leave."

"That's not going to happen."

"I'm not going anywhere without you. You're mine."

"Yours? I'm not a pet that you own and command at will. You do realize, *Sheriff,* that I could file charges against you for kidnapping and rape."

"Kidnapping and rape?" Sam delighted in the way his mouth fell open at that. "Woman, are you out of your mind?"

"What do you call accosting a strange woman and then abducting her?"

"I did not accost you."

"You fucked me against your patrol car!"

"*That* was expedient."

"*That* must be your excuse for why you didn't take the time to even tell me your name."

"What the hell does that have to do with anything?" he demanded, looking confused, as if it were a strange thing for him to know the name of the woman he was fucking.

"Like a lot of women, Sheriff," Sam enjoyed sneering his title and the way it made his eyes narrow with annoyance, "I like to know the name of a guy I'm going to be intimate with. Of course, it's not like I was planning to be intimate with you. You sort of forced that issue, didn't you?"

"I didn't force anything. You wanted it."

"I was cuffed!"

"Doesn't mean you didn't want it. Besides, lest you forget, you begged for me to—"

"Shut up! Just shut up and go away!"

Sam could not catch her breath as her chest constricted painfully. His attitude hurt. It clearly stated what kind of man he was and what kind of relationship he liked. Neither of which should matter to her.

She just didn't like being used. Sam prided herself on being above that, better than the type of woman that meekly gave in to a man's demands. Her reaction to this man was beneath her.

"Look." Sam tried to calm down before she said or did something stupid, like attack the arrogant ass before her. "There's not going to be any repeat performance, so go harass some other woman."

"Like hell. Now you listen to me, Samantha, and you listen good. You are going to walk that pretty ass over to my car and get in like a grown woman or I'm going to drag you there and shove you in."

"That's called abducting, Sheriff!"

"Not for our kind, it's not!"

"Your kind? What the hell does that mean? Aren't you human?"

* * * *

JD watched her eyes go wide with her question, and her hand fluttered up to touch her shoulder. Her lips started to tremble, and he could smell her anger taking on the sour scent of fear.

"Oh my God. You aren't human, are you?"

"What do I look like?" JD demanded, insulted by the growing disgust in her eyes.

"What are you? A werewolf?" Apparently, his agreement was not necessary as she continued, talking more to herself than him. "And you bit me. That means I'm going to become a werewolf too."

"It's not that bad."

The woman should be happy over this news. Turning humans was against pack law, except for mates. Few were ever blessed with all the advantages of becoming a shifter.

"Not that bad? You turned me into a fucking dog."

"Not dog, a wolf."

"Call it what you want. I'm still going to have a tail and walk around on four legs."

"Not permanently."

"I could just kill you."

He watched her little hands clench into tiny fists. Not with those.

"That is enough. You should be proud and thankful for this gift, not threatening me."

"Get away from me. I don't ever want to see you again!"

With that, she turned and fled. Every one of JD's wolf senses flared to life as the beast beat at the reins of his control. She should not have run. He had thought nothing would ever turn him on more than his mate's blind submission, but he had been wrong.

He slammed through the cabin door. The lock didn't slow him down for a second. Almost immediately, he had to duck as a lamp crashed against the wall. If it had not been for his quick reflexes, the damn thing would have hit him in the head.

"Get out!" Samantha roared, her face flushed, her chest heaving. She was sex personified, and his cock swelled with the need to bend her to his will. First, he had to dodge the alarm clock she sent sailing at him.

"Cease, woman." JD hit the incoming hairbrush out of the way.

"Don't you come near me, you single-minded Neanderthal!"

She hefted a remote control at him as she looked around for something bigger and heavier. JD was not going to give her the chance to find it. With his mate momentarily distracted, he moved in fast and hard. Tackling her, he took her down to the bed. He might have had her pinned, but she was far from defeated.

"Get off me, you overgrown ox!"

One of her flailing fists caught him in the eye. The blow did not hurt, but it annoyed him enough to capture both her wrists and stretch her arms over her head. Still, she bucked and twisted, trying to throw him off.

Her fight, though, was winding down. He could see by the glassy look glazing over her eyes that the musk was beginning to take effect. Still, he waited until she fell completely still, her whole body relaxing beneath his.

"My name is JD McBane, and you belong to me, Samantha."

Chapter 6

With that declaration, JD slammed his mouth down onto hers. It was not simply an expression of savage passion. It was a declaration of ownership, of complete, ruthless domination. He thrust his tongue into her mouth and claimed her with such intensity Sam was lost.

There was no way to fight the need he roused in her. She did not even try. Capturing his tongue between her lips, she sucked on it, making him growl and his hands tighten on her wrists.

A moment later, she felt the cool air on her chest as he ripped her shirt open. She could feel the fine tremors coursing through his hand as it closed over her breast. He caressed the hard tip through the lacy fabric of her bra before tearing that last barrier out of the way so he could feel her soft flesh beneath his palm.

JD tore his mouth away from hers, leaving her panting as he kissed and nibbled his way down her chin, over her neck, toward her breast. Her flesh burned, fueled by the feel of his mouth on her skin. He spared nothing in his assault as he licked, sucked, and bit her tender nipple. Instead of soothing her, his mouth ratcheted up the white-hot need sending sparks of pained pleasure down her spine and echoing into her pussy.

That was where she needed his mouth the most. Her pussy wept, demanding attention. Twisting into him, she spread her legs wider so she could rub herself into his thigh.

Her panties caught and caressed her hidden nub. Gasping, she arched her hips and ground herself against him. The motion drew a ragged moan from JD as he released her nipple and began kissing his way down her stomach.

* * * *

JD lost the reins of control over the beast prowling inside him. The scent of her arousal called to the wolf to come and take a taste. The beast wanted to spread her legs wide, bury his face into the pink, swollen folds of her pussy, and devour her.

He held her away from him, fighting not only her jeans, but also his mate. Samantha bucked and writhed against him, fighting to wrap her legs around his thigh and ride him to orgasm. She could ride his mouth if he could just get the damn denim out of the way.

Snarling in frustration, he felt his fingernails grow into claws, slashing the offending material and freeing his mate to his eyes, hands, and mouth. JD paused. Her pink and wet, bare cunt was the most beautiful of sights, and he shuddered as he lowered his head.

He could feel his tongue growing to the length of the wolf's as he lapped at her like the dog he was, his tongue stroking through her creamy slit in long, hungry licks.

Delicious.

JD closed his eyes, savoring the unique taste of his mate. She was like a pure shot of caffeine, energizing every cell in his body with the need for more.

Mine.

The wolf growled inside, staking its claim. She would remember no others after today. He would pleasure her and keep going until she could no longer recall the touch, the kiss of any other man. With that single intent, he unfurled his tongue, fucking it deep inside her clenching channel.

He heard her sob his name as the walls of her sheath clamped down on his tongue and her body erupted in tremors. He continued to eat at her cunt with greedy, carnal abandon, forcing her climax to expand, compress, and explode with redoubled strength as he brought his fingers into play, trapping her clit, rolling and flicking it.

She was crying. Her hands, now free, twisted in his hair, and she pushed on his head, trying to drag him away from her mound as her cunt spasmed hard and flooded his mouth with another wave of her sweet cream.

Growling in the back of his throat, the wolf slid its tongue out of her clinging sheath to lick its way up to her clit. The sensitive nub was trapped between his fingers as he ravaged the bud with rough, savage licks, making her scream and buck even harder against him. The untamed beast paid little attention to the ranting of its mate.

His thick fingers filled the void left by his tongue in her sheath, and he fucked them into her with rapid, hard thrusts. Her inner muscles contracted, pulling him deeper. JD could take no more, and he fought the wolf to reclaim control.

He wanted to feel her tight sheath sucking at his cock, milking his release from his body. First, though, he wanted to drive her insane, to bind her to him in such a basic, elementary way that once the musk wore off, she would not dream of leaving him.

With a growl, the wolf went down as JD ripped himself away from her weeping flesh, leaving Samantha sobbing that it was too much. Tears streamed from under her lowered lids. The fight went out of her the moment he released her pussy and she sank deeper into the mattress.

JD snarled. If she thought they were done, she was in for a shock. He had only just begun. Working at the zipper with fingers made clumsy with need, he finally managed to free his cock. Not bothering to remove any clothing, he bent back down to his mate.

* * * *

Tears of passion blurred Sam's vision as her eyes opened at the feel of his hard, hot length pushing into her. She shook her head against the invasion. Her arms struck outward to halt his progress.

Her ravaged flesh was still quivering from the aftershocks of her multiple orgasms. Her muscles, clenched tight, ached, and she just needed a moment. She needed to recover, but he was not giving her any time. In a repeat of last night's savage fucking, he forced her to continue, bathing her body in another round of devastating pleasure.

Colors danced before her eyes as his cock forged deeper, branding her tender flesh as he slowly slid all the way in. Sam cried out, trying to find something to anchor to as her world again began to expand and contract in consuming waves of ecstasy.

Expecting him to fuck her with relentless, driving intensity, she made a hoarse sound of frustrated pleasure and denial as he slowly began to rock inside her. He hooked his elbows under her knees, forcing her legs all the way back toward her shoulders and allowing him to penetrate deeper into her.

Sam whimpered and writhed beneath him as her world was reduced to the hot, erotic sensation of his slow thrusting. Each pull and stroke made the lips of her cunt tighten and clamp down on him as her pussy pulsed with ripples of ecstasy slowly rebuilding into a storm.

The slow fucking was a torturous lesson in rapture. Her body was so primed, so sensitized that she swore the next stroke would surely bring release. Instead, it only drove her higher.

"Damn you, JD," Sam growled, unable to withstand anymore. "Fuck me."

"I am fucking you, sweetheart." His voice sounded smooth and confident, but she could feel the sweat dripping from his body, knew that his restraint was costing him as well.

"Harder! Fuck me harder!"

* * * *

That was what JD had been waiting for. He stopped the slow thrusting, fighting every muscle in his body to stay still. It was sweet torture to be buried deep in her clinging warmth, the gentle spasms of her muscles teasing his cock to resume its motion.

Keeping a tight hold on her hips to stay inside, he rolled. Samantha's protesting murmur turned to a groan as her weight forced him a little deeper into her body. For a moment, he thought he was going to lose it and spill his seed into her. Grinding his teeth together, he fought for breath and sanity. Only when he was sure that he was in control did he dare to move his hands up her sides.

"Up, Samantha." With gentle pressure, he forced her to rise, kneeling over him as his knees bent to support her back. Now that was a sight.

Her breasts bounced enticingly as she panted. Her hard nipples tempted him to lean up and take a bite. Her full lips were swollen and red. They made his cock ache to feel them wrapped around his heated flesh.

Above him, Samantha growled and began to ride him. JD matched her growl and clamped down on her hips, holding her still. Samantha fought him, but she was no match for his strength.

"I need to move." She rolled her hips, trying to entice him to let her do just that.

"Later," JD ground out.

"No, now!" Again, she tried to move up his shaft, but JD held her still.

"Do not, Samantha, or I'll pull out and turn you over my knee."

It was a lie. He did not have the strength to follow through on the threat, but his mate did not know that. Given their short past, she obviously believed him as she fell still.

"Good girl." JD's praise sounded ragged to his ears. "Now give me your hands."

She did not seem capable of obeying his command. JD slowly let go of her hips, pausing for a moment to make sure she stayed still. He placed one of her hands over her breast and the other on her mound.

Samantha whimpered as her hands lay listlessly on her flesh. She was too lost in the haze of passion to understand. JD put his hand over the one resting on her stretched folds, singling out one finger to begin teasing her clit. Slowly, as her finger began to move on its own, he released her.

"That's it, baby. Pleasure yourself. I want to watch you come."

He did not know if she heard him over the passionate sounds she was making. Her movements became more frenzied, the circular motion of her finger quickening as she coaxed herself to orgasm. The hand on her breast joined in, twirling and pinching her nipple.

He could feel her inner muscles quivering, tightening and relaxing rhythmically. Then her climax hit, and her tight little sheath closed around him like a strangling fist. The beast inside him growled its pleasure as it clawed at his control, urging him to move.

JD no longer had the strength to fight the beast. Tightening his hands on her hips, he began to slam up into her. She tilted her head back and screamed as her orgasms came one after another.

He could not stop, lost in the enjoyment of feeling every ripple, every spasm of her hot sheath stretched around his engorged shaft. She might have been on top, but he was still dominating her, controlling her pleasure, bringing her to release after release.

The white-hot streaks of ecstasy boiled up from his balls, warning him that he was about to explode. For endless seconds, the tension coiling through his muscles bit painfully before his seed erupted and flooded his mate as pleasure racked his body in devastating waves of destruction.

As Samantha collapsed on top of him, JD's wrapped his arms around her so he could hold her close. In that moment, he knew his world would never be the same. Nothing else mattered beyond this, beyond Samantha.

She meant everything to him. That realization sent a shiver of fear through him. Mates were a means to an end, the path to family and home. He had never imagined that he would fall in love with his mate. He had never wanted to love any woman.

He could not tolerate that vulnerability. If he were to lose her, he would lose everything. Life itself would hold no meaning. His body responded to his thoughts. His muscles tightened in preparation for battle, his fingers curled into fists and the musk disappeared. Samantha responded immediately to the change in JD. She muttered and rolled away.

JD did not try to stop her, too absorbed in his thoughts to focus on his mate.

* * * *

Damn it, not again!

Sam took deep breaths, trying to clear the last vestiges of lust from her system. She was really going to have to figure out a way to defend against that lust-inducing smell the deputy generated.

No, sheriff, and his name is JD. I guess that's a step in the right direction.

Not really. A step in the right direction would be to get him out of her bed, out of the park, and out of her life. Samantha had enough problems without complicating her life with a set of over-sexed twins. There were the millions that Frank Morison had shockingly decided to leave to her instead of his own son, Brett.

Brett, that asshole, hadn't taken it well when he'd learned his father had left all of his estate to his live-in caretaker instead of him. Which meant the whining, annoying man had turned his unappealing charm onto Sam, convinced that she was dumb enough to fall for any and all of his tricks.

Still as irritating as Brett was, he wasn't the one who had sent her fleeing from Florida. Bruce had been the one who had played her and then horrified her.

Werewolf.

The word whispered through her head as the memory of watching him transform beneath the starlight replayed for the millionth time before her eyes. Sam considered herself to be rational, logical, but sometimes she'd wondered if she hadn't lost it.

Lost it good, because now here she was in the arms of another man who claimed to have the same supernatural linage. With JD she could accept reality a little easier, because the man certainly acted like a beast.

A quick glance at JD had her frown turning into a full-face scowl. The jackass had not even bothered to undress, *again*. She did not know if she was angrier with herself for not noticing or caring while they had been going at it or at him for not having the decency to remove his pants.

The sheriff did not even glance her way as she stomped off to the bathroom. Sam stopped to grab some clean clothes that were piled on the dresser. When she returned ten minutes later, the arrogant lug was still lying on his back, his cock hard and naked as he glared at the ceiling.

"You have to leave."

Sam stayed well away from JD when she made that announcement. He did not respond to her, did not look at her. She inched a little closer and nudged his leg with her foot. That got her a hard glare from those navy-blue eyes.

"You have to leave now."

"What?"

"I said, you have—"

The whoosh and whine of air brakes as a semi pulled into the parking lot outside drowned out her declaration. The sound distracted her, and Sam looked to see what was going on.

It was here!

Without a word of explanation to JD, Sam flew out of the cabin and raced across the parking lot to greet the truck driver as he made his way down the length of the tractor-trailer.

"Hey!"

"Hey. I'm looking for a Samantha Hark. I got a delivery for her."

"Well, you are looking at her." Sam could barely keep her

excitement contained as she danced around the truck, anxious to see the door open and her gift revealed. "You need help unloading her?"

"You're gonna need a forklift." The driver was holding out a clipboard toward her.

"I'll get it." Sam raced off toward one of the main hangars in an all-out rush.

"Hey, you gotta sign this!"

* * * *

"She'll be back in a moment." The driver turned to find a dark-haired beauty smiling after the woman who had disappeared into a large garage. "She's a little excited."

"I can tell. Can you hold this for me?" He handed the clipboard over toward the woman and went to open the back of the trailer. He had a feeling that when Miss Hark returned, she would be ready to wet herself if he did not have things set for her to pull the crate off the trailer.

When he had everything ready, he could hear the chug of a forklift coming closer. Its tires churned and ground over the asphalt. He turned back around to find a huge cop now standing near the raven-haired beauty. She was firing bullets at him with her steel-gray eyes.

The party was about to get bigger as several pickups came flying up a dirt path. Hopefully, this would not hold him up too long. He had three other deliveries to make and an hour drive to Charleston.

* * * *

JD stared at the large wooden crate and wondered what the hell it could possibly be to send Samantha into a state of near-hysteria. The sudden change in her scent from annoyance to excitement had pulled him from his thoughts. Before he could ask her what was going on, she had raced out the door.

He had watched her prance around the driver as if he were Santa Claus and she was five years old before she went running away again. When she had reappeared driving a forklift, he knew that whatever was being delivered, she had taken a personal interest in.

He was distracted from his curiosity by the sound of trucks approaching. He scowled as he mentally counted the number of men headed toward him. They were packed into the cabs, the beds and some were even standing on the tailgates. He was not leaving his mate here.

Samantha and the trucks all converged on the semi at the same time. JD eyed the men spilling into the parking lot with a critical eye. A woman would probably consider some handsome with their work-hardened bodies barely covered by jeans and shorts.

"Hey Vic." A large redhead separated from the crowd to come and drop a kiss on the viperous Victoria's cheek. "What's going on?"

"It's here." Vicky nodded to the truck. "And Sam's about to lose it."

"I wasn't talking about that." The man eyes darted toward JD, and he gave a slight nod in his direction. "I was talking about him."

JD's attention was diverted from those two as a large bare-chested man stepped up to the forklift to talk to Samantha. The way he leaned in close and smiled at her face triggered JD's hot button.

Ignoring everybody else he stormed toward the couple, reaching them just as the other man was holding a hand up to help her down. JD knocked his hand out of the way and forced the man backward.

"Don't touch her."

"Hey, peace, man." The blond Adonis held up his hands and backed off.

"What the hell do you think you're doing?" Samantha snapped at JD as she swung down to the ground. "Go on, Chase, the lift's yours."

Giving the sheriff a wide berth, the blond muscle head climbed onto the forklift. As he started up the engine, Samantha turned on JD.

"Don't you ever do that again!"

"You don't give me orders, woman!"

"I do when it comes to me."

"No other man is allowed to touch you, Samantha." JD grabbed her arm, pulling her closer.

"Any man I let can touch me. That doesn't include *you*." She jerked free.

"What is in the crate, Samantha?" JD let her comment go, knowing they could spend the rest of the day arguing about it. She could say whatever she wanted. Nobody was going to touch her but him.

"That's none of your business." Her chin tilted up.

"What is it?"

"It's a motorcycle. A Ducati. *My* Ducati. Happy now?"

"You are *not* riding a motorcycle." JD felt his heart seize painfully at the idea.

"Ah, but *Daaaad*."

"Don't give me any sass, woman! You could be seriously hurt or killed." He hated revealing so much emotion to her. It should be enough that he told her no. She wasn't listening, and that hated fear was back.

"Screw off. I'm not yours to boss around. Now go on and get out of here, Sheriff. I'm tired of you."

"I'm not going anywhere without you."

"You heard her, Sheriff." This came from the large redheaded man. The smart-mouthed Vicky was standing just behind him with a smirk on her face. "This is private property, and, unless you have a warrant, you're not welcome here."

"I'm not going anywhere without Samantha."

"Do you have a warrant for her arrest?"

"He doesn't have anything but a bad attitude." Samantha answered for him. "But you have made a mistake, Sheriff. Just because I like fucking you, doesn't mean I like you. So good-bye."

With that, Samantha went jogging off after the forklift. Every cell in JD screamed at him to go after her, to take her down and prove to her that just liking to fuck him was more than enough. He could not do that, not with his emotions so raw.

Tonight, when she was alone and defenseless, he would be back. By then, he'd be back in control.

Chapter 7

Caleb stared down at Samantha. She was so cute when she was sleeping. In the webbing of shadows and moonlight, her rich hair looked dark, almost black against the pale perfection of her skin.

His wolf eyes missed no detail, the stray strands that curled around her cheek, the sensuous curve of her parted lips, even the shadow her pert nose cast on her pillowcase. She was beautiful. He could just sit and stare at her all night if not for the ache in his balls.

That pain had been with him all day as he trained with a set of seasoned SWAT officers. It had been a long, grueling day, but not because of all the strenuous exercise or heavy gear. The entire day he had to work hard to focus on what was going on around him and not drift off into dreams of the night to come.

When the day had ended, he had paused long enough to catch a shower before he rushed home. He had fully expected to find JD already there, pleasuring their mate. At least, he had been right about JD being there.

Samantha had been missing. Caleb had been just as impressed as he was annoyed to hear that she had picked the lock on the cuffs and escaped. Their mate had some skills and the fire to use them. That was all the positive to be had out of the situation.

Obviously, Samantha needed a little taming before she learned that her skills and fire were better directed at people other than her mates. JD had agreed with the fact that Samantha had to be brought to heal, but he thought she needed a lot of work.

Their lunchtime encounter had left a bitter taste in his twin's mouth. Samantha had upset JD enough that it was hard for Caleb to get the whole story out of him. JD had wandered in the telling, constantly sidetracking on Samantha's viperous words.

As sassy and combative as Samantha had been, it was her parting comment that had cut his brother to the quick. Whether she knew it or not, Samantha had hurt JD when she had told him that she did not like him. Caleb did not like to see his brother hurt, even if it did amaze him that a woman had managed that feat.

His brother did not respond well to pain. That was why Caleb had argued with him most of the night about who should go to collect their mate. In his current mood, Caleb had been concerned that JD would do more harm than good to their cause.

Ultimately they were going to have to get Samantha to stay on her own volition. They could not spend the rest of their lives chasing their mate. JD's solution was to get her pregnant as fast as possible.

In his twin's prehistoric brain, a woman with children did not leave her mate. That was true of most werewolves raised in packs, but Samantha had not been raised that way. Caleb was sure she was not going to be so easily cornered.

No, what was needed now was a gentle touch and a little seduction. That was Caleb's specialty. He had wooed more women than JD had hairs on his head. More than one had claimed to have fallen in love with him, much to his annoyance.

It should not be so hard to make Samantha take the plunge. With that in mind, Caleb smoothed back the stray strands of hair from her face and began to place soft butterfly kisses along her cheek.

Samantha mumbled, her hand coming up to swat him away as if he were an annoying fly. Caleb smiled and captured her hand. Switching his attention to her fine-boned fingers, he began to lick and nibble his way down and up them.

"Stop," Samantha grumbled, trying to pull her hand back.

Caleb did not release her as he worked his way down to the sensitive skin of her wrist. He could feel her pulse kick up as he lingered there. Despite the delicate shivers cascading down her arm,

Samantha frowned, one eye opening.

"JD!" she snapped sleepily as she tugged on her arm. "I wanna sleep."

Caleb let her arm go as her eyes drifted closed. He waited, and seconds later her lids snapped back up. In a sudden rush of unexpected motion, she rolled away from him and right off the edge of the bed.

"Are you all right?"

Caleb leaned across the small twin mattress to check on her. She'd hit the floor with a thud, loud enough to concern him. Samantha threw off the fall and quickly scrambled to her feet.

"What the hell are you doing here?" She fumbled with the lamp on the nightstand.

"You didn't hit your head, did you?"

"You're not JD." Samantha managed to turn the lamp on.

"I'm Caleb, his brother."

"Well, no kidding. Let me take a wild guess. You're twins. Now tell me what you are doing here."

"I brought you flowers." Caleb gestured to the elegant bouquet sitting in the glass vase he had placed on her other nightstand.

"Flowers?" Samantha blinked and stared at the arrangement as if they were some alien things she had never seen before. "You brought me flowers at," her eyes darted to the digital clock, "two in the morning?"

"I wanted to surprise you."

"Well paint me red and call me shocked. Now get out."

"That's not very gracious, Samantha."

"Oh, excuse me. I'm not up on the proper social protocols when a man breaks into my room in the middle of the night to bring me flowers. I guess that's another of your little werewolf traditions, huh?"

"JD mentioned that you had figured out that we were werewolves. I was wondering how you came to that conclusion."

He had hoped to get to the seduction first. Once she was nice and relaxed, he had planned to ask her some questions. Given her current attitude, he might as well reverse the order.

"Is that what the flowers are for? A sort of 'sorry I turned you into a dog girl' consolation prize?"

"No. I'm—"

"Oh, wait." Samantha cut him off as she started to move backward. "I forgot. You're sorry you turned me into a four-legged animal with a tail, but you're still hoping I'll have sex with you, right?"

"Samantha—"

"Don't call me that! Only my mom ever called me that and only when I was in trouble. Everybody else calls me Sam."

"Sam—"

"Don't call me that either."

"Then what—"

"Don't call me anything. Just leave."

"I can't do that."

"Why? Because I'm going to turn into some bloodthirsty creature that is going to have to be caged whenever there is a full moon?"

"Where do you get these notions about werewolves?"

"Everybody knows the lore."

"There is a big difference between myth and reality, sweetheart."

Caleb stood and began matching her progression backward. Samantha had managed to make her way toward one of the doors settled in the back wall. Caleb was not sure what was through the door, but he did not feel like chasing his mate.

"I take it you're going to educate me."

"That's a rather long discussion. Better for another time, but I will say that you should be happy about the change. Few are ever bitten."

"What? You and your brother don't run around biting every woman you fuck?"

"We've never bitten any before you."

"Oh, I do feel so honored, just blessed to my soul."

"I know it's a shock, Samantha, but there are a lot of advantages to becoming a werewolf."

"Yeah, I can see that. Now I can lick myself, no need to put up with men, right? Now get out."

"You'll heal faster, and your body will be more resistant to injury and illness." Caleb ignored her snide comment. "Your senses will be heightened. You'll be able to see in the dark and at distances, to hear softer sounds and higher pitches, and you'll smell things you have never smelled before."

"Smell? So does that mean whatever that odor JD and you keep emitting is going to become more powerful?"

"No, the strength of the mating musk is purely based on the woman we're with," Caleb assured her, his grin reappearing.

"What does that mean? The woman you're with?"

"Just what I said. The potency is based on our attraction for the woman we are with. It is most potent when we are attempting to arouse our mate."

"Go arouse your mate, then, and leave me alone."

"I'm looking at her."

"What?"

"We only bite our mates."

"I'm your...mate?"

"Yes."

"Mate as in, like, wife?"

"That's a traditional human concept, but the idea is similar."

"That can't be. Sorry, you got the wrong woman." Samantha shook her head, obviously having difficulty with the concept.

"No, there is no mistake. Werewolves know when they find their mates."

"Well, maybe you need to get your antenna checked, because I don't like you."

"You don't mean that."

"Yes, I do. Unbelievably, I take a grim view of men who *abduct* women to use as their sexual plaything and then leave them *cuffed* to a bed. If that is not arrogant enough, an outright jerk then hunts down the woman once she escapes and demands that she return. Not to mention showing up in my bedroom at *two* in the morning. Not much to like, now is there?"

"Sam—"

"Besides, I'm married."

"You're what?"

* * * *

"Married."

There, that should do it. It was a lie, a boldfaced one, but as long as it got rid of Caleb, it was worth whatever time it cost her in purgatory. From the confused look darkening Caleb's face, she knew he believed her. His eyes cut immediately to her hand, and she knew he was looking for her ring. There was none, but that wasn't all that unusual.

"You're lying." There was a hard note to his statement. It came out more like a command than the question it should have been.

"Nope. Not everybody wears rings. Especially not in my line of work." Sam crossed her arms over her chest, pleased with the shift in the balance.

"You don't have any pictures up."

"I know what my husband looks like."

"Where is he? Why is he not in your bed?"

"Not that it's any of your business, but he is working down in Florida."

"You're getting a divorce."

"Excuse me? You don't tell me what to do."

"You don't love him."

"How the hell do you know what I feel?"

"I've had you in my arms. No woman who is in love with another man responds the way you did to JD and I."

"That was because of the musk."

His audacity was breathtaking. He drugged her to have sex with him and then turned around and threw her response in her face.

"You think your husband will see it that way?"

He was advancing on her, and Sam wisely backed up. There was no way she was going to let him or his brother get another one over on her. The bathroom doorknob bit into her back, and she reached around to grab it.

"Are you threatening me?"

"If you don't divorce your husband, I'm sure JD and I can convince him to divorce you."

Her eyes widened at that threat. That was low. Admittedly, she'd made up the husband bit, but Caleb was quite serious about betraying her supposed affair. Now what the hell was she supposed to say? Bruce immediately came to mind.

"You think he'll divorce me because I fucked you? He wouldn't care. He likes to run around with his own little hot bitch. Trust me, he doesn't have room to complain."

"He cheats on you?"

That brought Caleb to a stop. He appeared shocked and angry on her behalf. That confused Sam even more. The man had just threatened to betray her, and now he was upset that another had already done that.

"All men cheat."

"JD and I don't. We'd never do that to you."

He said it with such sincerity Sam almost believed him. Almost. What else was a man who was trying to convince her to marry, no, mate him say? Divorce your husband and come fuck us; we'll be chasing every skirt that passes by behind your back? Not likely.

"Just leave me alone, Caleb. I don't need or want you." The conversation had gotten way out of hand.

"How can you stay with a man who disrespects you?"

"That's none of your business."

"You're wrong. Everything about you is my business, and you will divorce this man."

"I will not. Why would I divorce one dog just to marry two?"

That red flag sent the bull raging. Sam barely got the bathroom door closed behind her before he slammed into it. She silently thanked herself for installing all wood doors throughout the property, as it held under his weight.

It would not hold for long. She worked fast, flipping on the lights and grabbing the bottle of cheap perfume Vicky had lent her that evening. She sprayed herself and continued until the room stunk and the door splintered.

Caleb charged in and almost immediately reeled back as he hit the fragrant wall of odor. Responding like he had been punched in the face, his muscles tightened and he turned his head.

"God, woman, what is that stench?"

"Let's see that musk work now." Sam, assured that she had the upper hand, almost laughed at his disgusted expression. "This is my mating musk repellant."

"You think that is going to deter me?" he demanded from the relative safety of the doorway.

"You can't even step into the bathroom. It wouldn't matter if you did. Unless you intend on raping me, you can't make me want you. So why don't you leave?"

"You honestly think that the only reason you respond to me is because of the musk?"

"What the hell else could it be? I told you I don't like you. Why would I desire you?"

"You're lying to yourself, Samantha. You do like me, and you do desire me. You're my mate. The musk only heightens the sensation."

"In your dreams, fuzz butt. I'd never have done any of the things I did the other night without that musk."

"If you get in the shower and wash that stench off now, Samantha, I'll spare you the punishment your ignorant words have earned you," Caleb growled.

"If you get out of my cabin now, I'll spare you the silver bullet."

"That's it!"

Chapter 8

Caleb had had enough. Samantha was their mate. She could protest all she wanted, but nature would not have selected her were she not compatible with them.

Samantha needed a lesson in what it would cost her to deny the natural bonds that were already forming between them. That was a lesson Caleb was more than capable of teaching her. With a deep breath, he stormed into the bathroom.

"Stay away from me!" she shouted at him, holding her hands up to stop his progression. It was a flimsy defense, and he grabbed her wrists, using them to pull her into his embrace.

"Can you smell the musk, Samantha?"

"Let me go." Samantha fought against his hold. Caleb tightened his grip, transferring both wrists to one hand. The other he slid behind her back, letting it glide down to the hem of her nightshirt.

"Answer me, Samantha."

"Go to hell! Don't—"

Her protest turned into a shriek when his hand slipped under her nightshirt and he slapped her directly across the ass. Because of the strong, horrid stench of her perfume, Caleb could not smell what effect the spanking had on her.

She was squirming and spewing obscenities, but he did not let that stop him as he tugged her panties down. Samantha protested by clamping her legs tightly together, trying to hold her underwear in place and deny him access.

Caleb was not about to be denied and spanked her again for her imprudence. The slap had her whole body jerking. Her legs separated just enough for her panties to fall freely to the floor, and Caleb took immediate advantage.

"You're wet, Samantha." Caleb could not deny the satisfaction in his statement.

The truth was right there in his hand. It could not be discredited by the musk. Thanks to the wretched perfume she had drowned herself in, there was no way his mate could be overwhelmed by the mating scent.

"Don't touch me." She gasped and squirmed, trying to escape his touch.

"Admit it, Samantha. You're hot for me, and it has nothing to do with the musk."

"Go to hell!"

Caleb shook his head. Punishment was in order for her lying, but he was willing to give her one last chance. If she refused to be truthful, he would have to take a firmer hand with her. The mere idea had his cock twitching.

The hard flesh between his legs was already engorged with blood, longer, harder than it had ever been. It wanted out, ached to be buried balls deep in his mate's warm, wet cunt. It did not want to waste time playing games with Samantha.

Too bad for his cock, Caleb was still in control. He was not about to rush things and have her accuse him of any atrocities later. No, when he buried himself in her tight sheath, she would be begging for it. She would know that it was her decision and not one made for her by the musk.

* * * *

Sam twisted in his hold. Her traitorous pussy was alive with excitement. There was no way she could excuse her reaction to his touch on that stupid mating musk. No, her body was buzzing with desire simply because one of the sex gods was near.

She had been successfully fighting the effects since she realized who was in her bedroom. That first spank had begun to crumple her control. The stinging blow had sent pleasurable vibrations echoing into her pussy.

That such an act of domination could so totally turn her on mystified Sam. She was not a weak-kneed, submissive type of woman. She liked to take charge and be in control, but when these men touched her, all the rules changed.

Her response scared her as much as it excited her. There was no time to work through the contradiction. His head was already lowering, demand shining in his emerald eyes.

It was a hard kiss, his tongue stroking into her mouth and igniting an eruption of electric shocks through her body. Sam jerked under the impact. Panicked by the onslaught of lust, she bit into his lower lip.

Shocked by her own behavior, Sam tried to rear back, but he chose that moment to thrust two thick fingers up into her tender channel. The sudden invasion made her gasp, and Caleb took advantage of her distraction to stroke his tongue back into her mouth.

He tormented her by matching the movements of his tongue with his fingers thrusting into her clenching sheath. It was too much for Sam to take, and the last of her resistance crumbled around her. Despite her best intentions to fight him to the end, she felt her body melting into his. Her tongue dueled with his as her legs widened, giving him more room to tease her sensitive folds.

His thumb slid over her clit, and Sam felt as if she had been hit with a cattle prod. Her entire body lit with sparks and shimmers of electricity as he teased the little bundle of nerve endings.

He tormented her, spearing his fingers deep into her, making her inner muscles stretch with each greedy, exquisite stroke as he swallowed her cries of passions. The worst was his thumb, as he rubbed, rolled, and pulled on her clit, tightening the coil of tension that spread from her pussy throughout her body.

Just when she was sure that she could take no more and the coil would snap, he stopped. Sam moaned, her hips arching into his still palm in a demand for him to continue.

* * * *

Caleb pulled his mouth free of hers, his breathing ragged as he fought his inner beast for control. Another second and she would have come, an act that would have snapped the reins of his control and released the wolf to rut as it so desperately desired.

Man and beast battled silently. Caleb came out victorious, but just barely. If only she would submit, then he could give in to what they both wanted. He would bend her over the counter and ride her with all the frustration that had built up during the day.

"Do you submit, Samantha?"

She ignored him, rubbing against him in blatant invitation. Before he could weaken and break, he pushed her away from him. The motion had her eyes clearing slightly, coming to rest on his.

"Damn it, woman, submit!"

* * * *

Sam blinked.

Submit?

Her body was on fire, and she was so close to the edge, it would only take the barest of caresses to send her over. The urge to give him what he wanted so she could get what she needed was strong, but her pride came back with the cold air caressing her bared mound.

Had she not submitted enough? She had let them shave her, play with her, fuck her at their leisure, giving in to every demand. Why should she be the one to submit when he was so obviously close to submitting himself?

All he needed was a little provoking and he would snap. Sam pressed against him, delighted at the feel of his large, hard cock pressing back into her, even if the rest of him flinched away.

"Why don't you submit, Caleb?" The deep, husky sound of her voice surprised her. She hadn't known she could sound like that.

"What?"

Sam could not help but smile over his confusion. She pressed into him again, rubbing against his erection.

"Why don't you get out of these clothes, go lay down on the bed, and let me ride you? You know that is what you want."

"You're playing a dangerous game, Samantha."

His voice sounded like gravel as he forced the words through clenched teeth. Sam leaned up, letting her hard nipples press into his chest as her pelvis ground into his. She felt the shudder that racked his body and knew that he was seconds from giving in.

"I'm not playing, Caleb," she promised him as she traced the muscle twitching in his cheek. "I'm very serious about riding you. You know I'm wet and ready, and all I want to do is slide myself down your cock. I know you want the same thing. I can feel how hard and thick your erection is."

She let her hand slide down his neck and over his chest, past his pounding heart, and lower.

"Doesn't your cock ache to feel my heat swallowing every hard inch you have to offer me?" Her hand closed around the thick bulge in his jeans. He reacted as if she had shot him, jerking hard under her hand.

"I'll squeeze you tight and…Hey!"

Sam's seductively whispered promises turned to a screech of surprise as she found herself suddenly whipped around and shoved over the vanity. The laminate countertop bit into her stomach as her forehead hit the mirror.

She was struggling to get up when she felt the cool air on her backside as Caleb flipped up her nightshirt. A second later, fire licked up her skin as he spanked her.

"I told you, you were playing a dangerous game, sweetheart," he warned her as he hit her other ass cheek.

The smack sent a second wave of fire up her spine. It exploded when it reached the top, sending a fine shower of sparkling rapture back down her spine. Sam moaned as the tingling pleasure condensed into her pussy, making her cunt clench with the need.

"You do not give the orders." He paused between each word to land another blow on her hot backside. The words and smacks came faster, harder, and Sam felt every burning cell in her expand, dangerously close to exploding. One more slap and she would be pushed right over the edge.

"Please, one more. I just need one more."

"Who gives the orders, Samantha?" The hard-edged authority in his voice sent shivers of excitement through her.

"You do."

"Did I give you permission to come?"

"No."

"Did you ask for it?"

"Please, Caleb, let me come. Make me come. I need it."

* * * *

God, she was gorgeous. Caleb had always enjoyed submissive women, never had met a woman who did not give in to his commands. He had always thought that he would want the same in a mate, but Samantha was teaching him otherwise.

She challenged his male authority, refusing to concede defeat until the very end. He would never tire of this, of the challenge she represented. Her submission now was made all the more potent because it had been fought for.

He'd won it by the mastery of his skills as a lover and her undeniable attraction to him. The thrill was not over. It never would be. Once the lust passed and her body was satisfied, she would rouse to fight him again.

As much as that knowledge invigorated him, Caleb knew the rules had to change. It needed to change from fights between two strangers to the well-familiar pattern of two lovers who practiced the fine art of disagreement for a lifetime while always realizing that the end was inevitable.

"Damn it, Caleb. What are you waiting for? Fuck me!"

Caleb smiled at the demand in her voice. His Samantha would never truly submit, not without the musk. With that thought in mind, he lifted her off her feet and placed her in the shower. Not giving her a chance to react, he flipped on the hot water.

She sputtered and cursed as the spray came out cold at first, bringing her back to her senses. Caleb kept one hand on her neck, holding her under the showerhead, as his other quickly removed his clothes. By the time he joined her in the stall, the water had heated, and the bathroom was quickly filling with steam.

The moist air was saturated with the mating musk, and his little mate had lost her will to fight or demand. She was trembling with her desire as her eyes ate up his naked body.

Her nightshirt was plastered to her body, leaving nothing to the imagination. It was still too much, and Caleb ripped the offending material from her body. As he stared at the lush perfection of her body, the wolf inside stormed his defenses.

There was no controlling the animal lust raging through his blood. If he had any hope of teaching his mate the lesson he wanted, he would need release first.

* * * *

"On your knees, woman."

Sam could barely follow the hard command. Her mind was doped on pure lust, her body shaking with need. There was no hiding the thrill that shook her as he forced her down. His large cock bobbed in front of her face.

"Suck it, Samantha," he commanded. "Suck it now."

Sam licked her lips. Giving in to the hard shaft's silent demand, Sam leaned forward and licked her way around the head, tasting the salty liquid pouring from its eye.

"Don't tease me." Caleb groaned above her, his hands fisting in her hair.

Her lips followed her tongue's teasing caresses down the length of his hard cock until she had taken him all the way to the back of her throat. She felt the shudders that racked Caleb as her lips clamped down and she slowly traced her way back up.

"You're going to pay for teasing me like this, Samantha. You've just earned your second punishment."

Responding to his threat, she nipped him lightly with her teeth around the rough edge of his head. Caleb jerked and cursed. He took over, holding her head still as he fucked himself deep into her mouth.

Sam tightened her lips around him, enjoying the heated, silken feel of his hardness as he plunged even deeper. It was a short-lived thrill. He was pumping faster and faster into her mouth.

"Shit, baby, I can't take any more."

That was all the warning she got before he was slamming himself into her and jets of hot, salty liquid were flooding her mouth. Sam tried to take it all. Her nails bit into his thighs as she held herself in place for his pleasure.

Even after he stopped coming, he continued to stroke into her mouth, his motions slowly gentling as his ragged breath panted out in great heaves. Finally, he came to a stop and pulled her off his still-hard cock, though it had lost an inch or two in length.

Sam glanced up, proud to see the effect she had on him in the hard, taut lines of his face. She might be on her knees, totally at the mercy of his lusts, but she had just reduced him to her level. Despite the musk clouding her brain, Sam still enjoyed her moment of victory.

* * * *

Caleb saw the glimmer of satisfaction in Samantha's eyes and knew its source. His mate thought she had the upper hand now. The truth was just the opposite. With his lust momentarily satiated, he could hold out to do what needed to be done.

"Up." He matched his command with a hand on her arm, pulling her to her feet. Easily he manipulated her into position, with her face pressed against the tile stall, bent at the waist. He used his legs to force hers apart and reveal her pink, swollen folds.

Nothing tempted him more to take a taste than a naked pussy. Caleb went to his knees and used his thumbs to spread the bared lips of her cunt wide open. Without any preamble, he shoved his muzzle into the delectable folds and began to gorge himself on her wet flesh.

She was delicious. He would never get enough. Repeatedly he fucked his tongue into her tight cunt, savoring the exquisite clench of her inner muscles and filling his mouth with her sweet juices.

He ate her with greed, carnal abandon, letting his fingers flick and tease her clit until her hips were bucking and she was crying out her need for release. When he felt the beginning spasms of her inner muscles tickling the sides of his tongue, he moved away from her tempting folds.

Forcing himself to his feet and turning her around was one of the hardest things he had ever done. She obviously thought he meant to fuck her now and was trying to wrap her arms and legs around him.

"Listen to me, Samantha." Caleb grabbed her wrist and held her still, waiting until her passion-dazed eyes focused on him. "Are you listening?"

"What?"

"When you agree to divorce your husband and submit to our authority, we will fulfill your every desire." Caleb let her go and stepped back. "Until then, you'll suffer the pain of your lust alone."

With that, he turned and walked away.

* * * *

Sam blinked her eyes, her mind slowly clearing as the fog of lust followed Caleb out of the shower and bathroom. For several minutes, she stood there, not believing that he had left her like this.

Growling, she wrenched herself away from the wall and stormed out of the shower. The cold air froze the droplets of water draining down her body, reminding Sam to wrap a towel around herself before she followed Caleb into the bedroom.

"What the hell are you doing?"

He was already dressed and sitting on the bed to lace up his boots.

"I'm going home."

"No the hell you are not!"

"Yes, I am."

"You are not leaving me like this. Now you get those damn clothes off and back into that shower." She jabbed a finger in the direction of the bathroom.

"Sorry, sweetheart. That's not going to happen."

"Is this some sort of sick game to you? Get the little woman all hot and bothered, then walk out on her?"

"Are you bothered, Samantha?"

"Damn you, yes. It's all your fault, so you better be planning on doing something about it."

"If you're willing to submit, then you are more than welcome to come home with me. JD and I will take care of all your aches."

"I'll never submit."

"Never is a long time to be hungry." Caleb shrugged into his jacket as he stood.

"I'll find somebody else. One man is as good as the next."

"Any man who dares to touch you will suffer a horrible fate." Caleb leaned in to drop a quick kiss on her cheek. Sam flinched backward, annoyed beyond belief.

"That's not my problem." She knew she was being a bitch, but could not to stop herself.

"Trust me, Samantha. None of them will be able to satisfy you. We've ruined you for any other man. You'll never find release without us. That's the fate of taking a mate."

With that grim promise, he walked away. Sam chased him all the way to the front door and watched with disbelieving eyes as the bastard strolled out into the night.

"Damn you, Caleb, get back here and fuck me!"

His response was to turn and hold out a hand for her. She knew exactly what he was asking for.

"Never!"

Chapter 9

Tuesday

The persistent ringing of the phone finally dissolved Sam's dreams into the reality of her lying alone in bed. Groaning as the harsh world made its reappearance, Sam burrowed deeper into her pillows.

Life sucks.

Her body was still strung out from the combined effects of Caleb's surprise visit and the erotic dreams that had haunted her.

Damn him and his superior attitude.

The arrogant jerk had been absolutely right. She had suffered from her unfulfilled desires, and no amount of masturbating had relieved her tension. Frogs would grow beards and crow before she went to JD or Caleb for relief.

She was a woman of strength, not a woman to kneel down and beg just because of a little ache in her pussy. She'd suffered from worse unfilled desires than this and overcome them all.

When their father had run off with another woman and left her siblings and her with a drunken mother, who had dropped out of high school to support the family? When their house had been foreclosed and their mother committed suicide, who had moved them into a new apartment and kept social services happy? It had been her.

When they had found out their father had remarried and was living comfortably, had she gone on bended knee to beg for money? No. She'd stood strong, and she would do the same with JD and Caleb.

She was not a plaything. Never a plaything, not with her body. In many ways, Sam had always considered her shorter, rounder frame a blessing. It had protected her from all the jerks that chased Vicky around just looking to score.

Almost none of them ever looked beyond Vicky's perfect body to see the intelligent, hardworking, strong woman she was. Men like that had never bothered Sam. That was probably why it took her so long to figure out what Bruce was really after.

After years of warning Vicky about men, she'd been the one who had gotten duped. Not that Bruce wanted her for her body. It was the money he was after. The fact that Bruce was handsome enough to model underwear should have tipped her off.

Of course, so were JD and Caleb. Sam's lips curled slightly as she considered her luck. She'd run from one werewolf lover into the arms of two. What were the odds of that?

That answer sent a cold shiver racing up her back. Did JD and Caleb know about the money? They had given her no indication of that. Neither had Bruce, but there was no overlooking the similarities.

Bruce was hot. He'd been insatiable in his supposed need for her. He hadn't babbled out some nonsense about mating, but then she wasn't supposed to have figured out what he really was. Instead he'd professed his love so eloquently, had she not discovered the truth in time, they'd already be married.

She'd trusted him and had taken everything he said at face value. She wasn't going to make the same mistake with JD and Caleb. They were all werewolves, and the possibility that they knew each other could not be underestimated. In fact, it explained quite bit about JD and Caleb's sudden, intense interest in her.

The whole situation left her feeling paranoid. What she needed was a normal man, a human one. There was a park full of those kinds of men around her. Most of them were good people. Some of them were actually hot. Surely, she could find one who would be willing to scratch her itch.

The phone began ringing again. For a moment, she debated ignoring it, but it would not stop making that god-awful racket. Shoving back the blanket, she yanked the receiver off the base.

"What?"

"Hey, sweetheart."

"Bruce?" Sam felt everything inside her still at the sound of his honeyed voice. How had he found her? Had JD and Caleb told him where she was? "How did you find me?"

"Come on, Sammy baby. Don't be like that." She could hear a slight puffing sound and knew he had his habitual cigarette hanging from his mouth.

"I don't want to talk to you."

"Sam, you have to tell me what's going on."

His reasonable tone made her feel even more unreasonable, and she responded crossly. "I left you a note. It said it all."

"It barely said anything."

"It said good-bye, and that's all I have to say."

"I love you." He managed to make the words sound so sincere it was hard not to believe them. "Doesn't that mean anything to you?"

"No."

"I'm not giving up, Samantha." There, his smooth demeanor slipped slightly. The hard edge to his words helped strengthen her resolve not to be suckered by this charmer again.

"I'm staying at the Land's End Motel. I'll be here until you're willing to talk."

"Then you'll die there waiting."

With that, she slammed the phone down. Already the day had worsened, and she had not even gotten out of bed yet. One thing might save this day. Sex, lots of hot, sweaty sex and she had thirty men to choose from. With that motivating her, Sam dragged herself off to the shower.

Forty minutes later, dressed in a skirt and fitted top, Sam decided to bypass breakfast, technically lunch given the hour, and zero in on her target. While bathing, she had thought of the perfect man to help her with her sexual frustration.

Chase was tall, well muscled, blond, and a nice guy. She was not sure if he would go for her. He normally had his pick of women, but she was not above using her authority to manipulate the issue.

Sam smiled at the thought. Here she was, after so many years of fighting poverty, of being at the mercy of her employers, about to go harass an employee. Not harass, Sam corrected herself, proposition. That sounded better. It sounded rich.

She found Chase just where she expected him to be. He was working alone, assembling several of the dirt bikes that had been delivered four days ago. His shirt was off, displaying a beautiful ripple of muscles as he flipped through his toolbox.

Sam was grateful that nobody else was around. Now that the moment had come, she felt her nerve weaken. She had never come on to a man before, and she felt strange, out of her element.

"Hey, Chase." Sam cringed at the high-pitched nervous tinge to her voice.

"Sam, what's up?" Chase cast her a quick look over his shoulder, his head already turning back toward the tools before he stopped and gave her a second look. "Headed somewhere?"

"No." Sam could feel her cheeks heating and was helpless to stop her fingers from pulling on the edge of her skirt. "I just felt like wearing something different today."

"You look nice."

Sam hesitated. He had said that she looked nice, but not in the way a man said it when he was bowled over. He sounded more like a man trying to be polite, and Sam felt herself teeter on the edge of turning and fleeing. She had come here with a single purpose, and as awkward and uncomfortable as things were, Sam refused to back down.

"So, Chase—"

"Nope."

"No? You don't even know what I'm about to ask you."

"You're going to ask me out."

"I was not." Damn her traitorous skin. Sam could feel her face flaming. This was a disaster, and the only way out was to deny and retreat.

"Yes, you were. Trust me, a man knows these things. If you had asked a week ago, I'd have said yes, but I'm not into getting slapped into cuffs."

"Cuffs? I wouldn't—"

"Not you, that Conan who was here yesterday. He made it quite clear that nobody touches what is his. No woman is worth being arrested before you even go on the first date."

"He wouldn't arrest you, and I'm not his."

Damn JD and his macho attitude.

"Well, I'm not going to tempt fate. So, I suggest you hold your nose and go back to the man. After all, you do like fucking him, right?"

"Just shut up, Chase," Sam snapped, completely humiliated. Even though she had been the one to shout that tidbit to the whole complex, Sam had been pissed and reacted rashly to JD's dominance.

Not wanting to continue this conversation a moment longer, Sam stepped out of the garage and stormed her way toward the main house. Slamming into the kitchen, she threw herself down onto one of the counter stools.

Vicky stood over the stove, stirring something that smelled like tomato sauce. Ignoring Vicky and the grumbling of her own stomach, Sam buried her face in her hands.

"Having that good a day, are you?"

"I hate my life." Sam spoke into her palms.

"No luck trolling for men, huh?"

"What?" Sam's head snapped up. "I'm not trolling for anything."

"Sam, you're wearing a skirt."

"So? What is the big deal about me in a skirt?"

"You hate skirts."

"I do not." At Vicky's disbelieving look, Sam rolled her eyes. "Maybe I'm reformed. Have you thought about that? I can change, you know?"

"Don't get snippy with me just because you're frustrated."

"Frustrated? I'm not frustrated. Who said anything about being frustrated?"

"Oh? So you took care of things after Caleb, was it? Refused to come back and fuck you?"

"What?" Sam's eyes widened as she felt her cheeks heat again. Was she going to spend all day blushing? "How do you know about that?"

"A little word of advice, this complex kind of echoes, especially when you shout things in the middle of the night."

"Oh God." Sam buried her face back into her hands. "Does everybody know?"

"My guess is yes," Vicky said unsympathetically. "You're becoming quite the talk of the park given your new habit of shouting everything for everybody to hear. Oh, don't look at me like that. It's not that bad."

"Yes, it is."

"You'll survive this. You've survived worse."

"My pride hasn't."

"Ah, Mike wouldn't let the guys take it too far." Vicky put down the spoon and came over to confront Sam over the kitchen counter.

"Can we please talk about something else?"

"Sure." Her tone was nonchalant. "You want to talk about Bruce?"

"No!" Sam slapped her hands down on the table. "Definitely not."

"The man drove twelve hours from southern Florida to see you."

"How did you know that?"

"He called here this morning."

"Did you give him my number?"

"Of course."

"Why? You know I don't want to talk to him." Sam's annoyance turned to anger as she glared at Vicky.

"I know you ran out on him."

"Vicky—"

"He really seems to care about you, and you just skipped out on him."

"It's none of your business. Just stay out of it and away from Bruce."

"I think you should at least hear him out."

"And you should really mind your own business."

"I just want you to be happy and break this habit of constantly running away from relationships."

Vicky's arms crossed over her chest, her eyes taking on that stubborn glint. This was one of her kid sister's best nagging points, and Sam was not in the mood to hear it again. She shoved her chair back.

"I've got better things to do with my time than obsess over men."

"They're not all like Dad."

That was it. Without a word to her sister, Sam stormed out of the kitchen. She wasn't going to hang around for the lecture. What the hell did Vicky know about their father?

She'd been eight the last time she had seen the man. There were other more pressing concerns than a man who had walked out on them fifteen years ago. Like keeping Bruce away from Vicky, Sam cringed at that thought.

Ah, hell. She was going to have to talk to that bastard after all.

Chapter 10

Sam saw the lights in her rearview mirror a second before the sirens sounded. A quick glance down at her speedometer told her that she was speeding.

Ah, the perfect day. I have a stalker, was humiliated by Chase, annoyed by my sister, and now a ticket.

That was not including the coming confrontation that she was planning to have with Bruce or the hangover she had from the confrontation with Caleb last night. She could only handle one problem at a time. The by-the-books cop was the first on her list.

As she watched a mammoth body unfold itself from the cruiser parked behind her, Sam's stomach dropped. It figured it would be him. No reasonable cop would pull a person over for going only eleven miles per hour over the limit.

By-the-books my ass.

Sam reached for her purse and was dousing herself in the horrid perfume when he opened her door. Coughing because of the perfume, Sam was grateful for the fresh air that rushed in. She was not as pleased when a hand clamped over her arm and she was unceremoniously yanked from the car.

* * * *

JD froze when he got a full look at her. God, she looked good enough to eat. Her hair was done to perfection, curling around her face to highlight her big green eyes, high cheekbones, and full lips.

Slowly his eyes traveled down over the skintight tank top she was wearing. It was red and had a deep V-neck that showed off an ample amount of cleavage. The skirt was a little looser, while still showing off the perfect flare of her hips.

It ended too soon, barely covering what needed to be legally covered. The little black heels she was wearing helped accentuate the beautiful curves of her calves. JD swallowed hard as the blood rushed downward to his cock.

Not even the overly sweet stench of flowers that had enveloped her could deter his angry flesh from rising. It did help keep his mind clear and aware that this was not an outfit a woman wore unless she had something special in mind, something like a man.

* * * *

Sam swallowed hard. There was no doubt of the direction his thoughts were going from the darkening of his features. She felt her muscles tighten as her heart started pumping blood too fast through her body.

God, the man was making her hot with just a look. Sam groaned silently to herself. Her response to him was out of proportion. It was abnormal. It had to be thanks to Caleb leaving her in a simmer last night.

I wonder if he knows about Caleb's edict.

What was she thinking? He could be in cahoots with Bruce. No matter how wet he made her panties, she had to remember she didn't know him, didn't like him, and couldn't trust him.

Sam's concerns jackknifed in a new direction when his eyes finally lifted. There was no doubt she was in trouble. A cowardly part of her told her to flee, to get back in her car and get away as fast as possible.

Another part of her told her to go in the opposite direction, right into the eye of the storm that was slowly building between them. Whatever he did to her, the hated truth was she would enjoy it.

A car went whizzing by. The sudden sound and movement broke the moment. Sam remembered why she didn't even like this man. He was an overgrown, arrogant jackass.

"What the hell do you think you are doing?" they demanded at the same time. They glared at each other for a moment, sizing up the opponent.

"What are you up to, Samantha?"

"That's none of your damn business. Why did you pull me over?"

"You were speeding. What are you doing dressed up like that?"

"What do you think I'm doing dressed like this? You want me to run around naked? And what cop pulls a car over for going eleven miles over the limit?"

"A cop you pissed off with your completely disrespectful ways! Now don't tempt me, Samantha. Tell me the man's name."

"What man? Who said anything about a man?"

"That's one."

"One what? Jesus, I don't know what the hell you're babbling about."

"You've earned one punishment. Now tell me his name."

Sam stilled. She'd earned punishment already, and they had not even been talking for a minute. The idea made her pussy pulse and weep as her mind reeled at the thought.

"I don't know what you are talking about." Sam bluffed, waving a dismissive hand in his direction. "I was just headed into town for some groceries."

"That's two."

"I'm not lying. Why would you think that I would bother to lie?"

"It's the middle of February, and you're dressed like a streetwalker."

"Ahhh! How dare you! A street—"

"Women only dress like that and speed down the road when they're on their way to meet some man at a seedy motel for an afternoon of illicit sex."

Sam flinched. He had it right except for the sex part.

"I'll kill him."

"There is no man." At his hard look, Sam could read the statement in his eyes. That was three. Well, if she was damned anyway… "Fine. I'm going to meet my husband."

"Caleb mentioned your marital status to me. Divorcée or widow, the choice is yours."

"What?" Sam could feel her eyes bulging out. "You're not seriously saying that."

"I don't share what is mine."

"You're a cop, for the love of God!"

"That just means I wouldn't get caught."

"You're insane." This whole conversation was insane. Everything about this place was nutty.

"Your choice."

"Listen here, you backwoods Neanderthal. Whether I divorce my husband or not is not your decision." Sam jabbed a finger into his chest to emphasize her point.

"Make your choice." JD did not flinch away from her finger.

"Not that it is any of your business, but to spare blood from being shed, I filed divorce papers on my husband months ago. Happy now?" Well that wrapped up that lie, and she was back to where she started.

"Far from it." JD grabbed her wrist. "Let's go."

"I'm not going anywhere with you." Sam latched on to her open door with her free hand and held on with all her strength.

JD turned, pinning her into the door. Having his hard heat pressing against hers sent her body into overload, and Sam was hard-pressed to keep her legs sturdy beneath her.

"Let go of the door, Samantha, or I'll strip you naked right here myself."

"You wouldn't." Sam's head was tilted all the way back so she could glare up into his eyes. He leaned down until his lips were almost touching hers.

"Wouldn't I?" The threat sounded like a caress given in that low, husky whisper that heated all Sam's senses.

"This is kidnapping."

"So? Sue me. Right now you're going to let go of that door and come with me."

"Why should I?"

"Because I'm going to make you feel really, really good. I can do that back at my house or here in the middle of the road."

His hands came to lend credence to his threat. They settled on her waist. His thumbs slipped under the edge of her shirt to softly rub circles on the sides of her stomach.

It was a small touch, but it had a devastating effect on her libido. If Sam didn't find a way to get him to step back and stop touching her, she'd be the one stripping herself naked.

"I won't ask again."

"I'm not a pet for you to order about."

Despite her words, her body was melting under his touch. Her breasts were swelling, her nipples hardening, her pussy creaming, all begging for his attention. If she did not find a way to stop him, he would tame her into a pet.

JD did not respond to her comment, at least not with words. Sam shrieked as cold air suddenly washed against her bared chest. The sheriff had shoved her shirt straight up and ripped open the front clasp of her bra, leaving her breasts exposed for all to see.

Her hand instinctively flew to the hem of her shirt, pooled around her neck now, to shove it back down, but JD's head got in the way.

* * * *

JD bent to take one of her perfect, rosy nipples into his mouth. He heard her squeal at the sudden pressure as he gently sucked the little nub into his mouth. Moving from breast to breast, he lapped at her tender tips, sucking them until she stirred restlessly against him.

Her hands clenched his hair, holding him to her. JD growled, pleased with her capitulation. The small act had his cock aching to be buried inside her despite the horrid stench she'd drowned herself in.

JD closed his eyes and fought to slow down before he did strip her naked and fuck her right on the side of a public road. Despite his threat to do just that, it would not be in either of their best interests.

She flexed her fingers, her short nails scraping against his scalp, urging him to continue. JD growled again, this time with the ferocity of the wolf as the beast came alive inside him.

Forcing a knee between hers, his hand slid up to find her panties damp with her need. He ripped the offending material out of his way. Once they had Samantha trained, she would know better than wear anything that blocked their access to her sweet, delectable cunt.

Her thighs were slick with her desire, and without hesitating, he slid three fingers deep into her clenching sheath. Samantha cried out, her hips bucking and forcing his fingers deeper until she had taken them all the way in.

"Oh God, yes." She began to hump his fingers with carnal abandon.

JD groaned. He needed to get her off the street now before he undid his pants and pushed his cock into her eager little pussy. Once he started fucking her, he knew that nothing would stop him, not even the whole town lining up to watch.

The wolf snarled with frustration as the man forced his hand to withdraw. Samantha's eyes were wide, dazed with lust, her cheeks flushed, her lips rosy. She was stunning, so incredibly sexy, he could barely believe his luck that she was his.

Before the lust could clear and she found the strength to protest, he hefted her over his shoulder. Kicking her car door closed with his foot, he carried her off to the cruiser.

* * * *

Sam sat in the patrol car, silent and shivering, as JD sped toward their destination. She had little doubt where they were headed or what they would be doing once they got there. She knew she should protest, but the fight had drained away from her, leaving an array of emotions in its place.

Desire, fear, confusion, Sam did not know what she was feeling anymore. The only thing she knew for certain was, whether her mind approved, her body was eagerly anticipating the moment they would be alone together in that big house of his.

Right or wrong, the way JD and Caleb treated her turned her on like nothing ever had. Her body was so excited, Sam would not be surprised if she left a wet spot on his vinyl seat.

The only thing that could excite her more was to know that Caleb would be there as well. As great as the sex had been with each man individually, nothing compared to what it felt like to be taken by both men at the same time.

Sam shuddered and closed her eyes. The bottom line here was no matter how much she enjoyed sex with JD and Caleb, she had to remember that it was only that. She could never truly trust them, so there was no hope of any kind of relationship.

Even if they had turned her into a dog, she would end up being a lone wolf. There was no time left to debate the matter, to save herself from the destiny that seemed to be creeping up on her. The doors of the double garage closed behind them, and Sam knew that there was no escaping now.

* * * *

JD could smell Samantha's apprehension. He did not feel like chasing after her any more than he already had. Latching on to her wrist, he dragged her across the bench seat.

Samantha didn't struggle as he pulled her through the kitchen door and up the stairs. JD did not halt in the bedroom, but continued straight into the bathroom. When he turned and swung her into the shower stall, Samantha finally resisted.

He blocked her exit, holding her in the tiled enclosure with one hand while the other flicked on the water. Samantha shrieked as the rain-head fixture instantly doused her, clothes and all, in a steady stream.

"Damn it, JD!" She whipped her hair out of her face. "That was completely uncalled for."

"You needed a shower." JD grunted, backing up as she began to tear her clothes off. It was a lovely sight to be sure, and he relaxed against the vanity to enjoy the show.

"You could have let me take my clothes off first!"

"Perhaps you'll think twice before dousing yourself with that god-awful perfume again."

"You just don't like it because it stops you from using that musk thing you produce." She flung her wet shirt at him.

"Are you back on that?" JD dodged her shirt and the skirt that followed it. "I thought Caleb settled that argument last night."

"We settled no—"

"Leave the shoes on."

She looked sexy as hell wearing nothing but her high heels. The provocative image had his cock reminding him that it was still waiting. It was getting tired of waiting.

"What?" Samantha blinked at him. "I'm not wearing high heels in the shower."

With that proclamation, she kicked her shoes off and at him. JD growled, annoyed and excited by her show of defiance. She snickered in response to his sound. Turning her back on him, she tossed her head as if she were not the least bit concerned about his anger or the fact that she was completely naked and vulnerable to him.

The dismissal had his hands ripping at his shirt. If she decided to underestimate him, provide him with an opportunity, he would be glad to show her just how vulnerable she was. With his eyes trained on her sexy backside, he quickly divested himself of all his clothes. That ass was built to be filled, but right now JD wanted to pound into a different tight channel.

He knew he would find her pussy wet and ready. The sweet scent of her desire tinged the steam rising out of the shower and taunted his senses. It was Samantha's own mating musk, and it was just as powerful of an aphrodisiac as any there ever were.

JD did not bother with a slow, sensual seduction or even a second of foreplay. Samantha had forfeited the right to demand those when she had turned her back on him. Without a sound, he stepped into the shower and fitted his hands to her hips.

"What are you…Hey!"

Samantha shrieked as he forced her to bend with a hand on her back. A thigh shoved between hers pushed her legs wide enough for him to fit between. The position left her pussy exposed.

The odor of her arousal wafted up, strong and mesmerizing. JD looked down, admiring the way her spine curved into her ass and the pink folds beneath. They were, as he knew they would be, swollen and wet with desire.

Not hesitating a moment longer, he fitted the head of his cock to her opening. He heard Samantha's indrawn breath a second before he impaled her with one strong stroke. She squealed under the impact, her inner muscles clamping down on his heated length.

JD snarled. Nothing had ever felt this good. This heaven was all he would know the rest of his life. His lips pulled back in a snarl of carnal triumph as he began riding his mate fast and hard.

The feel of her small human channel pulsing around him, milking him with every stroke, drove him into frenzy. He pounded into her harder, deeper, her cries not piercing the single-minded focus driving him to fuck.

Then she was screaming as the tight fist of her sheath convulsed around him. The pressure was too much. It pulled his seed from his body. JD tipped his head back and let out his own roar of satisfaction as the mind-shattering orgasm washed over him in a lava-hot eruption that left him feeling strong and powerful.

* * * *

Well, damn. The man certainly knows how to end an argument.

Sam panted underneath him. Her hot cheek plastered to the cool tile kept her anchored in a world that threatened to spin away with her. Her body felt weak and her mind tired. All she really wanted to do was curl up and take a nap.

That was apparently not what JD had in mind. As he stepped back, his still-hard dick sliding free of her body, he lifted her off her feet. He dried her off with quick, rough motions that made her sigh.

It was probably wrong of her, but she couldn't help but compare JD to Caleb. Caleb had been gentler when he toweled her off, turning the strokes into caresses. Caleb was also a little more into foreplay, drawing out the moment of passion.

Sam sighed. JD might have a different style of loving than Caleb, but her response was just as intense. Caleb might be a tender lover, but her body ignited at JD's urgent touch.

It wasn't her body that was the problem, Sam admitted. It was her heart. As much as she knew JD wanted her, he made her feel like a means to an end. He treated her like she was a good fuck, one he couldn't get enough of.

The feeling chafed, and Sam admonished herself for caring. This wasn't about a relationship. Her only interest in these men was the pleasure they could give her, nothing more.

Sam was pulled from her worries when JD dropped her on her feet. With a hard look, he silently commanded that she stay. The order grated on her nerves.

"I'm not a dog, you know."

As defiant as she felt, Sam still stayed. Running would get her nowhere. Not only was she limited in where she could go, naked as she was, but Sam was sure that JD would catch her before she even made it to the door. That would only make her appear weaker when she needed to present a strong front.

JD did not bother to respond, but returned carrying a bottle of cologne. Sam recognized the brand as being a popular, well-known scent. She watched him uncap the bottle and was mildly surprised when, instead of putting the scent on himself, he dabbed generous amounts on her.

She blinked under the strong smell, immediately recognizing it as part of the volatile mixture that JD himself smelled of. The smell did funny things to her insides, warming her and relaxing her muscles.

"What was that for?"

The arrogant man still did not respond. She watched him warily as he put the bottle back into the drawer and turned to the wardrobe. Her vow not to run was tested as he opened the ornate wooden doors.

The morning she had made her escape, she had looked through those wardrobes in her search for clothes. What she had found had been a large assortment of sex toys. The variety was so immense, she did not even know what most of them were.

At the time, she had vowed that she was not going to hang around long enough to find out. Her eyes darted toward the door. She wondered if she had time to make it to safety while his back was turned on her.

Chapter 11

"Don't bother." JD's hard tone drew her eyes back to him. He was walking back toward her with several lengths of black fabric in his hand.

"I would just have to hunt you down, and that would mean more punishments."

"Punishments? Whatever for?"

"Pay close attention, Samantha," JD instructed as he stopped in front of her. "You have been disobedient, flippant, and outright combative. These are not traits that I will tolerate in my mate."

"Well then I suggest you go find an—"

"Silence!"

Sam snapped her mouth closed and glared at him. He might have the upper hand at this moment, but it wouldn't last. When their roles were reversed, she'd get her revenge.

"Good. Now from this moment on, you will obey my every command. Do you understand?"

Sam nodded, taking perverse pleasure in not giving him the satisfaction of a verbal agreement. From the narrowing of his eyes, she knew that her tactic had worked. He made no comment, accepting her small act of defiance.

"Give me your wrists."

She merely raised an eyebrow at his waiting hand, not bothering to respond to that command in any other way. JD sighed, his lips tightening with displeasure.

"Samantha, you've already earned four punishments. Do you wish to add to it and spend the whole night in suffering, or would you rather spend it in more pleasant pursuits?"

When he put it like that, Sam had to agree that as much as she liked being spanked, she didn't want to spend the whole night bent over his knees. Why was she bothering to fight anyway?

The softening of her pussy, the telltale moisture dampening the tops of her thighs told her what she really wanted. With a sigh, she conceded defeat and lifted her hands to his.

He made short work of binding them together with the ties he'd brought. The action didn't surprise her. She had assumed that was his intent. Sam was a little shocked when he lifted her.

A moment later, she felt the cold slide of metal over her hands. When he released her, she realized he had dangled her from a hook. Hanging her from the ceiling, JD surveyed her for a moment before reaching for the hook. He twisted the fastener, turning it so that she rotated down toward the floor.

Slowly he lowered her until her feet were barely touching the wood beneath. She was forced to stand on her tiptoes, a fact she could see clearly now that she was facing the full-length mirror set into the wall. Sam swallowed as she took in her predicament.

The sight sent thrills down her spine. Her eyes darted toward JD, watching him for signs of what came next. Whatever it was, it required something from the wardrobe full of playthings. Sam waited tensely as he looked through his collection. When he finally turned, she could see in the mirror what he had selected.

Sam felt her mouth go dry even as her pussy pulsed. Despite her body's already excited response to the harness he was holding, Sam suddenly rethought her decision to accept this situation without complaint.

"Uh, can I—"

"Silence." JD smacked her hard on the ass. The blow sent her up, off her toes, and for a moment, she swung. "You are not allowed to speak without permission. Do you understand?"

"Yes," Sam squeaked, finding the floor again with her toes.

"Yes, what?" he demanded, his hands sliding around to hold her tight against him.

"Yes, JD?"

She tried to think of what he wanted, but with his breath tickling her ears and his hand resting mere inches from her pussy, her mind could only focus on what she wanted him to do. It had nothing to do with the harness he was holding against her stomach.

"You're going to need a lot of training."

She saw his smile reflected in the mirror. Even in reflection, it looked arrogant, satisfied. Sam opened her mouth to respond to that comment, but his eyes narrowing made her close it. No way was she going to be that rash and end up with even more punishment.

"Tell me, Samantha, can you smell the musk?"

"No."

"No, what?"

"No, JD."

"If I have to remind you of that again, I'm going to punish you. Understand?"

"Yes, JD."

"You can't smell the musk, only the cologne I put on you, right?"

"Yes, JD."

"Then you know that they way you respond now is your own response, not forced or drugged. Right?"

"Yes, JD."

"So tell me, what are you feeling?"

"Feeling?"

"Your nipples are red and puckered."

One hand moved up to fondle her tender tips. Sam moaned at the touch, her back arching to thrust her swollen flesh into his palms. He chuckled, pleased with her response.

"Are you going to deny that you want my touch here?"

"No, JD."

"You want it elsewhere, don't you?"

"Yes, JD."

"Where? Tell me."

"I…my…" The words would not come out of her mouth.

"Tell me, Samantha."

"Lower."

She compromised her need with her dignity, but he was not willing to accept that. She shrieked again as another blow landed on her tender backside. The shot of pain blossomed into sparkles of pleasure.

"Every time you deny me, you will be punished. Now tell me where you want my touch."

"My pussy." Sam closed her eyes as the words fell out of her mouth, unable to take the image in the mirror anymore.

"Are you wet?"

"Yes, JD." Sam could barely hear her whispered response, and she tensed, expecting another spank. Apparently, he was satisfied, though.

"Then beg me to touch you."

"Please, JD."

"I can't hear you."

"Please. I need you to touch me."

"We have a lot of work ahead of us, sweetheart. But don't worry. We'll get there."

Sam was not sure what that meant. To hell with him. Since when did she care about pleasing a man who had her dangling from a hook, literally?

The question was lost as he knelt. Lifting her legs, he instructed her widen her stance. Sam was not sure how to do that with only her tiptoes resting on the floor, but tried to obey.

JD took over, forcing her to bend her legs and rest her weight on his thighs as he knelt beneath her. Sam's face flamed at the view he must have, but that worry lost as he gave her a quick lick through her slit, letting his tongue tease her clit.

Oh yeah, I could get used to this position.

Sam groaned, letting her head fall back and her weight sink down deeper onto his legs. Despite her invitation, he stopped the teasing caress of his tongue. Sam whimpered, wanting him to continue.

"Open your eyes, Samantha. I want you to watch."

She obeyed him, but it took a moment for the image in the mirror to come into focus. She shivered, half-afraid and half-excited, as she watched him lube up the butt-plug end of the harness. When he turned, lube in hand, toward her ass, she could not stop from tensing.

Her reaction earned her another smack, this one directly on her pussy. The stinging blow made her cry out as her whole pussy vibrated with the impact. The sensation was magnified as he used first two and then three thick fingers to spread the lubrication deep into her ass.

The sensation bordered on painful, her body still too new to this type of penetration. That did not stop or even slow JD's actions. Sam held her breath as she watched him slip the harness into place.

The smooth, rounded head of the plug pushed against the tight ring of muscles at the entrance to her rear. Sam flinched as he slowly worked the toy past the puckered flesh, gently pushing it into her until it filled her ass.

Sam had to bite down on her lip to keep from moaning. Whether in pain or pleasure, she was not sure. The sensations rioting through her body were too much for her distinguish. What started as pain echoed back as pleasure, leaving her confused and uncertain.

In his usual style, JD was not giving her any time to adjust to the strange feeling of having a plug up her ass. He aligned the thick rubber cock at the front of the harness with the opening to her cunt. There was no slow penetration this time.

JD thrust the toy deep and hard into her, making Sam scream out at the sudden intrusion. It was too much, being filled in both places. She was stretched to her limit and so close to coming, all she needed was a little movement.

JD slid out from under her, making her close her legs to remain standing. The positioned tightened both her channels, making the toys feel bigger, thicker, and she moaned at the pressure.

Her ass throbbed, and her pussy pulsed. Both wanted the same thing, a release from the tension that was winding its way through her body. It felt good, erotic and naughty. She had tumbled headfirst into the sexual abyss he had ripped open at her feet and no longer knew who she was. She no longer even cared.

JD fastened the harness tight around her waist to keep both toys secure in their positions deep within her. Pausing behind her, he met her eyes in the mirror. His were steady and dark with promise. Hers were watery and glazed with lust.

"You may not come without my permission. Do you understand?"

"Yes."

A sudden sharp explosion across her ass had her screaming as her body bucked and writhed on the toys. The normal burn of the slap was intensified by the plug filling her ass, making her inner muscles ripple with pained pleasure that vibrated down to her pussy, making it clench on the dildo.

"What was that?"

"What?" Sam could not focus on his words.

"A lot of work. Well, we'll get to those punishments later."

"P...pun—"

Another smack and another cut off her stumbling question. The blows came harder, faster until every cell in her body began to detonate. Sam screamed and bucked as her pussy and ass squeezed the fake cocks.

Still he did not relent. All thoughts of punishments or rules and orders slipped from her mind as the tension broke, her body igniting into an inferno of devastating ecstasy.

When the world finally righted itself and her heart stopped trying to pound its way past her ribs, Sam became aware of JD watching her. His arms were crossed over his chest, his face drawn in taut lines of disapproval.

"You came without permission."

Sam did not have to guess why he was so upset. She lowered her eyes, bowing her head in the hopes that would appease him.

"Samantha?"

"Yes, JD. I came without permission, but this is all new to—"

"No excuses. It is obvious that you are new to this, just as obvious that you require intensive training."

Damn, there was that word again. Sam didn't know which was worse, the way he threatened constant punishment or bandied the word training about. She had a feeling they both meant the same thing.

* * * *

JD kept his smile locked away. He could see the worry on her face and guessed its reason. Samantha would no longer be able to hide behind the mating musk. She knew now that her response to him was her own.

His secret smile disappeared for real when he heard the tingling sound of his cell phone. With a growl of annoyance, he went into the bathroom and fished the small gadget out of his pants.

"What?"

It was the worst of news. A shoot-out had taken place down at the old Barber Shop, which was not actually a barbershop. It was where the local gangster wannabes gathered to boom their music, talk trash, and deal some drugs.

His deputies spent a lot of time patrolling the place, but since the little soda shop didn't have a rule against loitering, there wasn't much they could do until after bad shit happened.

Of course, normally there weren't any problems until nightfall. The crack dealers and potheads must have gotten an early start to their day. After assuring dispatch he would be headed that way as soon as he dressed, JD disconnected.

JD didn't bother putting on his clothes as he walked back toward Samantha. Their plans were going to be delayed, but he couldn't just leave her hanging from the ceiling. Instead, he decided to start her first training session.

It would leave her primed for when he got home. Lifting her off the hook, he rid her of the harness and carried her to the bed. It took him less than a minute to tie her ankles to the posts and her wrists to the headboard.

Intentionally he diverted his eyes from the beautiful body on display. The image of her gorgeous curves was already burned into his mind. His cock was hard and causing him pain, but there wasn't enough time for a quickie.

Finding the butterfly and vibrator that hooked up to an automatic timer, he carried the gear back to the bed. Setting the timer unit down on the nightstand, he sat down beside Samantha.

She was watching him with anxious eyes. JD turned his gaze toward the naked pussy spread wide for his pleasure. Her pink nether lips were split open, revealing her weeping passage and the little nub of her clit.

He couldn't help but to take a quick taste. She jerked beneath his tongue. Her back arched as much as her binds would allow, offering her pussy up for more of his caress.

JD smiled. When he returned, he would make a feast out of her. For now, he needed to get moving. Wasting no more time teasing his mate, JD quickly slid the vibrator into her.

Samantha gasped and wiggled as he worked. Her small movements did not slow him down as he finished attaching the butterfly and setting it so that it covered her clit.

"This will be your first lesson, Samantha." JD stood. "Hopefully when I return, you'll be able to control your climaxes."

"Wha…"

Her question ended in a shriek as the vibrator and butterfly clicked on. JD watched her writhe, for a moment, mesmerized by the sight. With a shake of his head, he went to the bathroom.

When he returned fully clothed, she was panting, twisting against her binds. Her eyes widened at his state of dress.

"You're leaving me?"

"Gotta go to work." JD finished fastening his gun belt.

"But…"

JD saw the tears gathering in her eyes and felt his heart kick over. Crossing to her side, he dropped a chaste kiss on her forehead.

"Don't worry, sweetheart. I'll be back shortly."

"You can't leave me like this."

Her eyes pleaded with him, and JD was hard-pressed not to give in to her demand. That fact annoyed him. Even if she was his mate, she was just a woman. He'd left many women tied to his bed and never felt a moment's doubt.

"You'll be safe here." JD gave in to the awkward need to reassure her and dropped another quick kiss before standing. "Caleb will be home shortly."

Not risking another look in her direction, JD walked out of the room. His prediction about Caleb turned out to be truer than he had suspected. His twin was walking in through the kitchen door. JD paused long enough to tell him that Samantha was there and in what condition he had left her.

"You left her like that?" Caleb gave him a disbelieving look.

"What?"

"That's just a little cold."

"You've left women tied to the bed before."

"Samantha is not other women. She's our mate."

"Whatever. It would be nice if you would let her stay like that for at least a half hour. Perhaps then she'll learn her lesson."

"Yeah, yeah, yeah." Caleb waved him away. "Perhaps I'll go sit with her."

"Can you sit and not touch?" JD raised a dubious brow at that.

"Don't you have work to do?"

"Don't you have any control?"

"Tell me something, JD. Did you fuck her before you tied her to the bed?" Caleb taunted his brother.

"I'll be back shortly." JD yanked open the kitchen door.

"Don't rush on my account," Caleb called after him.

Chapter 12

Caleb didn't agree with JD's handling of their mate, but his brother had a point. Samantha did need to learn a few lessons. JD had also been right about what would happen if Caleb went upstairs.

So he settled down onto the couch, turned on the TV, and had a beer and a few slices of pizza. He checked his watch every five minutes until twenty-five had passed. He reasoned that five minutes here or there really didn't make a difference.

Taking the steps two at a time, he rushed up to the prize waiting for him strapped to the bed. Caleb remembered his promise to Samantha to leave her wanting unless she agreed to the mating. It would be cruel to adhere to that now.

JD had set her up to be in great need. It would be ungentlemanly to leave her in that condition. More than ungentlemanly, it would be inhumane not to ease to his mate's condition.

Besides, however JD had gotten her to the house and strapped to the bed, Caleb was willing to bet that it had not helped their standing with Samantha. She was probably already adding more negatives to her already low opinion of them.

He had to do something to reverse that.

* * * *

Sam couldn't tell how long she'd been tied up. Time became irrelevant as waves of pleasure ebbed and flowed through her. She was at the mercy of the tides of rapture, spurred to the edge by the torturous toy JD had left her impaled on.

Every time, when she was sure she could stand it no more, the vibrator would stop, leaving her panting with need. If she had the energy, she would have been enraged that he had done this to her. At first, she'd fought her bounds, desperately trying to escape the ceaseless frustration.

It had been pointless, and her strength had failed her when the butterfly lit up her clit with another round of spasms that echoed throughout her body. All too soon, it stopped, and she was left on the brink once again.

Just when she was sure she could stand it no more, she heard footsteps in the hall. Tilting her head, she watched as Caleb walked in. He came slowly toward the bed, his eyes sweeping over her body in heated strokes. She could see the bulge grow in his slacks until his pants looked deformed they were so tented.

"Please." Sam's voice broke. There was no breath left in her lungs or moisture in her mouth for more.

"Please what, sweetheart?" Caleb settled onto the edge of the bed.

"Make it stop. Please."

"Stop." Caleb appeared to be considering it. "I can only do that if you've learned your lesson."

"I have." Sam nodded enthusiastically, hoping that he would do something soon. By her mental counting, she had just moments before the torment started over again.

"Why don't we test your newfound skill? Then I'll know if more training is needed."

Sam didn't respond. She would pass this test. Then when she had the opportunity, she would reverse their roles. That was the only thing they had gained with this cruel little trick they'd played on her, her vow of vengeance. Now, though, was not the time to bicker.

Silently she watched as he turned off the timer. She sighed, relaxing. Her moment of relief was short-lived as he moved to settle himself between her legs. She was not fooled into thinking it was just to remove the toys from her pussy. The slow slide of the vibrator past her sensitive inner muscles had her grinding her teeth to keep from letting the sensation push her over the edge.

He discarded the toys on the side of the bed. Sam waited, her anticipation growing as he remained still. Her suspense was ended when she felt the warm brush of breath against her overstimulated pussy.

Before she could draw breath, a warm and soft tongue licked her. With long, slow strokes, it lapped at her cream, delving into her core before flicking up to rasp against her clit.

Sam fought for breath, fighting back the need to come. She couldn't orgasm. If she did, he'd probably leave her here again, and that was not acceptable. Even as she fought her own internal mental battle, her body responded, arching into the talented tongue slowly trying to drive her insane with slow, deep explorations that sent bolts of pure energy rocketing through her body.

"Please, can I come?"

"No, not yet, sweetheart."

* * * *

Samantha cried out as Caleb lifted away from her body. He felt the fast pounding of his heart echoed in the throbbing pulse of his cock. As he kissed his way up her body, he had to fight to only teasingly flick at her breasts instead of devouring them as his mouth watered to do.

"More," she whispered, causing his heart to clench as she rubbed against his erection. His cock jerked, hungry for the feel of her tight little channel squeezing around him, bathing him in the hot wash of her liquid desire.

"Samantha," Caleb growled in warning. "Damn it!"

So much for teasing her and testing the limits of her new skill. She was shredding his control with every grind of her pelvis. If he didn't get out of his clothes now, he wasn't going to make it out of them in time.

Caleb would be damned if he was going to disgrace himself that way. It was the hardest thing he'd ever done, but he managed to get out of the bed with no damage done.

* * * *

For a second, she feared she had pushed him too hard and instead of the relief she needed, she was about to get more punishment. Caleb was not JD. She let out a pent-up breath as she watched him shed his clothing.

Surely when he was done undressing, he would take care of the ache causing her pussy to clench painfully.

"I'm going to release your wrists now. You're to remain still. No trying anything."

"I'll be still."

He undid her ankles first and then made short work of the binds around her wrists. As her arms were lowered, she groaned in pain as blood came rushing into her limbs. Rough hands gently massaged their way from her wrists to her shoulders.

Caleb's lips followed in the wake of his hands. Nibbling his way along her flesh, he paused to tickle the sensitive inside of her wrists, her elbows. Sam sighed, enjoying the tender, gentle attention.

Her sigh turned to a groan as his lips nipped over her shoulder, pausing to lick at the bite mark there.

"Do you know how hard it makes me to see my mark on you?"

To prove his point, Caleb shifted, pressing his thick, hot length against her thigh. Sam squirmed, rubbing her leg against his cock to try to entice him to hurry. She was past the point of foreplay.

Her pussy was drenched in cream, her flesh so hot it amazed her that she did not burn him with a touch. All she wanted was to feel him filling her, stretching her wide as he rode her hard and fast.

He lifted his head. One hand cupped her cheek, while a finger on the other went to work on her breasts, the needy tips puckering painfully beneath his teasing touch. The rolling, pulling motions drove her insane, and she arched her back, forcing her sensitive nipples deeper into his palm.

"Do you like that, baby?"

"Please, Caleb."

A part of her secretly wished it were JD with her. He only seemed to have two settings, pussy eating and fucking. Either one would be welcomed right now, just as long as he didn't stop.

"Take my hands, baby." He pulled her fingers from where they were clenching the bedsheets. "Show me how you want to be touched."

Sam felt wild with her need. There was only one touch that would soothe the flames burning through her. Gripping his hands, she pulled them both to her pussy.

Without hesitation, she guided three fingers into her drenched sheath and began fucking herself on them. She ground his other palm into her clit so that, with each thrust of her hips, she rubbed herself against his callused skin.

It felt good, and all too soon, she was mewing as her climax tightened up on her. At the last minute, she remembered.

"Can I come?"

"Not yet, baby." Caleb pulled his hands free and rolled over onto his back. "Mount me, sweetheart. Take what you need."

She growled her acceptance and quickly moved on top of him. Without a word, Caleb held his cock up, lining it up so she could lower herself down his length. God, he was so thick, so hard, it was a tight, perfect fit.

Sam clenched her teeth, fighting the urge to buck, impaling herself deeper on him. When she was sure she had her body under control, she opened her eyes. He was staring at her breasts, the golden globes hanging inches from his face.

She whimpered softly, bending down to offer him more of her sweet flesh. Sizzling heat speared through her as his rough tongue flicked over her nipple before sucking it past the hard scrape of his teeth and into the hot confines of his mouth.

Electricity shot out from her breast, lighting every nerve ending in her spine before exploding in her pussy. She felt herself tighten around his cock. The full feeling intensified, and she couldn't stop her hips from rotating, enjoying the electrifying spasms her motions caused.

It felt so good, better than anything. Sam closed her eyes and rocked against him again. Faster, harder, her motions quickly escalated until she was out of control, riding him with rough, hurried motions.

Caleb was no victim of her aggression. His hands came to help steady her, his hips thrusting upward, embedding himself deeper inside her.

Sam felt poised to burst, her body spiraling toward a climax made more intense by the agony of holding back, waiting for his permission. Her teeth sank into her lip, the small pain helping her to win the battle.

"Caleb!" she shouted, knowing she could no longer hold on to the leash of her passions. "Can I come?"

"Yes, baby. Come for me."

Sam exploded around him, her fingers biting into his shoulders as her body lit up like a Fourth of July firework display. Weeping from the power of her orgasm, Sam could not stop her body from riding him through to the very last sensation.

"Oh God. Samantha!" he roared a moment before she felt his hot seed flood her pussy.

She slumped down on top of him. Her sweaty forehead made a soft splat as it settled against his equally wet shoulder. Sam was done.

Her exhausted muscles ached to the point where they might be permanently damaged. Her heart certainly was. If the theory that a heart only had so many pumps in it for a lifetime was correct, she had surely burned off a few years in the last few minutes.

The mush of her mind could not be bothered with that worry. It held only one thought: sleep.

* * * *

"You all right, sweetheart?" Caleb asked as his wits came back to him.

"Sleep now."

"A little food and you'll be rejuvenated." Caleb couldn't help but touch her. He reached out to gently stroke her side.

"No." Sam flinched away from him, sounding grumpy enough to bite.

"Did I wear you out, little one?" Caleb grinned, more than pleased with her complaint.

"Don't sound so smug. Your brother did all the hard work."

"Ah, that's my Samantha, back in fine form." Caleb chuckled before pulling her up into a sitting position. Nothing she said could dampen his mood. "Come on, let's get a shower. Then I'll take you out to dinner."

That got her to open one eye. She squinted at him as her face bunched up in a pout.

"Considering everything, don't you think it's a little late to go on a date?"

"Up."

Chapter 13

The Firehouse was a small brick building tucked between the post office and a gas station. It fit the stereotype of a small southern diner with its fluorescent lights and maroon vinyl booths worn and cracked by age.

The pattern on the linoleum floor had long been eroded to a mere shadow by time. The walls, once white, were now a dingy yellow. The Firehouse didn't rely on its décor to draw customers in. The heavy scent of fried foods was all it needed to pull Sam past the door.

The place was packed full of people, and all the booths were taken leaving only tables open. There were precious few of those, and Caleb chose one that was in the middle of the restaurant. It should have been a thirty-second trip from door to table, but it turned into nearly five minutes as people constantly stopped them to greet Caleb.

Sam felt uncomfortable and conspicuous on Caleb's arm. It was obvious that he was very popular, and she had a feeling that was the motive for his sudden desire to take her out. He was staking a very public claim.

While Sam did not know the finer points of werewolves and their social behavior, she knew something about men and dogs. Both liked to mark their territory. Perhaps she should be happy that he hadn't pissed on her, Sam thought glumly.

As she sat silently contemplating the menu, Sam became aware that Caleb was looking down, past the plastic edge of his own worn-out menu. Her eyes dropped down, and she cringed. The already short skirt had shrunk in the drier, and it was bordering on being indecent.

"Stop leering at my legs."

"Can't help it, babe."

Before Sam could respond, an annoyed voice asked what they were having. Sam turned her eyes upward to find a blonde woman looking down on her with absolute disgust.

"I'll have a sweet tea." Sam kept her voice even, trying not to upset the already angry waitress.

She didn't know what the woman's problem was, but she didn't want to add to the woman's bad day. It soon became apparent that it wasn't her day that was the problem. It was Sam.

Right in front of Sam, the woman proceeded to try to flirt shamelessly with Caleb. To his credit, Caleb didn't respond. He barely looked at the woman. Two things became apparent in that moment.

The first was that Caleb and the waitress had had an intimate relationship, a fact the woman went out of her way to comment on. The second was that she blamed Sam for Caleb's lack of interest. With a parting glare, she stormed off to get the drinks.

"Well, I'm so glad you talked me into this."

"It's not that bad."

"Maybe you can get me a shirt that has 'Property of JD and Caleb McBane' printed in bold letters across it. That way all the men know not to talk to me and the women know to throw stones."

"You're forgetting the leash. I'll get you one of those with a tag that says, 'If Lost, Return To—'"

Two glasses of tea slammed down on the table, interrupting Caleb and sloshing over the edge to pool on the already sticky top. This time the waitress didn't even bother to be nice to Caleb. She took their orders with obvious annoyance before stomping off.

"You know, as a general rule, I don't like men who take me to places where their ex-lovers have a chance to spit on my food before serving it to me," Sam commented as she watched the blonde sashay away.

"I can imagine not. It's just…"

When his voice trailed off, Sam could guess at what he was going to say.

"Let me guess, there is no place we could go to eat where we wouldn't be served by one of your former conquests. Right?"

"I would like this chance to emphasize the word former."

"Whatever."

There was no point in harping on the matter. She would sound like a jealous bitch. Jealousy implied a depth of emotion. That was a dark and dangerous area considering this was only supposed to be about sex.

From all the women giving her side looks and frowning at their table, she knew she wasn't the only one having a problem with the current situation. It was like looking into her future. One day it would be her casting vengeful looks at another woman. Only for her, it would be worse than a simple broken heart. She would know then that they had not truly been attracted to her, but to her money.

"So, what do you do for a living?" Caleb's voice had a forced cheery sound to it, and she knew he was intentionally trying to draw her attention away from the other women. "Paint cars?"

"What?" Sam blinked before she remembered what JD had caught her doing. "No. I'm just helping my family out."

"Family?"

"Yeah, my brother, Mike, runs the park, and my sister, Vicky, is in charge of the spa."

"A spa? At a race park?"

"For the wives, and any man who likes to be naked and rubbed down by a beautiful woman."

"Ah, when you put it like that—"

"You're interested in making an appointment."

"Only if it's…" Caleb's eyes narrowed as the conclusion of that though suddenly dampened his mood. "You're not working in the spa."

"Was that a question or a statement?"

"Samantha—"

"Trust me. Not even a ham wants me to give it a rubdown."

Sam put a stop to that argument before it could get started. No doubt, he was about to say something arrogantly grating. She was so not in the mood for another round of control-freak smackdown, especially when the argument always seemed to end with her naked.

Caleb was obviously hesitant to let the matter drop. His eyes remained narrowed on her, and she could tell he was trying to figure out if she was serious or just being flippant. She was being both, but the waitress interfered before he could press the issue.

* * * *

Caleb scowled as their food was dropped unceremoniously on the table. After swapping plates with Caleb to assure he ate whatever had been spit on, Samantha dug in.

He knew that she was thankful for the interruption, but he didn't let the matter drop. As much as he pressed her for answers about herself, her answers became more and more obnoxious and flippant.

Samantha's defenses were fully up, and all his traditional angles were hitting walls. All those years of cultivating the perfect lines and she was forcing him to start from scratch. Finally, he managed to irritate her enough to get a straight answer, even if it was given with a good deal of annoyance.

"So you want to know about me. Let's see. I'm thirty-one." Samantha put down her burger and pursed her lips. "I have two siblings. I'm the oldest. Then there is Mike, followed by Vicky. My mom died when I was eighteen. I dropped out of high school at fifteen. I worked a long list of dead-end jobs, sometimes two at a time. I like things that go fast, action-adventure movies, the color blue, and I love to swim. I think that is about it."

"What about your dad?" Caleb knew she was being smart, but it was a start. Now he at least had something to work off of.

"What about him?"

"You didn't mention him."

"That's because he's not worth mentioning."

Her hard tone made a lie out of her statement. Whatever was between Samantha and her father, it was definitely something that Caleb wanted to know about. With the danger sign already flashing, he approached the subject cautiously.

"Is he dead?"

"As far as I am concerned."

"I'm sorry." Caleb understood that she wasn't being literal, but the pain was real. That was something he could relate to. "I know how hard it is to lose a parent. JD and I lost our fathers a few years back."

"Fathers? As in plural, two dads...or more?"

"Two. JD and I had two fathers, just as your children will." Caleb slipped that last bit in, knowing her focus was on the first part of his statement.

"So this sharing thing, it's hereditary?"

Caleb didn't want to get into that discussion now. In her current state, Samantha would no doubt use the reality of their condition to her advantage. So he shrugged and responded with a nonchalance he didn't truly feel. "It's a tradition in our pack."

"Ménages are your pack's ritual?"

"Look around."

Caleb watched as her head turned slowly, her eyes widening and snapping from one table to another as she took in what he knew she saw. Couples packed in the dinner, couples made up of male twins and a single woman.

He could sense the shock in her, knew that it weakened her defenses. As much as he hated to discussing something that had been almost too painful to endure, Caleb pressed the conversation forward.

"It's hard enough to lose one parent, but to lose two..."

"Sucks."

Samantha finished with a word that didn't do justice to the emotion he'd felt. He didn't correct her though. Her eyes were back on him and he could see the understanding, the sympathy in them.

"Yeah, it does." Caleb paused. When she didn't question him about the matter, he volunteered the information. It was difficult for him to talk about it, especially in detail. "They were murdered."

"Oh." Samantha fiddled with her fries for several moments before curiosity obviously won out. "Did you catch the guy?"

"Yeah."

"So, they're in jail."

"They should be so lucky."

"Why did they do it? Was it a robbery or something like that?"

"I don't know." Caleb shoved his half-eaten plate away. He'd lost his appetite. "There was never any explanation."

"Hmm." Samantha returned to playing with her food, nibbling occasionally on a fry.

Well, that had backfired. He'd wanted to have a pleasant dinner. He'd planned to charm her into telling him all about herself, and instead he'd ruined not only his own appetite, but hers as well.

"At least you know they didn't want to leave you." Samantha finally spoke, her words measured. "Mine just left."

"He walked out?" Caleb wasn't sure how to proceed now that she was finally opening up. He was afraid that one misstep might bring her defenses up.

"He said he'd had enough of this shit first." The twist of her lips angled up like a smile, but it was the furthest thing from it. "I guess he had better things to do with his life."

"I'm sorry."

"Please. I'm sick of hearing that. He wanted a different wife, different kids, a different life. You know what I wanted? A different dad."

There was no hiding the bitterness behind that statement or the hatred in her eyes. Caleb didn't doubt the depth of her emotion, but he had feeling that the anger hid a great deal of hurt.

"At least you had your mother."

"Yeah, a woman who couldn't bathe herself every day without a bottle clutched in her hand. She was a lot of help." Samantha shoved her own plate across the table until it clinked against his. "I'd have asked for a new mom too, but life is what it is. You do what you must. The only thing that ever went right was Mike and Vicky. At least I didn't lose them to social services."

"That's why you dropped out of school." Caleb was already beginning to add the pieces together. "You supported them, raised them."

"That was no biggie." Samantha shrugged. "I hated school, and it wasn't like I was getting good grades. Besides, I got a GED a few years later. It helped me get better-paying jobs."

"You make it sound like it was nothing, but it must have been hard on you."

Things were starting to make sense now. Samantha's strong defenses, her constant rejection of authority, why she had even come to Collin County, it all added up. Her life had been hard, and she put her family first.

While he didn't like to think of Samantha hurting, he couldn't have been more pleased that she was so loyal to her siblings. It was what every werewolf desired in a mate, a strong woman who would always put her family and pack first.

It also gave him insight on how to proceed. Samantha may not take to being bossed around, but she might be lured into their home with the promise of security and happiness. It was something that had been lacking in her life and something they would give her no matter what.

Samantha would never have to work two jobs again. Nor would she have to struggle to provide for her family. JD and he would make sure her life was easy from now on.

Caleb eyed his plate as he felt his stomach growling. Whatever pain it had caused him to talk about their fathers had been worth it. He now knew how to capture his mate, and that knowledge brought back his appetite.

As he ate, Caleb kept up the conversation. He told her about his childhood, his family, anything he could think of that would begin the process of forming a real relationship with Samantha.

Samantha didn't reciprocate. He didn't think it was just her being stubborn. Caleb could tell that her mind was constantly wandering elsewhere. He thought he knew where too.

It had been a mistake to bring her here. Way too much of his past was openly staring at them, and Samantha was smart enough to know what those looks meant. Caleb told himself she couldn't be upset about the fact that he had an active social life before he met her, but women were funny that way.

There was little he could do but eat fast and keep his eyes focused squarely on her. Samantha wasn't going to have the chance to accuse him of checking out another woman. Not that he was interested in looking, but he still made sure his head never turned or angled in any direction other than hers.

Soon enough Gina was carrying off their empty plates, and Caleb was fishing some bills out of his wallet. His mind focused totally on getting Samantha back home and into bed. It took a minute for her question to register.

"So, I guess JD's going to be mad at you when you take me back to my car, huh?"

"Is that what you really want?" Caleb's hands stilled, and he looked up at her from under a thick forest of black lashes. "To go home alone?"

"Yes, Caleb. That is what I want."

"Why? When it would be so much more fun to come home with me?"

"This is just all happening too fast."

Caleb studied her silently. There was more to her comment than the normal female complaint. Samantha's father had left her. Her husband cheated on her. Her level of trust in men was probably nonexistent. Her resistance to JD and him wasn't just a contrary personality, but probably based on true fear of letting any man into her heart.

"You want to slow down, huh? Like what? Dating?"

"Caleb, I'm married, and I really need to deal with that before I can deal with your brother or you."

Married, he hated that word coming out of her mouth. It made his fangs ache to grow. Her husband was lucky he wasn't near, or Caleb might have eliminated that problem for her.

"You understand, don't you?"

"I understand that you're mine."

Instantly he regretted the rash words. They'd slipped out before he even realized what he was saying. The scent of her fear rose several notches, and it took a great amount of willpower, but he managed to apologize.

"Sorry, it's just the beast in me."

His gaze dropped to her hands. They were trembling ever so slightly around her coffee cup. The sight made him scowl. Hell, he didn't want to scare her. He didn't want to go to bed alone either.

Caleb grinned as the solution presented itself. He would take her home, and he'd stay with her. That way, they both would get what they wanted. Well, he'd get what he wanted. Samantha may not think she wanted it, but after a few kisses, she'd see the wisdom in his thinking.

"I'll take you home." He lifted his eyes back to hers. Caleb slapped some bills down on the table. "Let's get out of here."

Chapter 14

The second the glass doors closed behind him, Caleb bristled. The beast inside him growled as it rose to prowl through his senses. Something was wrong. He could almost feel the threat lurking within the darkened corners of the parking lot.

Spurred not out of a desire to mate, but to protect his own, Caleb's hands tightened on Samantha's arms, and he pulled her close into his chest. She protested, but his ears were already tuning out the normal night noises, searching for the foreign sound of danger.

He could feel the slight shift in his body before the world of color went black-and-white. The night brightened around him the shadows lightening as the wolf's eyes peered into the crevices and saw the glow of another set of beastly eyes staring back.

With deliberate slowness, the man stepped forward, still keeping to the edge of the shadows and the security they provided him. Caleb didn't need to see the other beast to recognize what it was. He was a wolf and trespassing on Caleb's territory.

Occasionally as tourists moved through the town during the summer, other wolves would come into the pack's domain. It wasn't the season for such idle passing, and this wolf did not smell of innocent missteps.

The large man reeked of rage and calculation, a lethal combination when combined with fangs and claws. Caleb felt his own gums ache as his own fangs began to extend. He'd have gone for the interloper without a word of warning if it hadn't been for Samantha.

He couldn't risk her getting hurt. Without even thinking about it, he'd shoved her behind him when the man had stepped up. It had been an instinctive act of protection, but now he had to get her out of the way completely.

His truck was closer than the diner doors, but there were pack members he could trust to keep her safe back in the restaurant. Before he could make his decision on what to do with his mate, she stepped around him. Caleb growled and reached to shove her back when her words struck him cold.

"Bruce? What the hell are you doing here?" Samantha walked toward the dangerous stranger. "I told you to leave!"

"Samantha." The man growled, his chin raising as he sniffed the air with obvious intent. What he smelled drew his gaze sharply to Caleb before snapping back to Samantha.

"You disappoint me."

"I really don't give a shit!" Samantha seemed completely unaware of the danger as she stormed forward. Caleb moved quickly to intercede. "I told you it was over. I'm not interested in ever seeing you ag…Hey!"

Caleb ignored Samantha's screech and her pathetic slapping on his arm as he spun her away from the other wolf. He managed to pass his truck keys into her hands as he shoved her back.

"What the hell—"

"In the truck!"

"This is not—"

"NOW!"

Samantha fell silent for a moment. Caleb didn't spare her a glance, but he was sure she was glaring at him. Thank the Lord above she decided to obey. Muttering about arrogant men and threatening not to let him in his own truck, she stormed off.

Neither of the werewolves paid her any attention. Both were solely focused on the other. It wasn't until Caleb heard the slam of his truck door that he relaxed ever so slightly. Now he had the advantage. Nothing stood in his way.

"You are on my territory." Caleb paced forward.

"You stole my woman." The man shifted to the side.

"She's mine." Caleb matched the other wolf's movement, keeping his path to the truck blocked.

"Then you are prepared to die for her."

"Are you? I saw no mark on her when I placed my own in her flesh."

"A technicality I won't overlook again."

"A technicality you won't have the opportunity to correct."

"You don't know what you are getting involved in, friend. Let the bitch go before it costs you more than you're willing to pay."

"Never. Nobody else touches what is mine. Not you. Not her husband. Nobody."

"Husband?"

That made the man pause for a moment, his lips kicking up slightly. His humor was cut short by the sound of people coming out of the diner. Caleb didn't look. He recognized the smell of more wolves spilling onto the scene.

There were muted words and the quick, light steps of women fleeing. Heavier footfalls approached. Three of his pack members were coming close, a fact that made the interloper shift backward, deeper into the shadows.

"Everything all right, Caleb?" Duncan fanned out to the right.

"We have an intruder."

Caleb didn't expand. There was no need. The men all understood what was at stake. Trespassing wolves were given two choices normally, leave or die. Occasionally they were folded into the pack, but that was rare with a male.

"We should probably take this elsewhere." That suggestion came from Caleb's left. Todd's voice was slightly garbled, telling Caleb that he was more than ready to handle the matter right there in the parking lot if needed.

"Leave now, or die here."

"I'm just going to get my things from the motel." The invader held up his hands in the universal sign of surrender. "I'll be headed out then."

Caleb heard the unspoken words. This man would be back, back for Samantha. As he faded back into the shadows, Caleb scented the air, committing his challenger's scent to memory. If he were dumb enough to return, it would be his last mistake.

"Follow him." Caleb spoke without turning his head toward Duncan. "Make sure he leaves."

"He'll have a personal escort to the county line."

Duncan nodded at Todd, and both men headed off. Zane turned to see to the women. He didn't need to be asked. He would take Duncan and Todd's date back to her place, before heading home with his own.

Caleb watched as his pack members disappeared into the night before turning toward his truck. He could clearly see Samantha sitting in the front seat with her arms across her chest. Even at the distance, he could read her pissed-off expression through the shadows.

That was fine with him. He wasn't too pleased with his mate either. She'd lied to him. There was no husband, but there was another wolf seeking to claim her. It was time they had a little honest talk.

* * * *

The night flew past Sam's window. The blackness was pierced only by the occasional house light or passing car. She did not need the illumination to tell her that they were not headed back toward her home. That could only mean one thing.

Caleb was already breaking his word. That was the last straw. Her temper, already boiling from his attitude in the parking lot, ignited. It made no difference to her that his was near its flash point. If he wanted a fight, she was more than willing.

"What do you think you are doing?"

He did not respond to that demand. The only sound he made was the slight squeak as his fists tightened over the steering wheel. The bastard didn't even look at her. She knew he understood her question perfectly well, knew that she realized they weren't headed in the right direction.

When he hit the gas, accelerating to a nearly reckless speed, she did the only logical thing to do. She screamed at him to stop the damn truck. That didn't get her any further response. Well, she knew how to make him stop.

Without hesitation, she threw open the door. It worked like a charm. He hit the brakes so fast the back end of the truck skidded out to the side. The brakes whined as the tires smoked, but within a hundred feet, the ground beneath her eyes came to a standstill.

"What the fuck are you doing?"

Sam paid him about as much attention as he had her question. She already had her seat belt undone, and without so much as a glance in his direction, she hopped out of the truck.

She could hear him cursing as he threw open his door. That was just fine with her. He could cuss all night long. She wasn't going to wait around to hear his miserable complaints. Turning back in the direction they had come, she started walking, silently vowing to keep going until she found a phone.

"Where the hell do you think you are going?" His roar was too close, his footsteps gaining on hers.

"Home!" Sam picked up her own speed.

"Damn it, Samantha! Stop!"

"No!"

"Fine! I'll take you home. Just get in the damn truck before you get run over!"

His words sounded slightly garbled, the same way they had back in the parking lot. She knew just what that meant. He was about to have a serious snit. Well, she wasn't going to meekly obey his commands just because he was a little hot under the collar.

"Like I believe anything you have to say. You already said that, and where am I? Not at home!"

"You want to talk about lies? You want to tell me a little more about this husband you claim to have?"

"He's big. He owns a gun and tons of silver bullets. In fact, his favorite thing to hunt is wolf! We hang their skins on the walls, make them into blankets and rugs. I even have a coat!" She turned to hurl that last insult at him.

That was a mistake. She could see his eyes glowing in the night. They were gray now, lit by some weird inner light. His lips, too, were pulled back slightly. She could see the slight gleam of fangs in moonlight.

Oh God. He's turning into a damn wolf in the middle of the street!

Fear shivered down her spine. He was close, too close, and her feet stumbled backward. She spun back around, giving up her speed walk and breaking into a jog.

"Damn it, Samantha! Do not run!"

Yeah, right.

She wasn't about to hang around so he could eat her. With that concern firmly lodged into her throat, she broke into a full-out run.

* * * *

Shit!

She shouldn't have done that. He was having a hard enough time keeping the beast at bay. It had been aching to be released since he'd spied the interloper lurking in the shadows of the diner.

Now fighting with his mate was making the situation worse. The beast did not want to argue. The wolf demanded blind submission from its bitch. It had been all he could do to keep control of his senses.

He lost the battle the moment she started running. That was it. The wolf broke free, thrilling at the chase. There was nothing more that the wolf loved to do than run down its prey.

She was moving fast, but not nearly fast enough. He easily overtook her. She screamed when his arms locked around her. Kicking and clawing in a rage, all her impassioned fighting did was rile his own desires to a new height.

Her leg got between his and caused him to trip. He rolled with the fall, taking the force of the impact on his back and quickly turning until they landed in the soft grass and sand of the shoulder.

Samantha fell still, silent, obviously momentarily dazed by their sudden tumble. Caleb wasn't suffering any disorientation. He took immediate advantage of her stupor to roll her beneath him.

He made short work of shredding her top and bra with nails grown long into claws. Her skirt received the same rough treatment as he tried to shove it out of his way. She'd come back to her senses and was back to fighting him, squirming, bucking, and cussing at him. All it earned her were a few daring slits in her skirt as the fabric sliced beneath his hands.

Her struggles fueled the beast, controlling him, demanding that he conquer his mate and bring her to a heel. The wolf may not have cared if she resisted, but the man did. Caleb would have fought for domination if it hadn't been for the strong scent of her arousal filling the night air.

The sweet smell fired his own musk. In less than a minute, her thrashing subsided. The curses turned into soft moans as her body went pliant. Caleb snarled, sitting back on his knees so he could drag her ass up his lap. He lifted her off the ground, his hands biting into her hips as he forced her legs wide.

Even in the dim light, he could see her wet, swollen folds. The sweet sight and scent tempted him to rub his face against her softness, stroke his tongue over her creamy slit, and devour her with long, hungry licks.

The wolf inside him snarled, unwilling to resist the temptation. He began to fuck his lengthening tongue into her with carnal abandon, unable to get enough of her intoxicating taste. In moments, she was back to squirming.

This time she reared back, forcing herself onto his mouth. He barely heard her shout that she was going to come over the thunder of his racing heart. He felt it when her inner muscles clamped down on his tongue, trying to hold it deep within her.

Caleb didn't relent as she came, but continued to devour her softness with the zest of a starving man. His hands played with the bounty he had trapped before him. Manipulating her clit with expert precision, he forced her collapsing climax to bloom again, higher and higher.

His second hand slid around her ass, and he savagely trust his fingers into her ass. She screamed, and another tidal wave of cream flooded his mouth. It wasn't enough. He was not nearly satisfied. There was no stopping him from pushing her higher, harder, faster, until she bucked and sobbed beneath him as she climaxed again.

He barely heard her crying that she could take no more. She was clawing at the ground, trying to escape his grasp. Caleb's growl shattered the night as he was forced to return his grip to her hips and yank her back into position.

The feast was not over, and she was not escaping until he was done. He slammed her back down onto his tongue and began to roll and retreat the velvety length deep into her spasming channel. She screamed as another wave of delicious cream flooded his mouth.

He couldn't take any more. His own flesh had hardened to the point of pain, warning him that he could not last another round without pumping himself uselessly into his pants. It was difficult to hold on to her as he tugged on his zipper.

She was kicking at him, twisting and fighting for freedom. Caleb battled not only her, but also his fingers made clumsy by his haste. When he finally managed to release his cock, he did not bother to pause to shove his jeans all the way down before yanking her backward and embedding himself inside her with one hard thrust.

A raging inferno burned out of control inside him, one that flamed higher as he pounded into her tight, clinging sheath. His lips pulled back in a snarl as he forced her legs higher, wider, opening her up for deeper, harder penetration.

* * * *

Sam felt skewered on his thick, hard cock. Her pussy was stretched to capacity as he violently slammed into her. Instead of hurting her, his ferocity fed her own wild need. She cried out, arching her hips, lifting her pussy to take every thrust as deep as she could, taking his fierce fuck and returning it thrust for thrust.

It was too much, and Sam bucked mindlessly within his grasp, trying to both escape and get closer. When he shifted, reaching around to capture and manipulate her clit, the tension winding through her body broke. Every cell in her body exploded as great rippling waves of ecstasy rocked through her in rhythm with the thick shaft slamming in and out of her clenching core.

Sam screamed as her pussy convulsed violently and her body shuddered with release. Wave after wave of rapture rolled over her from her head to her toes, growing in speed and ferocity as he continued to pound into her.

* * * *

Caleb fought off the need to come. His testicles burned with the need to release his seed, but there was something else the wolf wanted, one last pleasure before he accepted the end of this amazing ride.

Sam whimpered as he pulled out of her sheath. The man hidden under the beast knew he was pushing her, but he didn't have the power to reign in his most base desires. He needed to know just one more of the delectable pleasures her body had to offer.

Thankful that his dick was already well lubed in a thick coat of her cream, he lined himself up with the clenched entrance to her ass. His hard invasion made her scream, and he didn't know if it was in pain or pleasure.

Truthfully, the wolf didn't care. It only knew the great searing rapture of thrusting into the tightest sheath it had ever found. As he felt her inner muscles fist around his cock, clamping him in a vise of intense pressure, the last remnants of his control vanished. He lasted six, seven more strokes before his release ripped out of his body.

Roaring with his pleasure, he felt his fangs slice through her tender skin. Sinking into the soft flesh of her shoulder, he pumped his full length into her as the last of his seed spilled from his body and bound them together in a perfect union.

His trembling muscles gave out and collapsed in a sweaty pile on top of her. Satisfied, the wolf slowly receded, allowing Caleb to return to his senses. It was a slightly uncomfortable transformation. His gums ached, and his muscles throbbed, but the worst was the realization that he had completely lost it.

A sniffle beneath him had him moving despite his body's objections.

Chapter 15

"Oh God." Caleb rolled to his side, lifting Samantha into his lap as he went. "I'm so sorry, baby."

She didn't respond except to sniff again. She didn't have to say anything to make him feel any guiltier. Her appearance was more than enough. From the twigs and stray bits of dirt clinging to her hair, to the ragged edges of her destroyed clothes, she looked like a ravaged woman.

Never before had he so completely lost it with a woman. Never had the wolf broken free of all binds and rutted on a woman untamed.

"Samantha?"

"What?"

She didn't look up at him. Her tone was hoarse from all her screaming earlier, but there was no indication of tears in it. Still he was not appeased. He wanted to hear her assurance.

"Did I hurt you?"

"You were an animal."

"I know, honey. I'm sorry."

"Sorry?" Her head jerked back, cracking against his jaw. That didn't stop her from glaring at him. "I do not appreciate being fucked by a wolf man!"

"I..." Caleb blinked, not at all sure how to respond to that comment. "It's..."

"It's disgusting!"

"You didn't think that a minute ago." Caleb's anger was renewed by her aggravating attitude. "In fact, you were moaning and coming all over me."

"It's that damn musk!"

"Are we back to that?"

"Yes, we are back to that. It was unfair, and you know it! I would never let a…a….whatever you were, touch me like that if you hadn't cheated."

"Cheated? I didn't cheat. This isn't a test."

"You know what I meant."

"And I'm not a whatever." Caleb stormed on indignantly, completely ignoring her growl. "I am your mate, and you will show me proper respect."

"Respect? How can I respect a man who runs me down and fucks me on the side of the road? A man who turns into some filthy, slobbering dog and rips my clothes to pieces?"

"I'm not a dog! I'm a werewolf."

"Wolf, dog, whatever. Both lift their legs to pee."

"If you don't want to be fucked by a wolf, then don't run from one."

"You're blaming this on me?"

Her expression would have amused him if it weren't for the smack she landed across his cheek. It was no girlie slap, and his head rotated under the force. Bright spots flashed before his eyes, and Samantha almost managed to escape.

She used everything she had to try to get free of his hold, kicking, clawing, even biting him, and damn if his cock didn't surge back to full-staff as the wolf began once again to prowl through his senses. Despite her struggles, he managed to get her pinned beneath him again.

This time they were face to face, and he was all too aware of her near-nakedness. The hard points of her breasts rubbed enticingly against his T-shirt, making him wish he wasn't so completely clothed. If they weren't lying on the side of the road, he might have done something about that.

"Get off me!"

Samantha tried to hit him again, this time with a closed fist. Caleb caught her wrist, pinning it to the ground before she could do any more damage. He wasn't sure if such a tiny thing would hurt, but he wasn't going to risk it, not in his present condition.

"Stop it, Samantha."

"I'll stop when you get off and leave me the hell alone."

"Damn it, be still!"

"Screw you!"

"That's about to happen to you if you don't calm down!"

"You wouldn't dare."

"I wouldn't, but the *dog* would."

That got her attention and an immediate response. She stilled beneath him, watching him with narrowed eyes. While her body might not be fighting him anymore, there was no denying the rage flaming in her eyes.

That was fine with him. He was far from pleased with his mate right now. With her normal dismissive attitude and outlandish comments, she had managed to completely sidetrack him from the argument they should have been having, but it was not forgotten.

"Now, we're going to talk."

"I don't have anything to say to you."

"You're going to tell me about your husband."

"What about him?"

"Anything. Everything. What's his name? Where did you meet? How long have you been married? What's your anniversary? What's his favorite football team? Whatever. I want to know about this man, so start talking."

* * * *

Sam blinked. He was serious. He really wanted to talk about her husband, her nonexistent husband. If she answered all his questions, she'd forget the answers. Sometime later, he would catch her in the lie.

Of course, if he were working with Bruce, he would already knew she was lying. That would certainly explain why, up to this point, he had appeared completely unconcerned about her marital status. If he was working with Bruce, then what had been with the show back at the diner?

Setup.

"Samantha?"

"I don't discuss my husband with my lovers. It's unseemly."

"Lovers? Just how many lovers do you have?"

"I don't discuss my lovers with my other lovers. That's unseemly, too."

"Unless you want to end up chained to my bed suffering punishment the likes of which you have yet to endure, you had better start talking."

"Really? Then I guess I better confess everything." Sam gave a smile could have turned water into ice. "I use a charting system to grade all men based on their abilities. Then I assign them a score for each one and calculate their overall ranking. Do you want to know what number you are? Or what number Bruce is?"

That got her mouth covered by his hand. It felt normal, but when his fingers flexed slightly, she could feel the nails grow a tad bit longer, just a bit pointier. She knew now exactly what that meant.

"Listen to me and listen carefully, Samantha, because I'm not going to warn you again. Any more snide or sarcastic comments come out of that mouth and I'll put it to better use."

* * * *

Caleb knew she understood exactly what he was implying. Samantha tensed even more beneath him. Her gaze became more spiteful as she glared silently up at him. He knew being rough with her like this played into all her prejudices and stereotypes of men, but he couldn't risk the wolf making a second appearance in one night.

"Okay." He lowered his hand slowly, pausing to see if she could be trusted to remain quiet. Thankfully, she did not hurl any more insults in his direction. "Let's start again. Tell me about your husband."

"Why?"

"I want to know."

"You already know everything there is to know."

"You haven't told me anything."

"Don't play dumb, Caleb. You know there is no husband."

"So you admit you lied to me. Why?"

"It was expedient."

"Expedient?"

"Yeah, normally when you tell a man you're married, he takes the hint and gets lost."

"So you just wanted to get rid of me."

"Geez, I'm glad I didn't have to spell it out for you or anything."

"Samantha."

"What? Am I supposed to be all happy pinned to the ground and forced to answer questions you already know the answer to?"

"I don't know the answers! Why the hell do you think I'm asking the damn questions?"

"It's all part of the play."

"What play?"

"This little contrived game Bruce and you are conducting...Don't look at me like that. I know all about dogs. They run in packs and are loyal to each other."

"For the last time, I am not a dog!"

"Wolf, right, less evolved than a dog."

"Werewolf." Caleb could barely get the words out. She was pushing it, and he only had a precious little patience left.

"Whatever."

"That's it."

He couldn't take any more of this. He jumped up and dragged her with him. This conversation was better conducted at home, where he had the advantage. He knew just what to do to get her talking.

"Where are you taking me?" Samantha was tugging on her arm, trying to wrest it free of his ironclad grip.

"Better you worry about what I'm going to do to you when we get there."

"Like that's going to make me trust you more."

That brought Caleb up short. He hated to admit she had a point. If he did what he wanted, he'd get his answers and earn even more of her distrust. That wasn't the foundation he wanted to try to build a permanent relationship on.

Ah, hell. He continued dragging her toward the truck, but this time he wasn't sure what he was going to do when he got there. The only thing he knew was he couldn't have her standing with all her goodies hanging out in the middle of the road.

It pleased him when he loaded her into the truck and slammed the door that she didn't attempt to jump right back out. He tried to build on that positive emotion as he walked around to his side. There was no helping the tension filling his body, but his mind was beginning to work again.

She didn't say anything when he put the truck into gear and started back off down the road. He was grateful for that concession. Still, he wasn't fool enough to think she was happily accepting the situation.

After a mile, he pulled into a dead-end driveway and parked. That got Samantha's attention, and she turned to study him with a mixture of apprehension and annoyance. Taking a deep breath, he tried to sound reasonable.

"Okay, let's try this again. Why do you think Bruce and I are in cahoots?"

* * * *

"You're both werewolves."

Sam saw his cheek flex, but whatever in her answer had irritated him, he kept to himself. He was trying to appear reasonable, that much was obvious. She didn't trust him. This was just a new attack.

"And what would we gain from working together? You're my mate, and, correct me if I'm wrong, he wants you as his."

"Oh, please. You know that's not what he's after."

"Pretend I don't."

"Fine." Sam was tired of this conversation. It was obvious that he wasn't going to let up until she played along. "Yes, Bruce and I were lovers. We were engaged until I found out about his less-than-human lineage and his interest in screwing other four-legged animals. Okay? Happy now?"

"You were engaged? Werewolves don't get engaged. We mate."

"Oh, I see. JD and you weren't planning on any form of official ceremony. How, then, would you get the money?"

"What money?"

"My money."

"You have money? I thought you said you dropped out of high school and had to work two jobs to support your family."

"So? I won the lottery. I'm rich."

"You did?"

"Is there something wrong with that?"

"It's just...I mean...it's a little odd."

Sam knew he was calculating what was the best way to handle the situation. He knew she was lying, but had enough sense not to accuse her of it. That would be the quickest way to reveal his association with Bruce.

"How rich are we talking here?" His eyes narrowed on her in obvious distrust.

"A hundred million. Give or take a few million."

"A hundred million? Dollars, right?"

"And you're not getting any of it."

"What?"

"You heard me. You're not even worth fifty bucks for the fuck on the side of the road."

Caleb roared. More like howled, Sam corrected herself as he began to pound his fist into the dash with inhuman strength. The hard plastic actually cracked, and she slunk back against the door.

She was very seriously considering the merits of getting out and making another run for it. Her ass was still sore, and there was no way she could outrun him, especially in wolf form. It appeared the beast was back as he turned glowing gray eyes on her.

"Listen very carefully to me, Samantha." The threat in his tone was magnified by the strangled sound of the words being forced past his elongating fangs. "I don't want your damn money. I want you!"

"Like I haven't heard that one before. Your buddy already tried that. He fell short, so don't think you'll do any better."

"You're referring to Bruce. He was after your money, and now you think JD and I are working with him."

"That's the gist."

"That's crap. I never met him until tonight."

"Of course not."

"Damn it, Samantha!"

"What? What am I supposed to think? Three months ago I was engaged to a man who professed his undying love to me. He was handsome, charming, and he couldn't keep his hands off me. Too bad he was a werewolf looking to steal my money.

"I come up here to get away from him, and suddenly I have two handsome, but not very charming, werewolves who can't seem to keep their hands off me and are professing that we're mates.

"Just to top it all off, out of nowhere, my former fiancé shows up and goes toe to toe with my current fling. Except they don't exchange blows, and I'm hustled off to the car so that I can't even hear what is really going on.

"So let me just lie down and accept my fate. Tell me what exactly is the plan. After I marry you, are you just going to drain my account, or are you going to kill me so you can enjoy it with the waitress from the diner!"

* * * *

Caleb growled and fought to keep the wolf chained. It was hard because as a man he was equally pissed off. Her words made him ache to put her across his knee and pound some sense into her backside. It was obvious that was what she was thinking with.

It took him several deep breaths before he tried to consider the rest of what she had said. No, it didn't work. That last jab about killing her and running off with Gina burned all rational thought away.

"Take that back!"

"Why should I?"

"I would kill anybody who even tried to hurt you."

"Right." She rolled her eyes, and he almost lost it.

"Fine, you want proof? You want blood? I'll hunt down your little furry friend and bring you back his head. Will that help?"

"Oh God. Don't do that." She paled, her expression relaxing into stunned horror.

"Whatever it takes, Samantha."

"What it takes is you driving me home and giving me some room to think."

"What would that prove?"

"It would prove you cared about my feelings!"

Damn, she had him with that one. Ah, hell, now what was he supposed to do? If he didn't do what she asked, he would be solidifying all her mistaken assumptions. That would only make things more difficult when they were already nearly impossible.

The problem was Bruce was still out there. For a hundred million reasons, Caleb didn't think the other wolf was just going to fade off into the night. Caleb would like nothing more than to hunt down that asshole and rip him to shreds.

Samantha had already been damaged enough by her father's desertion. The other wolf's betrayal had only reinforced her fears and insecurities, leaving JD and him the arduous task of healing her pain.

JD. Caleb could only imagine how his twin was going to react to tonight's revelations. That explosion just might seal their doom. Caleb sighed. He was screwed. He had no choice but to give her what she asked for and pray that JD didn't kill him for it. Caleb would need some kind of concession before he dealt with his brother.

"If I take you back to your place, what assurance do I have I'll ever see you again?"

"You don't."

"That's not going to work for me."

"Too bad."

"For you. I could just take you home and keep you chained to the bed."

"Fine, what do you want?"

"A date."

"A date? As in a dinner and a movie."

"As in a timeline for how long it's going to take you to think."

"What? God, what is with men? What kind of stupid statement is that? It will take me as long as it takes me."

"That's not going to work."

"Need I say too bad again?"

"How long?"

"Ten years!"

"I'll give you until Saturday."

"Gee, how gracious of you."

"There is a Valentine's Day dance Saturday night, and you're my date."

"Have you ever heard of asking?"

"Wear something that's easy to get off or you don't care if it ends up as a rag."

She snorted at that, but he wasn't kidding. After a few days without their mate, Caleb would be impressed if they lasted five minutes at the dance before they were dragging her off. Hell, she'd be lucky if she didn't end up being fucked in the parking lot, though he promised himself that they'd make it to the truck.

"Fine. I'll meet you there."

He didn't like the sound of that, but knew that she had bent about as much as she was going to. Still, she had a hundred million ways to run away. He'd have to keep an eye on her until Saturday, but at a distance.

He'd also have to do a little research into her past. If she somehow managed to escape, he wanted to know where to look. He also wanted to know about Bruce.

There was a lot to do in the upcoming days, and his mind circled the problems as he drove her home. Samantha appeared lost in her own thoughts, not even looking in his direction until he had parked outside the row of apartments she lived in on the racing complex. She paused then, looking down at her ragged, revealing clothing before looking over at him.

"A gentleman would offer me his shirt to cover up."

Yeah, a gentleman would, and he was stuck pretending to be one right now. Without comment, he pulled off his T-shirt and handed it to her. It was too big on her small frame, and it inspired a sense of possessiveness in him. It was a visible mark to anybody who saw her that she was taken.

It softened his mood, and before she could fend him off, he pulled her into his arms and kissed her.

* * * *

Sam went still beneath the gentle assault. Her heart tripped over itself, slamming into her rib cage as it began to pump overheated blood throughout her body. The taste of him crashed through her defenses.

The intoxicating scent of his musk began to fill the cab, but this time she didn't fight it, didn't want to try. The whole night had been too much, and she was worn thin. It may be the dumbest thing she ever did, but she wanted to feel special, even if it were musk-induced.

Her mouth parted at the teasing suggestion of his teeth nibbling on her lips. His tongue lazily slid inside to stroke the fire burning up her body. With his urging, she eagerly crawled into his lap, leaning into his chest.

Their mouths mated with wild perfection. Hot, hungry, deeply intimate, the kiss spiraled out of control. She wound her arms around him, sliding her hands into his hair; the cool silkiness of it contrasted with the warm hardness of his neck.

His body was hot and hard, inviting her to press into him and enjoy the feel of his thick muscles against her softer, more rounded flesh. He was solid, more than strong enough to hold her against him as her body began to tremble and writhe in his embrace.

His arms clenched her even tighter as she began to rub against him, and Caleb forced her down, pushing her against the hardest part of him. Sam gasped, breaking off the kiss at the feel of his overgrown erection pressing into her cunt.

What was left of her little skirt was shoved up to her waist, leaving nothing but denim between her needy flesh and his more-than-ready cock. Hypnotized by the pleasure, she ground herself against him.

Every stroke teased her clit and made her pussy spasm and weep. She could feel the wetness saturating his jeans and knew she was leaving a wet spot on them. Sam didn't care. She just wanted more.

With a suddenness that had her growling in protest, he shoved her back on her side of the truck. Sam blinked, cold at the sudden loss of his body. The sensation was more than just skin-deep. It reached all the way into her heart.

"Damn it, Caleb. If this is your idea of a joke—"

"Trust me, it's not."

"Punishment?"

"I'm trying to give you what you said you wanted, woman. Space. You can't be mad at me for trying to drag you home for sex and then get mad at me because I wouldn't have sex with you. Now get the hell out of my truck before I change my mind and you're bitching at me again for giving you what you really want."

Damn it, he had point. Sam glared at him, more annoyed with herself than him. She'd asked for time, but was all too quick to give up her stance once he started kissing her. Distance, that's what she needed to get her head back on straight. Distance and a cold shower.

With jerky motions, she pushed open the truck door and jumped out. As she turned to slam it closed, she caught Caleb's slight smile.

"You're going to make the right decision, Samantha."

She kicked his door closed and was left hopping on one foot as he took off out of the parking lot. She really needed to invest in a pair of boots before she broke a toe. A nice pair of steel-toed ones that left them hurting and not her.

Sam turned to storm into her apartment. She managed to get a shower, a hot one, and ready for bed before the stupidity of what she was doing hit her. There were two brothers, and she shouldn't forget that. Given JD's predilection for storming into the race park and dragging her off, staying in her own room was probably not a god idea. He knew where it was.

* * * *

All the normal night creatures quieted down, sensing the predator in their midst. The sound of clicking claws over the wooden walkway in front of the small row of wooden apartments echoed loudly in the still air. None of them had reason to fear, this wolf was after a very specific prey.

He knew exactly where he would find it too. Still, he sniffed the door, reaffirming that it was the right one. It was, and he backed up before rearing onto two feet. With his front paws braced on the sill, the wolf peered through the window.

The curtains were open, and he could see straight through to the back window. It was more than enough light to tell him the bed was empty. Falling back onto all fours, he looked around, his head high as he sniffed the air.

He found the scent he was looking for and traced it all the way to the main house. He pranced around the porch, checking in window after window until he heard her voice. Following this new trail, he made his way around back where a light and a new window revealed what he was looking for.

He growled slightly at the sight of the other bitch. That one he did not like, but she presented no danger to his mate, and so he retreated to the tree line. Settling himself into a spot that allowed him to watch for anybody or anything that approached the house, he rested his head on his outstretched front paws. He appeared asleep except for the glowing silver eyes that never once closed.

Chapter 16

Wednesday

The gift was waiting for her the next morning. Wrapped in happy pink paper with a large white bow on top, it had a simple card attached with just her first name on it. Vicky had given it to her over breakfast.

It was a visual reminder of her predicament. Caleb, JD, Bruce, a hundred million dollars, her mind telling her one thing, her heart telling her another, it was all complete chaos. Sam didn't know which way to go.

They were all werewolves. It was logical to be concerned over whether they were working together. Their actions were all similar. On the surface they all had the same goal, even if their techniques were different. Bruce was smooth, JD was raw, and Caleb was somewhere in between.

JD said what he thought, did as he pleased, and took what he wanted, when he wanted it. If JD were after her money, what would he do to get it? Abduct her, fuck her, and chain her to his bed until she agreed to marry him?

That sounded right, but it didn't feel it. Sam was having a hard time seeing him as the type of man who went after a woman for her money. Was that her mind or her heart thinking for her? She didn't know, wasn't sure that it mattered. Neither could be trusted to make this decision.

What she needed was a professional investigator. Sam liked that idea. Even as she warmed to the concept, she began to wonder where to find a trained investigator. It couldn't be just anybody out of the phone book.

The private eye might discover JD and Caleb's secret lineage, and she was guessing they'd become completely unhinged if that got out. What she needed was somebody that was not only good, but also discreet, the type of private eye who solved delicate problems for rich people. The problem was she might have the money, but she didn't have the connections.

Jameson did. The lawyer who worked on the trust funds she was now in charge of probably had all kinds of contacts. A quick call and she found out he didn't know anybody offhand that worked in South Carolina. He was willing to find out for her, though.

With that matter as settled as it could be for the moment, Sam turned her attention to the mysterious gift. Sam lifted it up and, as her habit was since a child, shook it.

Nothing rattled inside. It was light. Frowning, she began running through her guesses of what could be in it. Her imagination was guided by her assumption that it was a gift from Caleb.

Who else would have left the gift? It had been hand-delivered, no postage, just left on the doorstep early in the morning. It could have been Bruce, but Sam doubted it. For all his charm, Bruce had never been this type of romantic.

Sam also doubted JD had come up with the idea. His idea of a romantic gift would be along the lines of crotchless panties. She snickered at her own thoughts. Oh, if he did that, she would throw a tantrum the likes that would make a hurricane look like just another summer storm.

She might as well admit it to herself even if she didn't do so to anybody else. She kind of liked arguing with the big brute. Those arguments were never personal, not the way it had been last night with Caleb. In a weird way, shouting at JD was almost like foreplay.

They spurred him on to being even more aggressive and dominating than he was naturally. Sam had to admit that made for some of the hottest sex she'd ever had. The only thing better was when the men worked together.

Shaking those thoughts from her head, she tried to distract herself with opening the gift. She tore through the wads of tissue paper to find a beautiful necklace hidden in their folds. A large, strange stone was set in gold and strung on the fine chain.

The smooth surface seemed to shimmer and shift, the color swirling to life before her eyes in a sea of greens and blues. It was mesmerizing.

The jarring ring of her phone brought her back to the moment, and she realized that she had been sitting there for some time.

"Hello." She expected it to be Caleb, trying to add to the gift with sweet persuasive words to convince her not to wait until Saturday.

"Hello, Sam. Did you get my present?"

"Oh, it's you." Sam was annoyed to hear Brett's voice on the other end of the phone. "What do you want?"

"To apologize."

"Yeah?"

Like I believed that.

Brett was a narcissistic, spoiled brat. He was only motivated by one thing, money. There was only one person standing between him and his inheritance, her. That made Brett her problem.

"I'm sorry about the way I behaved over the past few weeks. I don't have any excuse for my behavior but that I was grieving for the loss of my beloved father."

"We were all upset."

Beloved father, bullshit.

Brett had never treated Frank as a beloved anything. He had only ever come around to try to charm money out of Frank. When Frank wasn't so easily fooled, Brett would throw a tantrum, more than willing to say anything that would hurt his father.

"It was just such a shock," Brett stated with the right touch of sadness in his tone.

Somebody schooled him.

Even when Frank had been diagnosed with lung cancer, Brett hadn't shown an ounce of sympathy. Just the opposite, he had all but rubbed his hands together and asked how long before Frank died and the money went to him.

"I know I said some mean things to you."

Like manipulative bitch, conniving whore, gold-digging tramp.

"I really feel bad about that. I was just so angry about the loss of my father, and I took it out on you. That wasn't right of me."

He had certainly been angry about the loss of something, but it wasn't his father.

"Sam?"

"I'm here."

"I know it was a little enough offering, but I hope you got my gift."

"The necklace?"

"It's a peace offering, and I hope you will accept it as that."

"How did you…Are you in town?"

"Uh, I'm in Savannah, actually."

"What are you doing there?"

"I know you're in charge of the trusts now, and that is a heavy responsibility. I just wanted to offer my help in any way that I could."

"Help?"

Sam shook her head. Did he really think she was that dumb? To hell with playing this game. He thought she was a low-class bitch with no sophistication, and she was about to live up to that image.

"You're not getting any money, Brett. The trust pays your allowance as your father wished, and I'm not going to change that."

"I wasn't even thinking that way." There was the slightly insulted tone that normally preempted one of his tirades. "I was concerned about the charitable trust."

Ah, hell.

He wasn't trying to break into his measly little two-hundred-million trust. He was going for the gold, all the way for the five-hundred-million-dollar fund. She should have known. Why settle for two when he could have five? It had taken him long enough to come up with that one.

"That's nice of you, Brett, but I don't need any help. Your father left a list of charities that he was most interested in donating to and detailed instructions of how he wanted the money allocated."

"But the principal needs to be conserved. Otherwise, the fund will run out of money one day, and my father's legacy will die with it." There was the haughtiness she had come to know Brett for.

"Again, your father left idiot-proof instructions on how the money was to be managed and invested."

"Anybody who knows anything about investments knows that the market is always changing." His voice was like a cat's claw on a metal door. It made her cringe with the need to go off on him. "You can't expect his instructions to maintain the wealth of the trust. You need somebody who is aware of the current market trends and pitfalls."

"That's nice. I don't need any help."

She wasn't about to waste her time explaining to him again that the trust had not only employed one of the best money managers, but also had its own accountant and financial whiz to make sure the manager did his job. The truth was the trust pretty much ran itself.

They submitted reports for her to review, and she was already studying them to learn all the nuances needed to make sure the trust wasn't defrauded. In his last months of life, Frank had taught her a lot.

He'd been so sick and weak, but his mind had been as good as ever. Sam had taken care of him, trying to make him comfortable, but the thing he loved most was having her read him articles from all his investment newspapers and weekly editions.

He'd go into lecture mode and play teacher to her pupil. At the time, she'd thought she was just entertaining a very sweet man who was dying a slow, horrible death. It hadn't been until his lawyer contacted her to be present for the reading of Frank's will that she realized he might have viewed her as something more.

Even then, it had come as a shock when Frank had written that he viewed her as a daughter and was leaving her in charge of all three of his trusts. Brett had lost it completely in the lawyer's office, threatening her with all kinds of legal action.

Unfortunately for him, there was nothing he could do. If he tried, he would forfeit his own trust fund. Frank had understood his son better than anybody and anticipated his reaction.

"Sam, I know you think…"

She stopped listening. It wasn't worth the effort. Brett could think whatever he wanted about her. The fact was she was in charge and he wasn't. Nothing was going to change that.

"Sam?" Brett's loud question made her realize he wasn't talking anymore.

"I'm hanging up now." She'd had enough.

"Wait—"

She wasn't waiting and slammed the phone down on his plea. She stood, intending to take Brett's gift and throw it out. The glimmer of the stone caught her attention, and she again found herself trapped within its amazing beauty.

Ah, what the hell. Brett may be an ass, but the necklace was beautiful. Pulling it from the box, she stepped up to her dresser mirror and slid the chain around her neck. The stone settled nicely against her chest, warming the spot.

The phone rang behind her, but she ignored it. Let Brett call all he wanted. That didn't mean she had to talk to him. Barely touching the magnificent stone, she smiled at her reflection. Brett may be a lot of not nice things, but he had excellent taste in jewelry.

"Sam!" Vicky's bellow forced her to turn away from the captivating image in the mirror. With an annoyed jerk, she opened the door and shouted back.

"What?"

"Jameson's on the phone for you!"

Oh. Whoops.

Well, she'd answer her phone in the future and just hang up if she heard Brett's voice. That was a rude thing to do, but not an uncalled-for one, Sam assured herself as she ran down the steps.

Five minutes later, she was barreling back up them with a name and phone number in hand. Lilly Masterson was supposedly the best of the best when it came to investigators. Sam was in luck, too, because Lilly lived just down the road in Beaufort. She questioned her so-called luck the minute the woman answered her phone.

"Yeah?"

That wasn't the professional greeting she had been expecting. It wasn't even welcoming.

"I'm trying to get in touch with Lilly Masterson?" Her uncertainty turned her statement into a question.

"Whaddya want?"

"Is this Lilly?"

"Who the hell is this?"

"Uh…I'm Samantha Hark, and I was…"

"Hark?" That eased the annoyance in the woman's tone to a more thoughtful tone. "Samantha Hark? As in Sam Hark?"

"Um, yeah."

"Wow, you own that racing park that's opening up outside of Holly Town, don't you?"

"Yes, and I need—"

"So, what you got up there?"

"Pardon me?" This was not going the way she had expected. Whoever this woman was, there was no way she could be Lilly Masterson. Maybe she had dialed the wrong number.

"Race stuff, that is the point of a racing park, isn't it? So what you got to race?"

"A little bit of everything." There was some strange vein of authority in the other woman's tone that made Sam answer reflexively. "Cars, bikes, dirt bikes, go-carts, we even have some souped-up four-wheelers."

"Huh. That's too cool. So what you need?"

"I'm looking for Lilly Masterson."

"And you're talking to her."

"Maybe I have the wrong Lilly."

"There is only one of me in the whole state. So what do you need?"

"I have a—"

"Problem that you need somebody to discreetly look into for you and offer you a solution to. I know. That's why people like you call me. So, what is the problem?"

"I don't know if the men who are interested in me are more interested in my money." There, she said it, and she felt pushed into saying it by Lilly's mannerisms.

"Ah, one of the oldest problems there is. So, you want me to check out your boyfriend, or is it boyfriends?"

"Friends."

"Okay, give me the names, and I'll make short work of it."

"JD and Caleb McBane." That got an instant response. Obviously, Lilly had been drinking something, because she choked on it.

"As in Sheriff JD McBane?"

"Yes, he and his—"

"He's not after money."

"It's a lot of money."

"Well, that may be, but trust me, that's not what he's interested in. He's only has two settings with women, a good time and…well, if you've hit that other setting—"

"You mean mating."

"So, you know."

"Yes, I know, and he claims that is exactly what he is interested in, but I'm still—"

"Has he bitten you?"

"Excuse me?"

"If he's bitten you, then, well...How should I put this? You're screwed."

Sam blinked. That hadn't been tactful or discreet. It wasn't comforting either. "Listen, Miss Masterson, I want to hire your services to investigate him and his brother. Are you interested in taking the job?"

"I guess I better. I can't have you hiring another investigator who causes problems. God knows the dog boy will blame me."

"Thank you." Maybe hiring Lilly wasn't such a good idea.

"Yeah, I'll stop by tomorrow so we can have a meet and greet."

"The morning would be good for me."

"Fine."

"Do you need directions?"

"Nope. See you then."

Before Sam could respond, the line went dead. Well it would definitely be interesting to meet this supposedly great investigator. Hopefully, she wouldn't screw up things too bad.

If she did, her bags were already packed. Sam didn't want to worry over it anymore. She'd spent all night lying in bed worrying. It was beautiful out, unusually warm for a South Carolina winter day, but still a little cool for a girl from southern Florida.

Perfect for wearing leathers.

What she needed was to go for a ride, to go for a fast ride and burn off some of her pent-up annoyance. Without talking to a single person, Sam suited up and headed to the garage.

For over an hour, she lost herself in the rhythm of the ride. The track she'd chosen was one of the more aggressive ones with sharp curves and steep inclines. Sam took them fast, pushing herself, challenging the fear that tinged her stomach.

Sam cleared a curve and came into a straightaway that was dappled with light filtering through the thick growth of oak trees that wove their limbs together above the track. It had been an argument between Mike and her about what to do with these trees.

Spanish moss liked to grow in thick piles and hang down from the branches. It was not cohesive to racing to have debris falling from overhead and littering the track. While it would cost more in maintenance, Sam had eventually convinced him not to cut back the trees.

As she sped down the road, a strange cracking noise echoed above her. A flash of motion was all the warning she got before suddenly she was airborne. The ground rushed up to meet her, and she tumbled across the sand embankment as she heard her bike crashing down the asphalt.

Chapter 17

Thursday

JD paused at the study door to see if Caleb was still hunched over the computer. At least he was off the phone. Caleb looked run-down. His eyes reddened, his beard starting to peek out, and he could do with a shower or at least a change of clothes.

JD didn't have any sympathy for Caleb, though. No, thanks to his idiot brother, JD was just as sleep-deprived. Actually, it was thanks to his mate and not in a good way. Samantha wasn't here to punish, so Caleb took the blunt end of JD's displeasure.

After all, Caleb had dug this hole and dragged JD into it with him. After Caleb had told him all the details the other night, JD realized he had made a stupid mistake.

He'd left Caleb with too simple a set of instructions. Obviously he should have been more specific. Samantha was supposed to be where he'd left her, in their bed. If Caleb were suffering from his irrational behavior that night, it was his just reward.

"Well? Found anything yet?"

"Not a damn thing on Bruce or Samantha." Caleb leaned back in the oversized desk chair and rubbed his neck. "I'm beginning to think her name's not Samantha Jeanne after all."

"Are you saying she lied to us?"

"No. I don't know. Maybe she just left something off. Maybe it's her maiden name and she forgot to tell us she was divorced. God knows we can't trust anything she told us."

JD eyes narrowed at Caleb's comment. "Have you tried Samantha Hark?"

"Hark? Why…Oh, Samantha Hark. You think she owns that park?"

"She certainly has the money if she wasn't lying about that. Her brother is managing it, isn't that what you said?"

"Shit. I've been at this too long. That's too obvious."

"You miss a lot of obvious things, and I have to play right along with you."

"I did the right thing Monday night, JD." Caleb was tired of hearing it from his brother. "And you know that or you would have gone up there and brought her back."

"I wouldn't have allowed the situation to get to that point."

"No, of course not, because you wouldn't have even let her out of bed."

"Damn straight."

"Forget that it would only make her even more annoyed with us."

"Oh? Was she so much happier being screwed on the side of the road by a wolf man?"

"Let's not argue about it anymore." Caleb forced the words out from between clenched teeth. "We're not getting anywhere by bickering."

"Fine." JD glared silently at his brother for a moment. Caleb wasn't paying him any attention. He had gone back to playing with the computer. JD could only assume that he was looking for Samantha Hark now.

"So, what are we going to do about the interloper?"

"Zane tracked him all the way to a hotel in Savannah. I sent Tex down to relieve him. He said he'd keep an eye on the guy for us."

"Tex? What the hell is he doing in town? I thought he was off fighting wars for the Marines."

"He got out and was waiting for me when I got home last night. I mentioned it."

"No, you didn't."

"You weren't listening."

"Calvin wasn't with him, was he?"

"Out in three more months."

"Great, just what we need, those two running around and stirring up trouble."

"They probably wouldn't stick around for long. Tex was just stopping by for a few days before he headed out to Arizona."

"Arizona? What's out there?"

"A hot bitch, and I quote, 'She just might be the one.'"

"We can pray." But JD wasn't buying that for the moment. Tex was a weird wolf, falling in love left and right. That was part of the reason he was always causing trouble. Fortunately, Cal was little more sensible about mating.

Cal always slept with the women Tex selected, but he dismissed them just as quickly. JD honestly thought even if Tex found their mate, Cal would dismiss her. That was one wolf not interested in monogamy.

"Ah, here she is. Samantha J. Hark was the live-in caretaker of Franklin T. Morison…Upon his death, he named her as trustee of his FTM charitable trust. A five-hundred-million-dollar trust, the FTM donates money to many causes ranging from animal rescue and shelters to college scholarships…Miss Hark, a high school dropout, has been challenged for control over the trust by Mr. Morison's only son, Brett Morison."

"That article you are reading doesn't mention anything about this Bruce guy, does it?"

"Not this one. Let me see." Caleb clicked away on the computer for a few minutes. "Here…ah, this isn't much…It does give me his last name. Bruce Crane. Now, I just have to find out what pack in Florida he belongs to."

"Not many of them left down there." JD rubbed the back of his neck. It was stiff from two nights of sleeping on the ground. "You might want to check Georgia and Alabama. A lot of packs fled the congestion over the years."

"I know that. Are you just going to stand there all day and make useless comments?"

"No, I'm going to work. I just wanted to let you know I am calling a meeting for tonight."

"You are?"

"Given everything, I think we should drop tradition and let the others know about Samantha and this Bruce guy. I want her as protected as if she were a full member."

"Okay. That's a good move."

"If you can tear yourself away from that thing, it'd be nice if you could pick the guys up some beer and food for the meeting."

"I'm going to be glad when you have Samantha to boss around," Caleb muttered.

"What was that?"

"Go away, JD."

* * * *

"Hey!"

That obnoxious greeting was followed by a hard rock of Sam's mattress. She snarled at the annoyance and ignored the intrusion. She felt like shit, and she'd rather not feel anything at all.

"That's a cute little puppy growl. Whatcha going to do, bite me?"

Again, the bed shifted hard to the right. This time Sam had had enough. Whoever had dared to invade her room and pick on her was in for it. She shot straight up and roared.

"What the hell do you want?" Instantly she regretted her actions. Her body sent out shards of sharp pain. The searing sensation was contrasted by the sharp pounding in her head. She gripped it, not that that helped. "Ah, shouldn't have done that."

"Growls like a puppy, but croaks like a frog."

The chuckled comment drew her eyes to the stranger standing over her bed. The woman was short, pretty damn short for Sam to think that. And skinny, she hated skinny women, especially ones with big boobs and flared hips. If it wasn't for those very distinguishing marks, the girl could have been mistaken for a kid.

"Who the hell are you, and what the hell are you doing in my room?"

"Lilly Masterson at your service." Lilly did an elaborate bow. "And you must be Samantha Hark, multimillionaire and soon-to-be dog girl."

"That's not funny." Sam did not like Lilly any more today than she had yesterday.

"Depends on your point of view." Lilly shrugged before pulling up Sam's reading chair alongside her bed.

"Do you mind?"

"Nah, stay in bed. I heard you had a quite a tumble."

"Then you heard I need my sleep."

"I'm impressed that you're in bed, your own bed specifically. Would have thought JD and Caleb would have hit the roof when they heard about your accident. Guess I overestimated them."

"They don't know," Sam stated hesitantly after a pause. She hadn't thought of their reaction until now. It made her head ache worse to think what they would do if they found out.

"And how long do you think that's going to take in this small town?"

"I'm really not liking you."

Sam stretched back down on the bed. The motion made her ache, and she mentally began to catalog her pains. Something was missing. Sam's hand flew up to her chest and around her neck. It was gone.

"You're really not hiring me to be friends. You hired me—"

"Where is it?" Sam narrowed her eyes on Lilly.

"Where is what?"

"My necklace! Did you take it?"

"You think I steal jewelry from my clients while they are sleeping?"

"Where is it?" Sam shouted, sitting back up. If that woman had touched her necklace, she'd take the little investigator apart piece by piece.

"Hey, now." Lilly held up her hands in defeat. "I don't know what you are talking about, but perhaps it would help if you thought about where you put it last."

"It was on my neck. I never take it off."

"That important, huh?"

Sam ignored Lilly's smirk and stumbled onto her feet. The quick motion made her temporarily light-headed, and she swayed as the world went black for a moment. A hand on her arm drew her blinking gaze to Lilly. She'd jumped out of her chair and was frowning at Sam.

"I don't think you should be out of bed."

"I need my necklace." Sam tried to shake off Lilly's hold, but it was impossible.

"Fine." Lilly forced her back down to the mattress. "I'm an investigator. I think I can manage to find it for you. When did you have it last?"

"I never take it off," Sam repeated, glaring at the investigator.

"Oh, is that your way of saying you last had it when you crashed your bike?"

"Yeah." Her head was pounding, and it was growing increasingly hard to concentrate. "I had it then."

"Well, then it's probably in this bag."

"What bag?" Sam's head snapped back up to watch as Lilly moved toward the dresser. There was a small white plastic bag tossed on top of the wood surface. "What is that?"

"That's the bag they send you home with from the hospital. They put your personal effects in it…Ah, this is it."

"You have my necklace?"

The little woman didn't respond. Her back was to Sam, and not being able to see was killing her. She wanted her necklace back and was afraid the investigator would steal it. It was that beautiful.

"Give it to me." Again, Sam forced her weak legs to support her weight.

"Yeah, sure," Lilly muttered, but didn't move.

"Now!" Sam was almost on her when Lilly turned. Her eyes went immediately to the amazing stone. At the sight of it, she felt her tension begin to relax. It was safe. It was within her grasp.

"It's very pretty," Lilly commented as she handed over the piece of jewelry. "Mind if I ask where you got it?"

"It was given to me by somebody very close to me." Sam sighed as she clasped the necklace back around her neck. Her aches and pains diminished and with it her energy. She wobbled again.

"You really need to stay in bed." Lilly helped Sam back to the mattress. "No necklace is worth getting hurt over it."

"This one is." Sam wasn't sure where that came from, but it sounded right.

"Huh." Lilly studied her for a moment before taking her seat again. "You've had it a long time, then."

"Feels like forever." Sam closed her eyes. She was tired and didn't want to talk anymore. "Do you mind? I need my rest."

"I believe you had a problem that you wanted help on. If that is no longer the case, then I will be glad to go. Of course, I doubt once JD and Caleb hear about your unfortunate mishap you'll be getting much rest."

Sam sighed. She didn't feel like focusing on that problem, but that wasn't going to make it disappear. In fact, Lilly had a point in suggesting that it could become more aggravated in the short order.

"Fine, I got a problem."

"Yeah, I'm glad it yours and not mine."

"Excuse me?"

"Hey, I get down every night and thank the good Lord above that no dog boy has decided that I'm his one. I can't think of a fate worse than some overbearing, overmuscled, arrogant, flea-infested, fuzz butt deciding that he's the ruler of my life and trying to put a leash on me."

Sam couldn't help but smile at that. She certainly did know JD and Caleb, though they didn't have hairy butts and certainly not fleas.

"At least they wouldn't want you for your money."

"Ah, hell, honey. I told you yesterday that isn't a worry for you. JD and Caleb wouldn't ruin their chance to breed just to bite a bitch for her money. Children aren't something you can put a price on."

"What are you talking about?" That got Sam's eyes opening and wiped any memory of a smile from her face.

"I thought you knew."

"Knew what?"

"That they were Covenanters."

"I thought they were werewolves. What the hell is a Covenanter?"

"It's a breed of werewolf."

"There are breeds?"

"Yeah, lots of breeds, three in this area. We have the Narin. They're a little further north toward Charleston, the Rouffi hang around Beaufort, and then the Covenanters. JD and Caleb are alphas of that pack."

"So what? They all look different? Different coats or ability to retrieve a ball?" Sam's snide comments got a hearty laugh from Lilly.

"I like that. I'm going to use that in the future."

"For what?"

"To irritate the guys. If you're gonna live in this area, surrounded by these jackasses, you have two choices. You can get annoyed, or you can be annoying."

"I can already tell which choice you made," Sam stated dryly.

"Yeah, well, it came naturally to me." No matter what Sam said or how grumpy she was, it didn't shake Lilly's good mood. "But to answer your question, different breeds have different lineage, and some of them have evolved different abilities."

"Abilities?"

"Yeah, the Covenanters are noted for two special abilities. One I'm betting you've encountered is their mating musk."

"Been there." Sam nodded slightly, wincing over the movement.

"I bet you have. Never had the misfortune, but most women say it's a pleasurable trip. Anyway, their second ability is to be able to half transform."

"Half transform?"

"Yeah, some weres can only go human to wolf in a matter of seconds. Covenanters can pull on certain wolf traits without actually forming into a wolf."

"Like growing claws on a human hand?"

"Mm-hm, their eyes can click over. They'll glow, and they'll have great night vision."

And their tongues grew longer, and their cocks got bigger. Oh God, she'd been right.

Last night when she'd accused Caleb of screwing her in wolf form, she'd hadn't really thought he'd been a wolf. She'd just assumed that he'd…well, he'd…

"When they're like that, who's in control?"

"Pardon me?"

"Who is in control of their body, the wolf or the man?"

"Hell if I know. I'm no fur ball. I'm just saying, you don't want to take on a Covenanter in a bar fight."

"Okay." Talking to Lilly was making her feel worse. "Is there anything else I should know?"

"Depends on what you already know."

"Pretend I know nothing."

"All right, top of the list would be that you are the only woman who can bear their children, so there is no way in hell they'll ever let you go."

"So, it's my womb they're after, not my money." Sam wasn't sure exactly how she felt about that revelation. It wasn't good, though.

"They're lucky if they ever find a woman who can breed with them. That's why they're considered a diminishing breed. Most of them join the military to get a free ride around the world in search of their mates."

"Caleb said he was in the Marines."

"So was JD, until their dads were killed."

"You know about that?" Sam narrowed her eyes on Lilly. She had to admit she was curious about the details, but hadn't had the courage to ask Caleb for the specifics the other night.

"Everybody knows about that. Before that, it had been nearly thirty years since a cop was killed in these parts. The last time was some psycho a Beaufort deputy was transporting. He got free and…well, it was an open-and-shut case."

"Wow." Sam paused, not sure how to proceed. "I guess it was big news considering the circumstances."

"Are you fishing?" Lilly cocked her head and smirked. "No need to be subtle. You want to know something, just ask."

"How did they die?" Sam caved after several moments of heated silence.

"They were decapitated."

"What?" Of all the possible responses to her question, Sam was stunned into confusion by Lilly's blunt answer.

"Yeah, their bodies were found on the side of the road in front of Marcus's car."

"Marcus?"

"JD and Caleb's father," Lilly expanded before shrugging. "One of them that is. Of course, both their heads were found—"

"Never mind!" Sam cut her off, feeling her stomach roll. "Forget I asked."

"Hmm, I guess it is kind of gruesome."

"Ya think?"

"Ah, well. Sorry."

She didn't sound it, not in the least. Sam's dislike for Lilly was taking on a whole new level of animosity. Despite Sam's natural distaste for Lilly's bluntness, she couldn't fault her for not being honest.

"Caleb said he didn't know why…" Sam couldn't help but press. It was easier to ask Lilly than it would be to ask either twin given the nature of the crime.

"Nope, nobody ever found out why. My guess is drugs, but it's still an open case."

"Yeah, that's what he said."

"You can trust him. That's what I've been trying to tell you. So you want to tell me why you thought they were after your money, or are you just a paranoid person by nature?"

"It was because of Bruce."

* * * *

"Bruce?" Lilly scowled. She felt those prickles that served her so well in life. It told her that the meat was at hand. "Tell me about this Bruce."

"Why?"

Boy, she was turning out to be a difficult client. Lilly couldn't have been more happy for JD and Caleb. They deserved a woman who complicated basic conversation. Those two had had it too easy for too long when it came to women.

"Because I asked and I'm sitting here. You aren't in any condition to do anything about that."

"I could call my sister on you."

"Vicky?" Lilly smiled. "She's a sweet girl."

"Vicky?"

"What, you don't think your sister's nice?"

"It's not that. She's just protective is all. Don't tell me she let you up here."

"Of course she did."

"How did you pull that off?"

"Who is Bruce?"

"You're as single-minded as a—"

"Dog? Say what you will, but I can find out whether or not you tell me."

"Why would you do that?"

"Call it a hunch, but I'm thinking your problem isn't with JD or Caleb. It's with this Bruce guy."

"I thought he'd leave me alone if I left Florida." Samantha caved. "But the damn man followed me."

"Stalking?"

"He just wants my money."

"And you know this how?"

"We were engaged. I really thought I hit the jackpot, hot and sweet. Boy, was I stupid."

"So, he had a secret agenda, and you found this out how?"

"I went to his house to surprise him one night. He thought I was out of town, but my plans got changed at the last minute. I thought he was supposed to be having dinner with an old friend. Instead, I found him doing something altogether different with a not-so-old friend."

"Ah, he was pounding the sheets with another woman."

"More like the grass and then they went furry and did it again."

Lilly couldn't help herself. She burst out into laughter. She'd heard a lot of strange stories about how the innocents found out they were no longer alone on their planet, but this one was classic. The dog and his boner, Lilly shook her head. Figured.

"Thank you! I really appreciate your sensitivity! Now will you get out?"

"Sorry!" Lilly held up her hands. Sometimes she forgot other people weren't as thick-skinned or warped as she was. "So, werewolf Bruce followed you here."

"You're still here?"

"And I'm not leaving."

"Fine, he followed me here, and Caleb and him almost got into it last night."

"Caleb knows?" Lilly sucked her lower lip as she thought about that one. "Probably ran him out of town."

"Hopefully you'll join him."

"Yeah, yeah." Lilly stood. "Just one more thing."

"What?"

"Bruce's last name?"

"Crane."

"Good to know."

Lilly had gotten as much as she needed to start her investigation. Samantha might not know it, but she'd hired herself a private investigator to solve her real problem. The entire situation unnerved Lilly. An interloping werewolf was bad news. Normally that would be a pack problem and Lilly would stay out of it, but there was more going on here than territory wars.

That wasn't the only thing bothering Lilly. There was magic in this room, radiating out of Samantha's precious necklace. Her own twisted heritage made her sensitive to evil, and she knew black magic when she felt it.

That crap about the necklace coming from Samantha's mother had been a lie Lilly had easily sensed. Somebody else had given that necklace to Lilly and recently if Lilly's guess was correct. The question was why and what did they hope it would do to her? Whatever the answer was it wouldn't be good news for Samantha.

There was no point in taking the jewelry away until Lilly knew the particulars of those answers. Messing with the culprit's plans would only make whoever was after Samantha strike back harder.

Right now, he was in charge of the game, but not for long. When Lilly played, she played to win.

Chapter 18

Saturday

"Would you like to dance with me, JD?" Sally asked, smiling sweetly.

"I'm sorry, Sally but I don't feel like dancing."

"Oh, go dance with the girl, JD." Caleb gave him a shove, earning him a dark look. "Don't worry, I'll keep my eyes open for Samantha."

"I bet you will. Why don't you go dance with Sally?"

"She didn't ask me."

"You know I am standing here." Sally's smile dipped.

"Oh, yeah." Caleb gave her a quick smile. "Sorry, babe. You know how it is."

"So it's true."

"What's true?"

"Gina said you two had mated some outsider." Sally shrugged. "Said she saw her at the diner with Caleb."

"Yeah, you tell Gina the next time we come into the diner to watch herself too. Samantha is going to be head bitch around here, and I wouldn't tolerate any insult to her."

"You wouldn't tolerate? I'm the sheriff."

"We wouldn't tolerate it. Are you happy now?"

"Fine." Sally interrupted them again. "I'll tell Gina to put it back on the leash."

"Never mind that." JD waved Sally's offer away. "I'll tell her myself."

"Okay. Now about that—"

"Actually, I think you should do it." JD turned on Caleb again.

"Me?" Caleb's gaze blinked back from the door he had been watching. "I got better things to do."

"I'm not the one who slept with Gina. There is nothing going on right now, so you might as well clean up your own mistake."

"But Samantha—"

"Is not here right now."

Caleb growled softly before giving in. For the past hour, both brothers had been unsociable, staying to the corner where they could wait and watch for Samantha to show up. During that time, JD had tried no fewer than five tactics to get rid of Caleb.

Caleb knew that JD was still ticked that he had let Samantha go. To add insult to injury, Caleb had reaped all the benefits of his brother's lesson plan. JD felt like he was owed some alone time with Samantha, and he was probably right.

That didn't mean Caleb was going to bow out of the way for the night. Nope, they had a lifetime over which JD could make up his one lost night.

Still, Gina needed talking to, and here where there were witnesses was for the best. Caleb knew Gina liked to make up stories on the occasion. He didn't want her spreading any rumors about him that got back to Samantha. Their position was already unstable.

JD watched Caleb walk away before turning his gaze back toward the door. He knew that he was making a fool of himself, but that didn't stop him. Everybody was probably already whispering about how their mate had them by the short hairs.

Damn it! They were right. It had been almost five days since he last saw Samantha, last buried himself in her heaven, and it was driving him insane.

"Well, JD?"

"Oh, Sally, uh…"

"You're being very rude."

"Listen, Sally—"

"It's *just* a dance. Don't tell me you're out of the market for that too!"

"I just don't want Samantha to get the wrong idea if she walks in, is all."

"God, what a wuss." She muttered it as she turned to storm away.

JD's eyes narrowed. His instincts were triggered by the insult. It was in his nature to demand respect, especially from the members of his pack. Sally knew that. After their long relationship, she probably knew exactly how those words affected him. Normally that kind of talk would end up with a spanking and lead to some long hours of her apologizing while he fucked her in as many positions as possible.

Instead of shoving off the wall and chasing after her, as Sally no doubt intended, JD decided to save all his annoyance for Samantha. It really was her fault. If Samantha weren't being so difficult about everything, then his pack members wouldn't be acting like JD couldn't control one single bitch.

Well, the final mating would put that to rest. JD smiled as that thought soothed him. Whether he had to drag her kicking and screaming or she chose to behave with some dignity, nothing would stop the final mating.

His smile faded away as he spied Samantha stepping through the door. JD's breath caught in his throat. She looked elegant wearing a demure black cocktail dress. The severity of the color showed off her vibrant hair color as it fell in gentle waves around her face and shoulders.

His hands were already itching with the need to thread through the soft-looking tresses. Then he would peel that dress down and touch, kiss, lick each delectable inch of her that was revealed until she was naked and his head was buried in the soft skin of her pussy. Then they'd get around to her punishment for making him wait.

JD's thoughts were cut off as a big blond man stepped in behind her and took her arm. He recognized the man instantly. His eyes narrowed as a growl worked its way up his chest.

The man had been warned. Apparently, not well enough, because he had his arm around Samantha's waist, and she appeared to be leaning on him as they followed the others to a table.

* * * *

Chase helped Sam into a seat, while Jimmy took Vicky out onto the dance floor, and Mike went to find a beer. When Sam asked for a glass of punch, Chase jumped on the opportunity to go. He liked Sam, but he'd already caught the sheriff's glare when they'd stepped into the room.

The man appeared to be making a beeline toward them. Chase personally didn't want to end the night in jail. Sam didn't notice JD at all, too focused on how crappy she felt.

Vicky had been right. This was a bad idea. She'd suffered through putting a dress on that required way too much wiggling for her sore body, a car ride that has nearly too long for her rolling stomach, all to come to a dance when she could barely walk. For what?

For JD and Caleb. Sam sighed. The horrible truth behind all her rational arguments was simple. Fear and jealousy were the true motivations for her stupidity.

Her brain told her that the odds were if she didn't show up at the dance, they would show up at the race park to find out why. That part of her was still in shock that they had left her alone for the past five days, especially JD.

For a man who had been so determined to capture and hold her, she'd expected more from him. Maybe he'd given up? Maybe, despite what Lilly Masterson believed, they were really after her money. Now that they knew she was on to them, they'd backed off.

They could have just been respecting her wishes. They'd never done that in the short amount of time she'd known them, so why start now? Unless they had a new woman to fill their time and bed with.

So many possibilities, they were driving her insane. The only thing to do was to go to the dance and see their betrayal with her own eyes. Now, if she could just find the energy to lift her head up and look.

"Samantha." JD's growl was followed instantly by an arm jerking her straight out of the chair she had just found safe harbor in.

"JD." Sam winced at the sudden movement. "It's nice to see—"

"Why did you come with that man?" JD immediately began dragging her back toward the door.

"What man?" The room was starting to spin around her, and if JD didn't slow down, she was going to trip and fall.

"That one, Samantha."

"Chase?"

"He had his arm around you."

"He was being polite. You know, like civilized people?"

To think she missed this, missed him. There must be something wrong with her. It hadn't even been a minute, and he was already threatening her.

"Are you implying I'm not civilized?"

"I've yet to see that aspect of your nature." Sam swayed and stumbled. "If you don't slow down, I'm—"

"What is wrong with you?"

JD came to a sudden stop, apparently realizing her difficulty in keeping up wasn't due to her normal resistance to his brutish manners. His arm came around her waist, pulling her upright and close to his side.

"What are you wearing?" He scowled, his hands running slightly up her sides.

"It's nothing."

"Is that a girdle?" JD gave her a strange look as he continued to size up what was hidden beneath her dress.

"Yes."

* * * *

"Why are you wearing one of those?"

JD felt his fangs ache to lengthen at the realization she wearing sexy lingerie. Women only wore those things to taunt men into taking them off, which meant that Samantha had plans for later with her date. That wasn't about to happen. If anybody was going to be taking off Samantha's clothes, it was going to be him and not some blond Adonis.

"I can wear whatever I want."

The words were right, but the tone was off. Samantha's normal contrary personality was being inhibited. Otherwise, she'd be blasting him good right now. What fun was it if she didn't give him her full resistance?

"That's not a girdle." JD corrected himself. It was too thick and stiff to be lingerie. He ran his hand back down to her waist. "Is that a bandage?"

"It's a girdle. It's a new style."

"What's that? That's nasty." JD turned her arm over, pushing the sleeve up to study the bruise. He pushed her sleeve up a little farther to discover even more bruises. "How did you get these?"

"What?"

"Don't play dumb with me. How did you get this bruise? And that one?" he asked, noticing the one on her other arm.

"I took a little fall."

JD studied her with narrowed eyes. She was trying to take deep breaths. With each one her eyes clouded bit by bit. Something was seriously wrong, and he meant to know exactly what was going on. The first thing to do was to get her someplace private to interrogate her.

JD took her by the arm and started back toward the door of the hall. He was intent on finding a nice private area to demand the truth from her. His bed would be the perfect spot. Then he would undress her and see for himself this supposed girdle she was hiding.

As they moved, he could tell she was having difficulty. She was moving very slowly and stiffly, leaning too much on his arm. Concerned about her condition, he matched his pace with hers and slipped his arm around her waist to provide her with more support.

Before they could make it ten steps, the fiery little vixen known as Samantha's sister was blocking their path. JD sighed. He wasn't in the mood for this. Vicky didn't look like she cared.

Her displeased gazed turned on JD. He matched it with his own dark glare. No pint-sized woman was going to intimidate him.

* * * *

"Why are you taking such deep breaths?" Vicky's scowl turned back to her sister. "You feel sick, don't you?"

"It's probably the medicine." JD was almost completely supporting her now, but Sam wasn't about to tell Vicky about being light-headed or in pain. She'd probably insist on taking her back to the hospital.

"Damn it, Sam!"

"Don't make a scene." Sam hushed. "We're trying to make a good impression here."

"What better impression than having you keel over dead on the floor?" Vicky snapped.

Mike stepped up to join the little group. He didn't look any happier with Sam than Vicky.

"Where's Chase?" Vicky turned her anger on her husband, a normal target regardless of whether or not he actually deserved her wrath.

"Dancing with every single woman that asks." Mike turned a tight smile on the sheriff. "Sheriff, nice to see you again."

"What's going on here?" JD eyed the three of them like the well-trained, skeptical cop he was.

"Nothing for you to be concerned about, Sheriff." Vicky turned on him, scowling at his intrusion.

"Samantha?"

Sam sighed. She knew that tone. He was probably only seconds from snatching her off her feet and carrying her off to bed. It would be his bed, but right now any bed would do. Besides, nothing was going to deter him. Trying would only make the situation worse.

"I told you I had a little accident."

"What kind of accident?"

"Really, Sheriff. Sam is not in any condition for an inquisition. She needs to be home and in bed. That's exactly what's going to happen. I'm going to have Chase take you home now."

"I'll take her," JD growled.

"Back to our place?" Vicky challenged him.

"I'll take care of her."

"Maybe we should ask Sam what she wants," Mike suggested quickly, sensing the tension between Vicky and the sheriff could easily spin out of control.

"Sam wants to go home," Vicky snapped at their brother.

"Vicky." Mike was the one growling now.

"Fine." Vicky turned on Sam, whose head was beginning to droop. "Tell them you want to go home."

Sam took a deep breath, looking between her siblings and JD. If she went home, Vicky would continue to mother her to death. JD probably wasn't a better option, though instead of nagging her, he'd probably just boss her around.

He would hold her too, and then there was that big jetted tub he had in his bathroom. Not to mention Caleb. Sam was betting that Caleb had a sweet bedside manner. He'd probably carry her up and down the steps, if JD would let her out of the bedroom. Besides, if she didn't go home with JD, he'd just show up at the park and move in.

"Samantha!" Vicky snapped.

"I'll go with JD."

"Samantha!"

Sam knew Vicky wasn't as upset as she was hurt. She didn't want to hurt Vicky's feelings, but she had had enough of the sister-knows-best routine. All she wanted to do was sleep and be left alone. JD was more likely to give that to her, so she was going with him. She would have to soothe Vicky's feelings when she was feeling better herself.

"Come on." Mike stepped forward to get Sam's other arm. "I'll help you out to the car."

"I've got her."

JD matched his actions to his words, knocking Mike's hand out of the way and gently lifting Sam into his arms. Ignoring the looks from the crowd, he carried her to his truck.

Mike followed them. After Sam was settled in the front seat of his pickup, she closed her eyes and leaned her head back. She'd passed out by the time JD climbed in. He reached across to gently pull her seat belt into place.

* * * *

Samantha didn't wake up on the drive to his place. She didn't make a single sound as he carried her from his truck to his bed. Except for a small sigh as she settled into the mattress, she gave no sign she was even alive.

JD frowned down at her. He didn't want to wake her. The answers he wanted would have to wait. For now, he'd have to be content that she had chosen to come home with him.

That had to be a step in the right direction. The next step would be getting that dress off her. Her shoes were easy, so were her pantyhose and underwear, but the zipper to her dress was in the back.

Careful not disturb her, he slid his hands beneath her and caught the little metal tab. Samantha murmured and shifted as he lowered the metal clasp. Her eyes flittered open when he tried to work the tight dress off her.

"JD?" She blinked sleepily. "What are you doing?"

"Trying to get your dress off."

"I'm too tired for that." Her complaint made him roll his eyes.

"I know, but you'll be more comfortable sleeping without it."

"Hmm, okay."

"I need your help, Samantha."

JD prodded her to move as he worked the sleeves off her arms and the dress over her hips. As he pulled the garment off her, his gaze was drawn to the litany of bruises. They covered her shoulders, arms, and legs, and it was a bandage wrapped around her rib cage, just as he suspected. JD felt his temper flare at the sight of his mate injured.

She probably told him the truth about falling. The real question was what type of fall. It looked as if she'd tumbled down a whole flight of stairs. It hit him then, her motorcycle.

"Why are you growling?"

"You fell off your bike, didn't you?"

"A limb fell down in the road. It wasn't my fault."

"You shouldn't have been on the damn thing to begin with. You're not getting on another one."

"Don't tell me what to do. I can ride a bike if I want to."

"I refuse to allow it, Samantha."

"Refuse?" Her snort turned into a yawn, but that didn't stop her from talking. "You don't have any right to refuse to allow anything."

"I am your mate."

"Oh, I forgot. I'm your breed mare. You have an investment in my womb."

"What?"

"Don't play dumb with me, JD. I know all about your predicament when it comes to having kids. I'm your one shot at having kids."

"Who told you that?" He'd wring the neck of whoever had explained those details to Samantha. That was for Caleb and him to tell her about.

"That's not important. What's important is that you've tried to trick me."

"I have not." JD felt his ears flame with his indignation. "I would never…What are you doing?"

Samantha struggled to sit up, trying to throw her legs over the side of the bed. JD quickly forced her back down. There was no way he was letting her add to her injuries. She was going to stay in bed and get better, and that, as his mother liked to say, was that.

"I want to go home." Samantha sounded on the verge of tears.

"You are home."

JD began to get concerned. Her cheeks were growing flushed, and she looked like she might be getting a fever. It didn't help that she was working herself up into a state of distress. Samantha was already injured enough, she needed to rest and relax, not pick fights with him.

"I want to go to my home."

"Samantha—" JD groaned as he watched the first of her tears begin to fall.

"Don't." Samantha sniffled. "I wouldn't be used by another man. I've already been engaged for my money. I wouldn't be mated for my womb."

JD couldn't take the sight of her crying. It made him feel vulnerable and helpless, two alien emotions that chafed. Not sure what to do, he stretched out on the bed and pulled her into his arms.

She struggled a bit at first, but relented when he tightened his hold.

"I hurt," Samantha whined between sniffles, burying her head deeper into his chest.

JD lifted her, arranging her on her stomach so that she lay directly on top of him. She took over, wiggling into a comfortable position. The small motions caused him to groan.

It probably was uncivilized, but ever since he had pulled her dress off, his cock had been hard. JD knew there was nothing to be done about it tonight. Maybe tomorrow, just a quick and easy session, one that didn't tax her strength too much. He promised himself he would do all the work.

Her necklace was biting into his chest. JD shifted, trying to get into a better position, but the large stone still hurt. She appeared to have passed out, and so he was careful not to disturb her as he reached for the clasp.

"What are you doing?" Samantha shot straight up the moment he touched the small metal closure.

"I was just going to take off your necklace so I could be comfortable." JD scowled at her as her face darkened, her hand coming to protectively cover the piece of jewelry.

"No. It never comes off."

"What the hell is wrong with you?"

"Don't every touch my necklace."

"What the hell?"

"It's mine."

"Of course it is. What do you think I was going to do? Wear it?"

"You're trying to take it from me."

"No, I was just trying to get comfortable."

"Find a new bed if you can't get comfortable in this one. I'm not taking off my necklace."

"What's so important about that damn thing? A lover give it to you?" He'd rip the damn thing off her if that were the case.

"My dead mother gave it to me, and I never take it off."

JD could smell the deception on her. He knew she lied. The necklace hadn't come from her mother and it had better not have come from a damn ex-lover. "You weren't wearing it before."

"Are you saying I'm lying?"

"Uh, no."

He wanted to take exception to her attitude, but he was not dumb enough to fall into that trap. There was no point in arguing about the damn thing. At least not tonight. Later, when she'd healed some he'd get the truth out of her.

"Just turn it around so it doesn't poke me in my chest."

"Fine, but don't you touch it." Samantha yanked the necklace around. "Now, do you mind? I'm tired."

"By all means."

JD helped her settle back against his chest, the mood ruined by her tantrum. Well, it was ruined for him. With a sigh and a little wiggle, Samantha was asleep in moments. At least she couldn't pick any more arguments with him.

Unfortunately, the front door crashed open, and Caleb was roaring their names. He'd better intervene before Caleb woke her back up. JD heaved a big sigh as he moved Samantha back off his chest. Having a twin could be a real pain sometimes. Caleb interfered in everything.

Chapter 19

Sunday

Sam woke up aching, taken from her erotic dream to the reality of a sensual embrace with fluid ease. The details of the dream had seemed so real they had left her body quivering with a need being driven higher at the hands and mouths of her lovers.

Her legs were spread wide, a hard body trapped between them as Caleb nuzzled her swollen, weeping folds. Sam groaned as his voyaging tongue curled into her, tickling her sensitive inner muscles.

He was relentless, his tongue flicking her clit with quick strokes as his fingers thrust deep into her pussy. Sam's hips pumped up toward the lips and hand driving her insane, but Caleb wasn't about to let her control the situation.

He moved his hands, wrapping his arms around her thighs to hold her still as his tongue slid down to fill her. Sam groaned in protest. He was just being mean, making her so hot and denying her release.

The aches and pains from her recent accident were drowned out by the pleasure and frustration flooding her body. Forgotten too was JD, but not for long, not when a second tongue joined the first, swirling over her abandoned clit.

Sam couldn't take the feeling of having two mouths pleasuring her so intimately. She needed release, if not from the sexual torment, then from the tormenters themselves. Again, she lifted and bucked, but couldn't dislodge either heavy male.

Her reckless motions did create an opportunity that one of the brothers took immediate advantage of. She didn't know which scoundrel slid his hand under her ass, but it didn't matter. Either brother would have done the same thing.

Sam arched and shrieked as she felt two thick fingers press into her back entrance. In minutes, they had her moaning and writhing with need. Despite the almost painful, stretched sensation in her ass, Sam's body was alive with the need for more, with a dark desire to have both of them filling her, fucking her until they released her from the tense heights they were driving her toward.

JD lifted his head. He watched her with a feral, hungry look in his eyes that gave her hope that soon they would end their teasing. It had been over a week since they had introduced her to the rapture of having two hard cocks stretching her, pumping into her fast and hard until she exploded into pleasure she had never known she was capable of.

Sam needed that now. They had awakened her to a whole new world of delights the one night they had spent all together. She had fought her body's craving for that kind of satisfaction, but could do so no longer.

"Please."

"Please what, baby?" JD stretched up to rub a tender kiss across her lips. The sweet, soothing gesture was at odds with the rough, erotic motions of the hand he had hidden beneath her.

"I can't take any more." Sam's neck arched as JD trailed kisses around her jaw. "Please, I need you."

That was all Caleb needed to hear. He surged up onto his arms, which he planted on either side of her. The quick motion forced JD out of the way, but she didn't have time to worry about him.

She felt the large, rounded head of his cock pushing into her, forcing her muscles wide as he forged deep into her cunt. Sam couldn't help the sigh of satisfaction that escaped as he seated himself fully in her.

It was a moment of pure perfection, surrounded by his heat, filled with his hardness, warm and protected under his heavy weight. With every breath, she inhaled more of the lust-inducing musk. Instead of sending her into a state of animal lust, it traveled through her body, melting and relaxing muscles that had been stiff for too long.

Sam moaned an objection when he moved. She didn't want anything to disturb the moment. All she wanted to do was exist in the warmth of his love. They ended up reversed, with him on bottom.

She issued another murmured complaint at the new position. Her back was already getting cold. JD rebuilt the protective cocoon for her, pressing into her with an intent that changed her annoyance to anticipation.

His hand returned. His fingers, well greased now, speared lubricant deep into her backside. Sam gasped, her head lifting, her back arching. Yes, that was what she wanted, needed.

"More."

Caleb chuckled unsteadily beneath her, but she didn't care if she was amusing him. She did care when he flexed his own hips, pulling slightly back from her. He didn't make it an inch out of her before she was growling and thrusting downward, recapturing the precious thickness he'd dared to try to withhold.

This time JD chuckled. She flipped her hair and glared at him over her shoulder, growling her annoyance. He grinned back at her and spread her ass cheeks. She lost her annoyance when he settled the broad head of his dick against the tight ring of muscles protecting her rear channel.

With steady pressure, he penetrated her with a soft pop. Sam closed her eyes, her fingers curling into tight fist, trapping the taught skin of Caleb's shoulders, as JD fed her inch after thick inch. It was torture being taken so slowly. The tingly sparks of rapture were almost ticklish, not fueled by enough speed to explode into true ecstasy.

"Don't tease me, damn it!"

She flexed her hips to take what she wanted. The motion made Caleb slip slightly out of her. Instantly she bucked, trying to keep him fully inside of her. Before JD could slide his full length into her ass, Sam was already thrusting between them. It wasn't as good as when they did it, but she needed something, anything.

"Ah, hell." JD groaned behind her, right before he gave up his efforts to tease her and slammed his full length straight into her. Sam screamed as his balls slapped her ass. Not to be outdone by his brother, Caleb began to fuck her pussy with rough urgency.

The world dissolved around her. Pure fire arced through her like lightning bolts, setting small flares that were fueled into bonfires by each pounding thrust of the cocks dueling to fill her completely. As the hits came faster, harder, the inferno raged out of control until it sucked her straight into the fiery abyss.

Her vision went dark, and she lost all ability to distinguish one sensation from another as her orgasm stretched endlessly onward. She was barely aware of the twin roars or of being flooded with hot jets of semen. All that she knew was that she was flying high one moment, and the next she was crashing downward literally onto Caleb.

Her muscles were limp, her body drained. This is what death would feel like if it weren't for her raging heartbeat echoing through her bloodstream. It reminded her that this was life, her life, and it was a damn good one.

* * * *

It was several minutes before JD could remember that they had meant to go easy on Samantha. All concern for her injuries or worries about hurting her had been forgotten the moment she started thrashing between them. Caleb and him had planned to be doing all the work.

They'd been aware that it was too soon for this kind of thing, but it had been so long since they had touched her, tasted her, and driven her to climax as they reached their own. With her naked and moaning their names in her sleep, it had been too much temptation.

Now, he cringed as he thought of the rough way they'd taken her. It was too late to undo what had happened. The best he could come up with was being gentle now. Even that was difficult with her ass still clenched around his dick. His unruly cock was still hard, still eager to go again.

JD's groan was matched by Samantha's moan as he tried to gently extract himself from her ass. Her body didn't relinquish its captive freely, but tightened down around his thick length in an attempt to block his motions.

JD managed to resist the temptation this time, and his dick popped free with an audible sound. Samantha muttered a protest and buried her head into the crook of Caleb's neck. Caleb snickered slightly before smoothing her hair back and out of his face.

Caleb's slight mirth was lost a moment later when JD lifted Samantha right off him. This time it was Caleb's hardened dick that popped free to bounce against his stomach, leaving a wet spot. His brother glared at him, displeased with the interruption.

JD didn't pay Caleb any attention as he carried Samantha off to the bathroom. Their mate needed soothing and cleaning. A dip in the large whirlpool tub was the perfect solution, and JD was just the brother to help her out with that.

Samantha didn't say a word, moaning and groaning out her complaints or compliments while he bathed her with massaging strokes of the washcloth. JD enjoyed the silence. It was a nice change from their customary arguing, but he knew it couldn't last. He wanted answers, and she was going to give them to him.

"Samantha?" She didn't respond but to sigh. JD pulled her hair back from her shoulder so he could talk to her. "Are you feeling all right?"

"Mmm-hmm."

"We weren't too hard on you?"

"No."

"I want to know who told you about our mating rituals." He kept his tone calm as he continued to nibble his way across her shoulder. He wanted to keep her relaxed, but knew the conversation ahead was probably going to rally her ire.

"What?" Her hands covered his, dragging them up toward her breasts.

"You mentioned that you thought we were mating you for your womb last night, remember?" JD didn't need her to tell him what she wanted, but he didn't want her distracted.

"No." She tried to force his hands to move. JD relented, beginning to slowly massage her swollen globes, careful not to tease the tips.

"Focus, Samantha. You were upset, because you think we only mated you because you could give us children."

"Oh, that."

"I think you may have gotten the wrong impression about—"

"You're inability to have children with any other woman." Samantha sighed and slumped slightly against him. "I really don't want to talk about this."

"Too bad. This is important."

JD was trying hard to remain calm and sound reasonable. He knew Caleb didn't think he had enough tact to have this conversation with their mate, but she was JD's too. She was just as much his responsibility as Caleb's, and he had just as much obligation to take care of her as Caleb.

"Fine." Samantha shoved his hands way from her breasts. "If you must."

"I think it's necessary."

JD wrapped his arms around her waist, snuggling her not-so-relaxed body closer. He searched for the right words, but hated to admit that they were hard to find. When he did come up with something, it sounded so greeting card that he had trouble even saying them.

"I don't think you understand how special mates really are to our kind."

"I think I do. If you don't find your mate, then your family dies off."

"True, but that doesn't mean she is simply a means to an end. Nature selects mates because they're the perfect match for us."

Okay, that didn't even sound like him. He almost strangled on the words. What he really wanted to tell her was that she was theirs, end of story.

"You mean the perfect match to create a stronger and healthier breed of wolves, right?"

"Yes." Instantly she tensed, telling him without words he'd screwed that answer up. "I mean, that's part of it, but there is more."

"Like?"

Like?

Ah, hell, he didn't know the answer to that question. This was just stupid and frustrating. JD had had enough.

"Damn it, Samantha! You're ours. This is not up for negotiations."

"That's just so romantic. I just feel so much better now."

"Samantha…" Talking to her was a trial at times.

"What? Is it so horrible that I'm not swept off my feet by the fact that you just want me for my womb? Is it so strange that I would have liked a man to actually fall in love with me for just being me?"

"Don't be dense, woman."

"Ah!" Samantha began fighting to break his hold as she yelled at him. "What the hell does that mean? You don't think any guy would actually fall in love with me for me? Let me go!"

"Nice going, JD." Caleb shook his head as he strode into the bathroom. "I see you handled the situation with your normal tact."

"Damn it!" Samantha's nails bit into his arms as she tried to pry them free, but he held on. "Go away, Caleb. I'm not done handling it."

"I am not an it, you insensitive bastard!"

JD had had enough. He was going to be the one to explain the facts to her, not Caleb. Samantha just needed to settle down and listen. She didn't appear ready to be listen to reason just yet.

The first slap to her pussy riled her up even more. By the seventh, she was fully relaxed in his embrace and moaning for more. That took care of his mate.

"Leave, Caleb."

"JD—"

"Now!"

That took care of Caleb. With a sour look of disapproval, Caleb left Samantha in JD's care. JD knew it was hard for his brother to trust him, but he was going to have to. Samantha didn't seem to notice Caleb's withdrawal. She was still recovering from her little round of punishment.

"Listen very carefully to me, Samantha." JD began when he felt her tense slightly and knew she was focused back on the moment. "There is nothing more important to a wolf than his pack. That pack begins with the family. You—"

"Oh, please. Answer me this one question, JD. If I couldn't have your kids, would you have mated me?"

"Of course not." The answer was instant and, he knew, wrong.

"That's all I need to know. I'm not—"

"That's not all you need to know. Mates are perfect matches. Why else would nature choose you to be the mother of our children?"

"Ahh, it's like going around in circles."

"Are you going to deny that you feel something more than just lust for me?" JD demanded and damned if he didn't tense in anticipation of the answer he wanted to hear.

"Like what? Love?"

"That would not be uncommon."

"All we've done is fight and have sex. What's there to love?"

"But you are still starting to care about me."

"It's just the sex."

"That's a yes, isn't it?"

"I have an addictive personality," Samantha stated so crossly he had to laugh at her.

"Oh, baby." JD rested his cheek on the back of her head and sighed. "You're too much."

"I didn't admit to anything."

"You are right about one thing."

He could already tell it was going to be hard for her to get those words out anytime soon. That was all right. He didn't need to hear them. He just needed her to agree to stay in their home, in their bed.

"I may die of shock."

"All we have done is fight and fuck."

"So you see my point."

"I see that we need to spend more time together. We need the opportunity to expand our relationship." JD thought Caleb would have been proud of that line and that he had come up with it himself.

"Expand our relationship? Is that your way of saying you're not going to let me go home?"

"See, you're already beginning to understand me."

Chapter 20

Thursday

The bastards took my keys!

Sam stared at her car in disbelief. They'd even found the spare she kept hidden in a little magnetic box under the exhaust for the times when she locked her keys in the car. It really didn't shock her.

Caleb and JD had made it quite clear that they wanted her to stay at home and rest. JD had been blunt in his opinions, while Caleb had been more tactful, suggesting that she needed to take it easy while she recovered.

Recovered. Sam snorted. She was too busy injuring herself to fulfill that lofty goal. In the last five days of living at JD and Caleb's house, she had suffered so many accidents she was beginning to think the place was cursed.

It had been just three days ago when she had tripped on some invisible object and would have taken a nosedive down the curved hardwood steps if Caleb hadn't grabbed her arm. As it happened, he hadn't been able to save her from busting her butt and cracking her arm bad enough to leave a nasty bruise.

At least it went with her collection. There hadn't been a day that had passed without her earning a new injury. Sam would have packed her bags and moved back home if it wasn't for the brothers compensating her with hours of mind-blowing sexy every night.

She had thought only the men in the movies or novels were capable of that kind of stamina. JD and Caleb had proved her wrong. Of course, she'd also thought it would have been a dream come true to have a man like that.

Now she fantasized of a full night of sleep. Gone were the days of waking up at six in the morning wide-eyed and refreshed. She was lucky if she rolled out of bed by nine. Even then, she stumbled around like a hungover drunk that was still half intoxicated. Not that she had much to do with her days.

That was the real problem. She was going insane being trapped in their house. Out of desperation, she had actually tried to tend the garden. That had been a disaster. She'd been better at cutting herbs and making perfumed soap with a recipe she'd gotten off the Internet.

Nothing was going to stop her from going to see Vicky to show off her soaps today. If her sister liked them, perhaps she could use them in the spa. That idea had led to the concept of a line of soaps, bath salts, candles and all sorts of scented things Vicky could use.

Sam knew she was grasping at straws, but she was bored, damn it! She'd been working since she was fifteen. It wasn't until she had gone to work for Frank at twenty-two that she had ever had a week off. All those years she'd wondered what it was like to be rich and never have to work.

Now she knew. It was beyond boring. What she needed was a job, perhaps her own business. Who knew? Maybe she could make a business out of perfumed soaps. Maybe not, but she needed some hope.

Right now, what she needed was a day of freedom. Nothing was going to stop her, not even her missing keys. JD and Caleb had underestimated her if they thought she was going to give up just because of that. She knew how to hotwire.

They hadn't thought of that, and they never would. She'd be home before them, and they would be none the wiser, leaving the door open for her to leave whenever she wanted.

Well, whenever they weren't checking up on her, like today. Caleb had left a note for her that morning on the kitchen table. It had been short and to the point. He wished her a good day and said neither

JD nor him would be able to make it home for lunch. She guessed they were actually going to have to eat something then.

Caleb had signed the note "love." He did that a lot. He said it too. "My love" seemed to have become his nickname for her. What was she supposed to think about that? They'd known each other for two weeks. For a man to use that word so soon and often only proved his insincerity. Didn't it?

He needed her. Both of them did. They would say anything, probably do anything to keep her. Sam sighed, recognizing her own lie. JD had certainly not gone out of his way to be either charming or romantic.

He was just as bossy and arrogant as he had been the first time she had met him. It was her perverse luck that she was discovering how much she enjoyed having a strong man to challenge her in her life.

Whenever he got to be too much, there was always Caleb to balance out the equation. It was almost humorous how different the twins were. Different that was outside of the bedroom.

Sam shook those thoughts out of her head. Being stuck at home all day, she had nothing to do over the past few days but obsess about her relationship with JD and Caleb. Now all she wanted to think about was starting her car.

Ten minutes later, Sam slid into the front seat and breathed deeply. The car hummed idly. The sweet vibrations were the most relaxing massage she'd gotten all week. She savored the moment before shifting into drive.

Five minutes later, she was singing along to the radio with her window down and the speed limit a distant concern. She didn't even notice the blue pickup coming up fast and hard behind her. When she did realize the guy was riding nearly on top of her bumper, she dismissed the truck.

She was already going fifteen over the limit and sleeping with the sheriff. If the other driver wanted to pass, he could risk the ticket and go for it. The first hollow thump of asphalt changing to cement bridge echoed up from under her front tires when the truck suddenly pulled out.

Sam barely had to time to wonder at the rash driver's actions when the impact slammed her forward, and the world started to spin before her eyes.

* * * *

JD's patrol car had barely come to a stop before he threw open the door. He forgot to pull up the hand brake, and the cruiser rolled forward, bumping into the car parked in front. He didn't care.

He stormed through the maze of cop cars, fire trucks, and first responder vehicles with a single destination in mind. As he approached the group of uniformed men hovering around the side of bridge, most of them parted, moving quickly to get out of his way.

The sight that greeted him had his heart freezing as his blood boiled to threatening levels. The tide had receded, leaving the accident below naked for all to see. Samantha's car was buried almost to the windshield in the soft mud.

Samantha herself was out of the car, lying on the embankment. Her face was turned away from him, but he could still see the blood trickling down her forehead. There was more blood darkening the mud to black.

She wasn't moving. JD wanted to shout, but his voice failed him. He wanted to jump down there and hold her, but his body had turned to stone. The man who he was couldn't grapple with the horrifying realization of what his eyes were seeing.

The wolf suffered no such dilemma. The beast recognized its loss. It didn't need detailed images of the future lost to react. It only knew the pain. It only desired to outrun the horrible sensation.

JD could feel the prickles of change race down his back. He'd have given to the urge, regardless of the consequences, if Samantha hadn't chosen that moment to move. Like a crippled snake, she tried to wiggle across the mud, closer to the car.

"What the hell are you doing?" JD found his voice, and it roared out of him loud enough to echo down the tidal creek.

Samantha turned her head slowly, and he could see her wincing from the motion. His hands gripped the edge of the bridge's wall, unsuccessfully attempting to crush the cement beneath his hands.

He could see clearly now the bruise forming around her eye, the airbag burn discoloring her nose and cheeks. Then there was the blood matting the stray strands of hair that had fallen in front of her face.

"What the hell does it look like?" He could tell it cost her to yell back at him. Her eyes squinted closed, and she grimaced.

"Damn it!" JD was flexing his muscles, preparing to leap over the bridge to the mud-bank below when TJ's arm shot out in front of him. "Get out of my way."

"That's not a wise move, boss." The deputy didn't appear the least bit unnerved by JD's growl. "You don't want to get stuck in that mud too."

"I don't care."

"Yeah, well, how much help are you going to be then?"

"Somebody's got to do something!"

"We are." That came from Jason, TJ's twin. He had his firefighter's helmet tucked up under his arm. "We got to get her back to the car, and then we can hoist her up."

"Why is she out of the car?" JD was not in the least appeased by either man's calm, matter-of-fact tone.

"She crawled out the window, floated to the edge, but the tide ran out on her, and she got stuck in the mud. That's where we found her."

"How did she get down there?"

"Looks like she spun out." TJ nodded to where a set of black tire tracks led to a hole in the safety wall where it had been penetrated by her car, leaving crumbled stone chunks littering the road and peppering the mud below. "Wouldn't know more than that until we talk to her."

"How the hell did you end up down there?" JD directed his anger at the woman who was the source of his anxiety.

"My car crashed! Ow!" Samantha's wiggling stopped as she lifted up her left side.

"What? What is wrong? Are you injured?"

"Damn oyster." She flicked the sharp-rimmed shell away.

"Don't do that!" His heart couldn't take much more of this.

"Do what?" Samantha demanded, lifting herself up by her hands, only to sink a little more into the mud. "Scream when I am hurt?"

"Flat!" Jason hollered down to her. "Keep yourself flat so you don't sink more than necessary."

"Yeah, yeah, yeah," Samantha muttered, dropping back to her stomach. JD's wolf ears could still hear her muttering to herself. "Stupid, arrogant jackass. He ought to—"

"I can hear you!"

"Come down here and wiggle around like a fucking snake!" She went from muttering to screaming at him again. "Do I look like a snake?"

"You look like an idiot!"

"That's it! You come down here and say that to my face!"

"FLAT!"

"Stupid fucking men. They want flat. I'll show them flat. Flatten his arrogant ass. Ow!" She dug underneath her and chucked another oyster out of the way. "Stupid fucking oysters."

"I still want to know what happened!"

"I had an accident. Duh!"

"What the hell were you doing driving?"

"Escaping."

"How did you get that car started? I took the keys."

"I knew it! I'm not some fifteen-year-old you have the right to imprison!"

"You were not imprisoned!"

"Nor am I some sex slave you have the right to lock in your house and keep for your depraved pleasure!"

"I did not lock you in the house!"

"You cuffed me to the bed!"

"Not in over a week!"

"You still did it!"

"God, how many times am I going to hear about this?"

"Fine, you don't want to hear it anymore, I'll pack my bags and go home. At least there I'm not likely to fall down steps, have windows explode on me or get burned just taking a shower!"

"You were burned when you broke that pot, not in the shower!"

"I didn't break that pot!"

"You're just clumsy!"

"OH! I'm so leaving your ass for that!"

"I'd like to see you try!"

"You are the most annoying asshole I've ever had the bad judgment to sleep with!"

"Uh, JD." TJ cut him off before he could come back to her last inflammatory comment. His deputy nodded to the gathered men who were all snickering. JD didn't really care. Almost all of them were in his pack, and if they wanted to step up, he'd take every single one of them down.

"What are you smiling about?" That wiped their smiles off. "I want my woman out of that creek! Now do your damn jobs!"

With that, JD stormed back off, knowing that if he stayed there, the situation would only deteriorate.

Chapter 21

The only sound in the car was the faint grinding of JD's teeth. There was a tic in his cheek that Sam had never seen before. He'd tucked his chin into his chest and was glaring at the road as if was he trying to force laser beams out his eyes and incinerate the asphalt in front of them.

Sam didn't know why he was the one all pissed off. She was the one sitting there covered in mud, cuts, and bruises even worse than when she'd left the house. It was like God was trying to eradicate her from the planet, but instead of just killing her off, he was enjoying torturing her bit by bit.

It was a full-on assault, with JD as His secret weapon, to drive her insane, and it was working. She'd never met a more madding guy in her life, and why she was so addicted to arguing with him was beyond her.

No. Sam sighed and turned to look out at the rapidly passing scenery. That wasn't the truth. She knew why she liked it when he went postal. The proof was in her wet panties. He was hot when he was mad.

His anger also seemed to drive him to be rougher, more insatiable than his normal randy condition. Sam appreciated those two things about JD. Truth be told, she'd picked a few arguments in the past days just to get him all worked up. He was so easy.

Now though, as much as her pussy might hunger for it, she really was in no condition for a three-hour sex-a-thon, especially not one that involved all his favorite toys, floggers, dildos, and that orgasm-inspiring harness. The man knew how to be creative.

As much as her body might crave being tied up and fucked, it ached to be soothed by a long soak in the tub minus the large, horny werewolf with an erection big enough to make a horse proud. Her wants were not relevant to him.

Sam knew that look when he threw the car into park and began to drag her across the seat. She knew what was coming. They'd be lucky to make it into the kitchen before he had her on all fours and was riding her like a convict that just got released after twenty years in prison.

"JD!" Sam grabbed on to the steering wheel as it went flying past. She held on with all her strength, which was barely enough to bring him to a stop.

"Let go of that wheel, Samantha." His growl was soft, a true indication that his anger was fully ignited.

"I'm not in the mood for this."

"Then you shouldn't have stole the car and fled."

"It's my car! How can you steal your own car?"

"Let go of that wheel."

"Not until you promise to leave me alone! I'm in no mood for your mauling."

"I do not maul!"

"What do you call shoving me onto the floor, ripping my clothes off, and shoving your dick into me in less than thirty seconds? A romantic interlude?" Sam demanded.

"You like it. You're always wet and bucking before I can even get all the way in." JD bent over until their noses almost touched. "Now you let go of that steering wheel now, or I'll show you a real mauling."

Sam wasn't about to back down. Either way it ended, she'd win, so there was really no incentive to let go of the wheel. Not that she would ever admit it to him, but she loved a good mauling.

That didn't stop her from screaming and kicking at him as he ripped her hand off the steering wheel with one of his oversized paws.

Nor did it stop her from trying to crawl back over the seat when he flipped her over. He yanked her back with ease, so she perched on the edge of the vinyl bench, her ass in the air.

Even though the feel of inhuman claws ripping through her denim excited the hell out of her, she still threw cusses at him over her shoulder, constantly wiggling for freedom. She didn't want to get free, but she didn't want him to know that either.

It was less than thirty seconds before he had her naked enough to shove his hardened shaft straight into her so deeply it touched her womb and ripped a real scream from her throat. Oh, it felt so good to be so completely filled. Sam's head dropped to the seat, and she moaned, wiggling again, but this time to get closer, to get just a little more of his hardness.

JD chuckled behind her, and she groaned. She knew that sound. He was planning something, and it wasn't going to be good. It was going to be beyond that simple emotion. If his diabolic laugh didn't give her a clue, the fact that he was remaining still did. It was time for her to pay in some small part for all the arguing back at the bridge and here in the garage.

"You're wet, Samantha." JD purred, his hand sliding around until his fingers circled her clit. He gave her engorged nub a quick flick. "And moaning, but I want to hear you scream."

With that grim statement, he began to torture her clit, circling, rubbing, pulling on her sensitive bud until the world shifted around her. Her mind and body exploded with ecstasy, and she rode the wave of rapture until it fizzled out minutes later.

He'd stilled the motions of his hand, allowing her to regain some semblance of sanity. It was a short-lived reprieve, one that ended the moment her breath finally caught up with her heartbeat.

"Again." His fingers resumed their teasing, tormenting motions. "Come for me again, Samantha."

"Oh, sweet mercy…"

Her moan turned into a gasp as her entire body arched with the power of the pleasure streaking through her. It was like being trapped in an electrical storm. Again and again he shot her straight over the edge of reality into the abyss of rapture until she was a sobbing, sweaty mess, begging him, pleading with him, promising him any and everything he wanted if he would just relent and fuck her now.

He paid her no attention. His cell phone ringing finally gave her a moment of peace. Between the great gulps of breath and her own thundering heartbeat, she heard him snapping at somebody on the phone.

"...I'm busy...Damn it! Derek, can't you....Fine...I'll be there as soon as I can."

He clicked the phone closed, and she felt his hands settling on her waist. She knew what that meant. It was time for the final course. The culmination of all her torture was at hand.

"Sorry, baby, I gotta get back to work, so we gotta make this quick."

Fast and hard, her favorite type of ride, is what he gave her. The garage was quickly filled with her high-pitched screams, his low grunts, and the erotic sound of his balls slapping into the edges of her spread pussy. Sam couldn't take it. Her whole body bucked with the force of her orgasm.

Above her JD snarled and slammed her back into place. A moment later, her scream of ecstasy was drowned out by his roar of release. For a time everything stayed still, the world frozen in some alternate dimension defined only by the searing flames of pleasure burning through her body.

When everything clicked back to life, Sam collapsed. She was done, worn out, in desperate need of a nap. Her only rational thought was a thanks to God that JD had to leave. Otherwise, this would have been the beginning, not the ending.

"Mmm." JD sighed above her and began to slowly roll his hips, pulling his still-thickened cock back and forth over her sensitive inner muscles. Sam moaned her complaint. The motion tickled, and she squirmed slightly to try to escape. There was no escaping, not with his hands on her hips holding her still.

"I think you liked that, Samantha. I think you enjoyed being *mauled* by me."

"Mm-hm."

"I want to hear you say it."

"Don't you have to go?" Sam roused herself enough to resist his demands.

"Not until I hear you say it."

"What if I refuse?"

One hand slid around her ass to slip in between her crack and press against her back entrance. "I don't know. I bet I can think of something."

"Yes!" Sam didn't have the stamina for that. "Yes, I liked your mauling. Now please, JD, stop torturing me. I need to rest."

"And you will rest."

JD stepped back, making her moan again when he slipped free. She may not have been up for another round, but she hated the empty feeling that always came over her when they pulled out. Often she passed out with either or both of her men still buried deep inside her. It was a nice way to assure sweet dreams.

Sam curled into his chest as he carried her into the house and up to the bedroom. She hated that he had to leave now when all she wanted to do was snuggle into his warmth and go to sleep. That wasn't going to happen.

She wasn't even going to get to snuggle into the bed, not covered all in dirt and filth. There was only one thing she was doing and that was bathing. JD carried her straight into the bathroom to set her down on the edge of the tub.

"Can you bathe without injuring yourself?"

"Ha. Ha." Sam rolled her eyes at that. He was so good at turning her warm emotions to annoyance.

"You are not to leave this house." He pointed a finger at her that tempted her to take a bite.

"Do I look as if I'm in any condition to go anywhere?"

"You didn't look that way this morning, but that didn't stop you."

"My car is buried in mud in some damn creek. How would I leave?"

"I'm going to call your sister," JD stated after studying her for a moment.

"Jesus, JD. You're my lover, not my father."

"Caleb is leaving work early. He should be here in an hour." JD ignored her smart remark. Ignored it, but was not unmoved by it. He paused at the door to give her a considering look. Sam suspected she knew just what he was thinking.

"You don't have to chain me to the bed. I'll be here when Caleb gets home. I swear."

His eyes narrowed for a second, but then he turned and silently walked away. Sam sighed and rolled her eyes. Why, oh why, did she love that man?

Ah, damn.

At least she hadn't said it out loud. That would be a mistake. Only bigger mistake she could make was in saying it around JD or Caleb. Sam wasn't sure of the progression of this werewolf thing, but she wasn't peeing on any bushes yet. She figured if she admitted her feelings, they'd finish whatever it took to transform her into a drooling fur ball.

She might love them, but that didn't mean she wanted to be like them. Sam brooded over that thought as she soaked away the caked-on mud and dried blood. The water felt good, too good, and she drifted off. Only the stinging sensation of water going up her nose roused her.

With slow, forced motions, she slid into one of Caleb's T-shirts. She'd been using them as her nightgown whenever she wore one. That didn't happen often when the guys were around. Even when she managed to slip into one, there seemed to be something about that outfit that drove Caleb and JD wild.

Half the time they didn't even let her get it off before they thrusted deep into her. Those thoughts, combined with the intoxicating scent of male musk engrained into the soft cotton, warmed her body, bringing her pussy back to pulsing life. Okay, so the shirts worked on her too.

She crawled into bed and admitted it was awfully big and lonely in there alone. Sam sighed and pulled the covers close. She was too exhausted, and the lure of falling asleep with their scent engulfing her was too much to deny.

It seemed she had barely gotten to sleep when she woke with a start. Sam sat straight up and blinked, trying to figure out what was wrong. A noise had woken her. Probably had been a dream. Sam smacked her lips as the scales tipped in favor of staying in bed.

She settled back into her pillows. They were so soft, and she turned one over to rest her head on the cool fabric. Try as she did, Sam couldn't seem to escape back into her dreams. There was something wrong.

Slowly her mind followed her body, rousing to the reality of the mid-afternoon day. The noise that she had thought came from her dreams grew, crackling and sizzling to life. There was a strong odor irritating her nose. Sam blinked as her eyes dried out.

Smoke, strong enough that it was already beginning to give her a headache, making her gag for air. She jerked back up straight, now wide-awake. This time she didn't hesitate, but shoved the covers out of the way as she rolled out of bed.

In her haste, she didn't bother to look where she was going and slammed her toe into the curved foot of the bedpost. She grunted, hopping around as the searing pain momentarily overwhelmed her attention. There was no ignoring the plumes of black smoke coming in under the door.

Instinctively she rushed toward the door and almost grabbed the doorknob before reason struck. She'd never been caught in a fire, but she'd seen enough TV to know not to touch a metal ball that was probably burning hot.

A towel from the bathroom solved that problem. It didn't help with the wall of toxic smoke that fell through the room the moment she got the door open. Sam stumbled back, coughing as the fumes chased her across the floor. Okay, that was obviously not the right thing to do. So now what?

Getting out through the door was obviously not an option. Between the heat and smoke, all Sam wanted to do was escape in the opposite direction. That meant through the window. She fought with it for a moment before giving in and using a nearby book to break it.

Relieving fresh air floated through the hole and fought the black smoke curling into every crevice of the room. It was an impossible task. The smoke was too thick and dense for the lighter clean air to defeat it.

She wrapped her hand in the towel and used the book to widen the hole until she could put her head through it without fear of cutting herself. Taking a deep breath, she tried to think rationally.

It was a straight drop to the ground, which looked far away from her perspective. With the glass broken, there was no way for her to grip the windowsill and try to drop down.

It was either break a few bones or burn up in a fire. Was there really a choice?

Chapter 22

JD burst through the emergency room doors, almost knocking down a woman who was trying to get out. He barely spared her a glance as he stormed through the waiting room. Mike and Vicky were in the middle of an argument that fell silent as JD came storming up.

"Where is she?" JD demanded curtly by way of introduction.

"They took her back there." Vicky pointed through a set of double doors. "We haven't heard anything yet."

"Can you find out…" Mike was talking to JD's back. He was already headed to the registration desk.

"Samantha Hark, where is she?" JD turned his barely controlled fury on the harried-looking nurse on the other side of the registration desk.

"Who?" The nurse frowned at her computer.

"Samantha Hark," JD barked, drawing the nurse's undivided attention.

"She's with the doctor. You'll have—"

"Where?" JD leaned over the desk.

"Exam two," the nurse quickly responded.

"Wait! You can't go back there." She chased after him as he headed for the double doors.

"Where is exam two?" The nurse's eyes went wide as she took note of the gray overtaking his blue eyes as his gaze turned feral. She decided to let somebody else deal with him. She pushed the double doors open and pointed out the room before quickly retreating to her post at the counter.

"You can't be—" The doctor's voice stopped as he looked up to see who had just barged into the room.

"He's with me." Caleb didn't bother to look up. His gaze was solely focused on Samantha.

The doctor looked from one twin to the other. His thin lips almost completely disappeared as he eyed the two large men, but whatever thoughts he had, he held them back. It was a pointless fight. He had more than enough patients waiting for him not to bother wasting his time.

JD ignored the doctor's scrutiny, his attention drawn to the pale woman stretched out unconscious on the bed. Her long locks were singed at the ends. There were black streaks from smoke on her face around the oxygen mask. Her eyes were closed, her expression blank.

The bruises peppering her skin made him flinch. She'd almost died, again. There seemed to be nothing he could do to keep her safe. How did a man protect his woman from her own accident-prone nature? Lock her in a padded room?

Samantha would never put up with that kind of treatment. He could only begin to envision the tantrum she'd pitch if he even suggested such an idea. That one could get physical. Not that he would ever hurt her, but JD wasn't sure the same could be said of Samantha.

His eyes dropped to her hand where the doctor was cleaning a cut. There were several small bandages wrapped around her lower arm. When he had gotten the call from the office, they'd said she'd been taken to the hospital. That was it.

"What happened?"

"The house burned down." Caleb still didn't take his eyes off Samantha.

"With her in it?" JD pressed, not at all satisfied with his twin's curt answer.

"The firefighters found her on the ground. It looks like she busted out the bedroom window and jumped." Caleb's tone held no emotion, as if he didn't feel anything about what he had just said. JD was not so reserved. His eyes devoured Samantha a second time, looking for any signs of a splint or cast.

"She didn't break anything."

"Just cut herself on the glass."

"Are they bad?"

"Three needed stitches." JD's question was directed at the doctor, but Caleb answered. "She got a lung full of smoke. Other than that she's fine."

"Then why isn't she awake?"

"She passed out when I started putting in the first set of stitches." The doctor looked up as he wheeled his chair back. He eyed JD for a moment, contemplating his uniform. "You're a cop?"

"Sheriff of Collin County."

"Huh?" The doctor cocked his head. "You want to tell me about all these other bruises?"

"She's accident-prone."

JD knew exactly where the doctor was headed. He'd headed in that direction on more than one occasion when he saw a woman with a little too much damage to be overlooked. In all the cases of domestic violence he'd investigated, he'd heard the accident excuse more often than not. Apparently so had the doctor. He was buying into it about as much as JD ever had.

"Well"—the doctor looked from one brother to the other—"I think I'd like her to spend the night here. Keep her for observation."

"You think her injuries are that serious?" Caleb finally looked up. JD could tell that his brother didn't understand the subtlety of the doctor's comments. There was pure fear in Caleb's eyes.

"We like to monitor a patient's breathing after they've been in a fire," the doctor answered. It was an evasion and an understatement of what was really concerning the man. "Keeping them on oxygen is a good thing."

"Then do it." JD wasn't about to add to the man's suspicions, nor was he going to deny Samantha any extra medical attention he could get her.

"We'll stay with her." Caleb's eyes had dropped back to watching every breath Samantha took.

"Yes, well, visiting hours end at nine unless you're family. You're not family, are you?"

"We are—"

"That's fine, doctor."

They could wait the night through in the waiting room. If the doctor needed to hear privately from Samantha that she wasn't being abused, JD would give him that. Not that he thought it would change the doctor's mind. It never had his. Women normally lied about that kind of thing.

The doctor nodded, and after a quiet word with the nurse, he left. JD caught the distrust and determination in the nurse's eyes. She wasn't leaving until they did. JD didn't think anything was going to get Caleb to move.

"You eaten?"

"How can you think about food at a time like this?"

"Because I'm hungry." JD turned toward the door. "I'll bring you something back."

He wasn't hungry, but it was too painful seeing Samantha like she was. As much as he wanted to fix her, there was nothing he could do.

* * * *

Caleb watched Samantha sleeping as the heart monitor rhythmically beeped. The hospital was a good deal quieter outside the emergency room. Up here, where patients were stored and watched over, the silence was only broken by the squeaking footsteps of nurses walking up and down the linoleum floors.

Occasionally there was a creaking or rhythmic thumping as patients and their IV's were wheeled about. Now and again, the murmur of low-toned conversations floated past. More frequently, the intercom system blared to life as some nurse or another paged a doctor.

None of the sounds penetrated Caleb's concentration. He was stuck in a morbid cycle of repeating images from that afternoon. When JD had called to tell him about Samantha's car accident, he'd been seized by the worst kind of fear that had not dissipated even when JD had assured him that she was all right. Only seeing her alive and healthy would diminish his anxiety.

He'd been in the middle of a training session and had to hike back over ten miles to get to his truck before he could even drive home. His boss, Alec, hadn't questioned Caleb's sudden distraction. Alec knew. He understood.

As a werewolf himself, Alec could not fault Caleb his single-minded need to get to his mate. Alec was a lone wolf, and while he had never said anything, Caleb had seen the hint of envy in his gaze as Caleb had spoken about Samantha.

Well, Alec didn't have anything to be jealous of. This was hell. If things kept going this way, they'd lose their mate. If that happened, Caleb wasn't sure he would survive the pain.

A part of him had died when he'd turned onto his street to see the flames leaping high into the sky. Then he had seen the paramedics loading an unmoving body, covered almost completely with a sheet, into the ambulance. He lost it, almost taking out several firefighters with his truck as he'd roared toward the ambulance.

None of the emergency response team had dared to deny him as he had shoved his way into the ambulance. He'd heard none of their reassurances or explanations as he'd felt for her pulse. Even then, he hadn't been able to let go, needing the constant reassurance that she was indeed alive.

Only when her eyelashes had fluttered up and she'd given him a halfhearted smile had he been able to relax enough to listen to the paramedic's explanation. With each word, Caleb had felt some part of himself shut down, unable to cope with another near miss.

That emotion had carried him through the rest of the day. He wasn't sure how JD or Samantha's family had found out about the fire. He certainly hadn't remembered to call them. All his training, all his experience, and what had he done? He'd panicked and shut down.

"What are you doing here?" JD's aggressive snarl was the first thing that snapped Caleb out of his trance. The sound of the female voice responding to JD's abrupt question had him standing up.

"Why, Sheriff McBane, how lovely to see you."

"Don't bullshit me, Lilly. What do you want?"

"I've come to see my good friend, Samantha." Lilly offered JD a bright smile before turning to find Caleb blocking the door. "Hello there, Caleb. You look like hell."

"And you don't have any good friends." Caleb felt the beast in him stir at the sight of the pint-sized detective.

Her short stature and feminine body was a disguise. Underneath she was the most feared and hated private investigator in the state. It wasn't just her ability to deliver whatever her clients wanted. It was the way she went after it.

There had been a time, when he had first met Lilly, he had flirted with the notion of seducing her. She was hot enough to command that kind of attention from most of their pack, but all too soon, they'd realized that she was more trouble than a fuck was worth. They'd even made a rule that none of the males in their pack associate with her. It hadn't been hard to enforce.

"What do you really want?" Caleb stepped up beside JD, presenting Lilly with a united front.

"Can't tell you. I have a thing about client confidentiality."

"Client? Are you saying that Samantha has hired you?"

"Oh, look at the little puppy growl. Aren't you just so cute?"

"What's that in your hand?" Caleb clenched his fist, feeling the need to hit. Despite her attitude, she was still a woman. He didn't hit women.

"Santa's list of who's been naughty and nice. Want to guess what column you're in?"

"I swear to God, Lilly. If I have to throw you into jail, you will tell me what you are doing here." JD's patience had snapped, and he backed his threat with a step toward the woman. With her usual arrogance, Lilly matched his step forward with two of her own.

"I may not have good friends, but I have rich, powerful friends. I doubt that you really want a bunch of outsiders scrutinizing Holly Town." Lilly tilted her head and batted her eyes. "You never know what they could discover. They just might find a wild dog pack that needs to be put down."

"It's just amazing the kind of damage a wild dog pack can do," JD snarled. "They are even capable of killing."

"Now you're talking. The sheriff threatening murder. I wish I'd brought my tape recorder."

"JD?" Samantha croaked, drawing his attention. Lilly took immediate advantage, squeezing right between the brothers until she popped out into Samantha's room. Caleb snarled and grabbed her arm, intent on throwing her back out. Samantha's voice stopped him.

"Lilly?"

"Hey, sweetheart." Lilly shook Caleb hold off. "How you feeling?"

* * * *

Sam blinked, surprised at Lilly's presence. She'd heard JD talking to somebody, but she would never have guessed it was her investigator. Her head hurt, her body ached, and her throat felt scratchy and irritated, but she'd still been able to comprehend the anger in JD's tone.

"Is everything all right?"

"You shouldn't be talking." Caleb was by her side before she could blink. Every time she'd opened her eyes, he'd been there keeping vigil over her. JD had never been far away either. She had to admit that they were good at making her feel protected when things were going horribly wrong.

"That's all right." Lilly had moved to the other side of the bed. "She doesn't need to talk. I can do just fine on my own."

"Later, Lilly," JD snapped. "Now is not the time."

"Proving yet again that the sheriff knows little about investigation, this is a time-sensitive issue."

Sam was amazed at Lilly's ability to sound downright cheerful as she insulted and pissed off a man almost three times her size. So it wasn't just her. Lilly was just blatantly rude to everybody and in such a cheery tone.

"Out!" JD pointed toward the door, but Lilly just raised an eyebrow at Sam.

"I'll talk to her." Sam pushed the oxygen mask back off her face.

"Baby—"

"Please, Caleb. This wouldn't take long, will it, Lilly?"

"Nah, and I'll do almost all the talking."

"Fine then."

Caleb crossed his arms over his chest, obviously intent on staying. That drew another raised brow from Lilly. Sam could see just where this was heading. She really didn't have the energy for this.

"Just give us a moment."

"Samantha—"

"You know the more you argue with her, the more you make her talk," Lilly pointed out much to Caleb's annoyance.

He gave her a look that amazed Sam for its ferocity. She'd never seen Caleb respond that way to anybody. It wasn't so shocking when JD gave her the same kind of look before dragging his feet toward the door.

Lilly watched them go with a blank expression. Once the door had slid closed behind them, she cast Sam a quick look out of the corner of her eye and smirked. Sam began to ask what she was doing when she moved toward the door, but Lilly held up a hand for silence. A moment later Sam heard the door click close. Lilly chuckled as she sauntered back over toward the bed.

"Men." Lilly shook her head. "They're all alike."

"Yeah." Sam agreed, a little confused at Lilly's presence in her hospital room.

"You sound like you swallowed a spiked frog." Lilly scowled. "Caleb's right. You shouldn't be talking. So let's go with one finger for yes and two fingers for no and get this over with. All right?"

Sam held up one finger.

"Good." Lilly dropped the folder on the bed and flipped it open. "Okay, now. I've been keeping an eye on your buddy Bruce."

"You have?" Sam couldn't help but interject. "I didn't…"

"Hey, you hired me because you had a problem, but you just didn't know what the problem was."

"I didn't…hire you."

"Sure, you did. Remember the conversation in your bedroom."

"But—"

"You should save your voice. So just be quiet and answer my questions. Okay then, as I was saying. I've been watching this Bruce guy…By the way, I'm not the only one. Your dog boys have one of their own mutts following him."

"They do?"

"Problem with dogs is their single-minded focus. You got to be more flexible to be good at this kind of thing."

"You do?"

"I told you not to talk." Lilly corrected her as she began to flip through the photographs. Sam strained her neck to see, but Lilly scowled at her and lifted the edge of the folder to block her view.

"Now, Bruce has been staying down in Savannah for the most part, went to Beaufort once. We'll get to that, but first. You recognize this woman?"

Lilly held up a picture of a couple in an intimate embrace. Sam scowled and held up one finger. Shit yeah, she recognized the big-breasted brunette in the picture. That was the woman Bruce had been sleeping with on the side when they were together.

From the picture Lilly was showing her, they were obviously still going at it. Figured that scum would bring his mistress along when he tracked her down to beg her to come back. He had no class.

"That's what I figured." Lilly dropped the photograph back into the folder and pulled out another one. "She's not staying with Bruce. As you can see in this picture, she's supporting quite a nice diamond, and my guess is the man she's with gave it to her. You know Brett Morison, right?"

Sam was so stunned by the image of Brett with the woman, Lilly had to prompt her to get her to respond. What was Bruce's bimbo doing wearing an engagement ring on one hand and Brett on the other? It didn't make sense. Not until Lilly began explaining her theory.

"I don't have the proof right now, but the way I read the situation is this. Bruce knows you got control of these millions. He was trying to worm his way into your life to benefit from that, but you kicked him to the curb.

"So the woman, Candice, worms her way into Brett's life. Now, you die, Brett gets control of the trust. She's his wife. He dies. She inherits. Pretty simple game, but given they all lose out if your death is eventually connected to Brett, they have to be a little more cunning than the average murderer.

"And I think they've been really resourceful." Lilly grinned. "Bruce took out five thousand in cash and went to Beaufort. Now, that area is a hub of mystical activity. A lot of Voodoo and witchcraft goes on down there. Given all your...accidents lately, I think he bought himself a curse."

"A curse?" Sam's mouth gaped open as she stared at Lilly in amazement.

"Uh-huh. It makes sense. Curse you with miserable luck and just wait for one of these accidents to take you out. Completely untraceable."

"That's insane." Sam couldn't even begin to wrap her mind around that idea.

"It fits." Lilly lifted another picture up. "See this band on Bruce's wrist? That's a common healing ring, brings the wearer good luck and all that. I'm thinking he picked it up as a bonus with your curse."

Sam closed her eyes. What did one say to the notion of a curse? Did she need an exorcism now? Or find a four-leaf clover? A leprechaun? What? As if reading her thoughts, Lilly spoke up.

"Don't worry. I got a friend that can take care of your curse. Once you get out of here, we'll go for a little ride. She'll probably want money, but...you got a lot of that. The thing is, they'll try again, and you have to start thinking how far you're willing to go to stop them."

"What do you mean by that?" Sam forgot to be shocked about the idea of a curse. She was too overwhelmed by what Lilly was insinuating.

"I'm just telling you like it is." Lilly lifted the folder. "Now you rest up."

Lilly sauntered toward the door, but came to a stop short of the entrance. Sam could see her head waving back and forth as if she were considering something. She muttered something that Sam didn't catch before turning back to Sam.

"You might also want to consider letting those two overprotective flea bags in on what's really going on."

"They'll freak out."

"Yeah, or they could accidentally get in the way and get hurt." Lilly shrugged. "Not that I would care, but I think you would."

Sam watched her walk away. Could it be? Could all the accidents be something more than just a run of rotten luck? Was she a danger to JD and Caleb? What would she do if anything happened to them?

It was too much to process, and Sam closed her eyes. Sleep eluded her, but at least she avoided having to deal with Caleb and JD.

Chapter 23

Friday

Sam watched as the small cabin came into view. It was set way back from the road, down a long dirt drive that was peppered in shadows from the great oaks twisting and winding their way overhead in silent celebration of the sun.

Sam shifted between Caleb and the gearshift that sprung out of the floorboards like an awkward limb. She wanted to ask where they were, but knew better than to try to speak. Every time she opened her mouth, one of the brothers closed it for her.

On the rare occasion she managed to make a sound, they'd lecture her about the doctor's orders. Sam itched to point out to them that the doctor had said to rest her vocal cords, not remain mute. It was pointless, though.

JD had memorized the list of instructions the doctor had given her and could quote it verbatim in an instant. With the intensity he'd shown, Sam was a little hard-pressed to wonder how the doctor could even consider that either Caleb or JD would hurt her. It had really shocked her when the harried-looking man had questioned her about her other injuries.

He'd obviously not been satisfied with her answers and pressed to make sure she was safe with the McBane brothers. Safe? That was a distant notion, but it had nothing to do with JD or Caleb. It was the Fates or a curse if Lilly was to be believed. Whatever, there was nothing the doctor could do to fix it.

JD pulled his pickup around the back of the small wooden house to park in a spot of well-worn grass. Without a word, Caleb dragged her with him as he got out of the truck.

Her feet never touched the ground as he swept her up into his arms and carried her toward the porch. JD strutted ahead of them, clearing a path over the cluttered walkway and opening the door as the steps groaned in protest under Caleb's heavy weight.

Sam barely got a glimpse of the homey kitchen and the cluttered eating area before the narrow pass of the hallway walls blocked her view. Pictures of men and women decorated the wooden slats. Hung at irregular intervals and erratic heights, she recognized Caleb and JD in some.

The three-dimensional photo album opened into a large, rustic bedroom complete with a gnarled wood dresser and a handmade quilt slung over the king-size bed. Caleb set her down on the bed and reached for the hem of her shirt.

Sam put her hand over his and frowned at him. She'd had quite enough of this. Despite all her recent mishaps, she was still a grown woman. Being taken care of was one thing, but being treated like an invalid was another.

Caleb backed off and went to get an overnight bag that was on top of the dresser. Sam recognized it as hers. When he produced her large nightshirt, Sam's eyes widened. The implication was not lost on her.

They actually meant her to rest. That was a first. She had begun to think that Caleb and JD had forgotten that was what a bed was made for. As if she needed it to be explained to her, Caleb made sure there was no misunderstanding.

"You are to rest." Caleb handed her the shirt.

"Yes—"

"Both your body and your vocal cords." He cut her off.

Sam rolled her eyes, but he didn't catch the motion. He was walking out of the room. It was probably a good thing. She wasn't in the mood for another lecture. It just might make her scream.

As she began to peel her clothes off, she could hear a blender turn on in the distance. Her stomach growled at the noise. She hadn't eaten much of the food they'd given her at the hospital. Not only had it been disgusting, but it had been hard to swallow too.

She'd managed to suck a lot of ice, though, and it was backing up in her bladder. There were two doors beside the one that led back into the hall. Her first guess revealed a closet full of female clothes.

Given the style, Sam was guessing they belonged to an older woman, probably JD and Caleb's mom. That would explain the pictures and the garden. For all the coziness of the house, there was something sad about being here.

It was a stark reminder that her men had lost their fathers. Sam shook off the sense of sadness. Her life was complicated enough without rehashing a past she couldn't change.

All she could do was focus on the moment and take things as they came. Right now, she needed to find the bathroom. The second door revealed what she was looking for.

The large, luxurious, and modern bathroom surprised her. It was in contrast to the rest of what she had seen of the house. Their mother obviously had her priorities straight. Sam was definitely in agreement and would soon be taking a soak in that bathtub, but at that moment, it was a different fixture that called to her.

Sam was just crawling into the bed when JD appeared in the door. He had a large Styrofoam cup in his hand.

"You're going to rest for the rest of the day, Samantha." He set the cup down on the nightstand and tucked the blankets securely around her. "I don't want any trouble out of you. Don't roll your eyes at me."

Sam dropped her eyelids, feeling a little annoyed that he got to be so heavy-handed and she wasn't even allowed to respond. That was an unfair advantage.

"Drink this."

JD shoved the cup under her chin. Instantly Sam realized what it was. It was her own special style of milk shake. Sam considered herself a chocolate milk shake connoisseur. Too often commercial providers made their chocolate shakes with vanilla ice cream and chocolate syrup. Even worse, they made them with soft ice cream.

This shake was made with true chocolate ice cream with extra chocolate syrup to assure an addict's addiction was well fed. The real trick, though, to making the perfect shake was using two flavors of chocolate, dark and milk. That meant getting good ice cream. No generic, store-bought, gallon-sized, artificially flavored crap.

This one had obviously been made to her specifications, even down to the Styrofoam cup that kept the shake cold, but not her hands. Sam wondered how JD knew about her special shake, but wasn't allowed to ask him. She really didn't need to. The answer was obvious. Vicky or Mike had told him.

The first cool sip chilled her annoyance with him. Whether he asked or her siblings offered, the fact that he had gone out of his way to get the ingredients and make it for her touched Sam. It was a sweet gesture and completely unexpected.

JD sat on the edge of the bed, stroking her hair and making sure she finished the entire shake. Only when she was done slurping as much off the residual off the bottom as she could get did he take the cup and rise.

"Sleep."

Sam didn't understand the logic of loading her up on sugar and then telling her to rest, but then again, men were not known to be logical as far as she was concerned. That was her last coherent thought as she slipped into the black abyss of unconsciousness.

There was no telling how long she slept. She woke up in phases, realizing slowly that she was shaking. The whole bed was shaking. Had the Fates conspired against her to cause an earthquake in South Carolina? Wasn't that a little extreme?

When did earthquakes become so constricting? She could barely breathe from the tight bands around her chest. The restraints contracted even more, making her wince from the pressure. They were arms.

From the feel of the calluses on the palms gripping her sides and the unique male scent, she knew they were JD's arms. Sam was about to wiggle, silently demanding freedom, when she heard him sniff softly. When he rubbed his cheek into her hair, she was instantly pissed.

Her head was not a snot rag. That's exactly what she would have told him if the sound of his voice hadn't stopped her. It was soft, barely audible, slightly wavery, almost watery.

"Please, God, don't take her from me. I couldn't take it."

He sniffed again, and it clicked. He was crying. JD was actually shedding tears, and they were because of her. He was afraid. Those two revelations left her paralyzed. She lay there limply as he tried to squeeze the life that he was begging God not to take out of her.

There was only one thing that could make a man as strong as JD this weak, love. There were no children with tiny toes and big rounded eyes yet for him to feel that deep of an emotion for. That left only her.

Sam felt something deep inside her shift. The hidden worry that she had been carrying around as an ache in her heart since she discovered JD and Caleb's true motivation for being interested in her evaporated at the evidence of JD's feelings.

It didn't matter that he hadn't said the words. She didn't need them. It wasn't in what a man said, but what he did. No man had ever cried over her. The last one she would have expected to do so was JD.

That it was him begging God not to take her from him touched her even more because it was so out of his character. Underneath the rough and dominating personality lurked a heart, and it belonged to her, just as he already owned hers.

He sniffed again, and she couldn't take it anymore. As moved as she was at the evidence of his emotion, she didn't want him to be sad. That certainly wasn't what she was feeling. She was afraid if she said anything, she would embarrass him and all his defenses would go back up.

She didn't need words. With that in mind, Sam leaned up and placed a gentle kiss on his lips. She'd meant it as a soothing gesture, but just as it did every time, the kiss went wild, hot, and hungry. In short order Sam forgot all about her aches and pains, what she'd woken to, and why she'd kissed him in the first place.

* * * *

JD pulled back and took several deep breaths. Samantha was astride him, somehow having ended up on top. She was rubbing her body against him in the most delightful, distracting way. If he didn't get a handle on the situation, they'd end up doing it and to hell with her fragile condition.

As much as his body didn't want him to, JD knew he had to put a stop to the embrace. The emotions boiling through him were too raw, too harsh. He was in no shape to be the kind, gentle lover she would need him to be.

There would be no stopping him if he didn't get her off his lap. Already he was a second away from breaking. Once he pulled back, she'd switched her attention to his neck. The sharp little nibbles and the hot, wet licking tongue were driving him to distraction.

So were her hands, already sliding beneath his shirt. She was tormenting his nipples, and when her arms flexed and his shirt popped open, he knew what was coming next. Her mouth was kissing a path to his abandoned pecs while her hand moved south to the buttons of his jeans.

Quickly he lifted her off and dumped her back on her side of the bed. Samantha glared at him, her full lips pressing into a pout. JD was about to command her to rest when she launched herself back into his arms.

Before he could utter a word, she latched on to his nipple, her hands busy trying to tear his jeans open. His dick was making it hard for her. Swollen and hard, it pressed outward, stretching the denim and leaving very little room for the buttons to make it through the holes.

That wasn't stopping her. Samantha attacked him like a woman possessed. Between kisses, she whispered how good he felt beneath her hands, how strong and hard he was.

JD sat semi-paralyzed as her comments became dirtier and she began to describe what she would do with her hands and mouth if there weren't so many clothes in her way. When her hands finally got his jeans open, his cock sprang forward to greet the warm grip of her fingers.

Ah, hell.

He didn't have the strength to resist anymore. If this was what she wanted, then he would give it to her, but it would be on his terms. Samantha seemed to understand his intentions when he rolled her off him a second time.

She retreated, her sexy smile making him growl and follow her. He was a little disappointed when she didn't put up too much resistance and allowed him to pin her to the bed beneath him. That emotion was quickly lost in the feel of her legs parting and wrapping around his thighs and her pussy rubbing against his erection.

Her nightshirt had ridden up, allowing him to feel how wet she was as she continued her erotic grinding. JD snarled and settled his hands on her hips, pressing her even closer. It wasn't enough. He needed more than just to feel her heat covering him. He needed to feel it surrounding him, squeezing him tight. He needed that now.

Flexing his hips, he brought the head of his cock to the entrance of her weeping cunt, and with one long, smooth stroke, buried himself balls-deep inside her. For long moments, he remained perfectly still, absorbing the perfection of possessing her body, skin to skin, liquid heat to velvety hardness.

He couldn't lose this, couldn't lose her. JD's arms slid from her hips, around her back, intent on hugging her close. She had such soft, silky skin, and he trailed his fingertips along her ass to the slight indention in her lower back. Samantha gasped, arching herself into him and wiggling from the contact.

"What's this?" JD smiled. Gently he caressed the small of her back, causing her to moan as her hips bucked slightly against him. Ah, that was amazing.

"JD!"

"A sweet spot." JD began to rain kisses down her neck as he continued to stroke her lower back.

All he had to do was lightly caress the small of her back and she was gasping and writhing against him. With every little movement, her inner muscles tugged and pulsed around his cock, milking him with the erotic motion. It made his balls ache with the need to move, to pump and thrust until they were emptied of the seed backing up in them.

He remained motionless but for the tips of his fingers driving his mate to distraction. It was too delightful of a torture to give up just yet. Samantha didn't agree. She was moaning out cusses and demands.

She wanted to be fucked, and there was only so much strength he had left. He held on, though, his mind reeling with how to make the moment even better. One answer came quickly to mind.

Caleb was there in less than a minute after his brother called for him. He didn't need to ask why JD had hollered for him. One look at the couple on the bed and Caleb knew what he supposed to do.

* * * *

Damn JD and his teasing! Sam couldn't help but wiggle as he continued to lightly stroke the sensitive skin at the base of her spine. Nobody had ever found that spot. Then again nobody had ever gone looking.

When he finally relented, sliding his hands up to her shoulders to hold her close, Sam sighed. The tickling sensation had ratcheted up her need, but been way too light to actually fulfill it. Surely, that would come now.

Sam groaned to herself when she felt Caleb's hands divide her ass cheeks. This wasn't going to be a two-for-one, but a two-in-one special. She buried her head in JD's shoulder as he held her open so Caleb could lube up the back entrance he was about to lay claim to.

Her teeth came out to sink into his hard muscle as Caleb began to feed thick cock into her. It was so tight. There was barely any room for Caleb with JD's large erection already stretching her wide. The two cocks pressed into each other, rasping the sensitive membrane trapped between their hardened lengths.

Finally, Caleb seated himself fully inside her, and Sam released JD's skin to moan out her pleasure at the situation. All she needed was one of them to move, just a little bit. Sam thought she was going to get her wish when she felt Caleb tense and his hips begin to flex.

"No." JD stopped him, making Sam snarl and bite him again in revenge. The jackass just laughed and moved his hands back to her lower back.

"Don't, JD," Sam groaned, knowing what was coming.

"Check this out."

Sam couldn't help but clench under the teasing administrations. The reflexive motion made both her channels tighten almost painfully down on the cocks stuffing her full. She heard Caleb groan at the motion.

"That's great."

"Yeah." She could hear the smile in JD's voice. "It gets even better."

"Ah. I see what you mean." Caleb's words sounded forced as Sam gave over to the need to wiggle. She couldn't help it.

Trapped as she was between her two men, there was little room to move. Every tiny motion jarred her stretched sheaths, making their dicks jab and rub against her quivering muscles. The erratic motions sent sparkles of pleasure through her at intermittent beats that left her panting and wanting something more rhythmic, something that pulsed long and hard through her body.

"Damn it, JD! Will you stop teasing me and fuck me already!"

That earned her two laughs that had her growling. Her cursing was stopped midstream as JD's hips flexed and his cock slid almost free before slamming back into her with enough force that jolted under the impact.

"Was that what you wanted?"

"Or was it this?" Caleb imitated his brother's motions, making her moan and arch into the blow.

"Yes!" Sam bounced and pumped her hips trying to force them to repeat their motions, but they held still.

"Yes what, Samantha?" Caleb purred into her ear. "You want me or him to fuck you?"

"Both. Now, damn it!"

That earned her another round of chuckles. Despite their amusement, they seemed to realize they'd pushed her to the edge. In moments, they had set up a tempo that challenged her to keep up.

Beneath, the bed threatened to give out. Its high-pitched, protesting squeaks were in harmony with the solid thump of the headboard banging into the wall as her lovers pounded into her with deep, hard strokes. The melody blossomed into a full chorus with Sam screaming in soprano with JD and Caleb grunting out the bass.

Sam lost the beat as her orgasm crashed down over her. She shattered beneath the weight. Her body imploded with such force that the cocks still drilling into her felt twice the size as her muscles contracted sharply.

The extra pleasure sent a second orgasmic wave crashing through her, and Sam cried out as her vision exploded into a sea of color flashes. It appeared to have a similar effect on her men. JD's roar was echoed by Caleb seconds later as they both went taut around her.

All three lovers collapsed in a sweaty heap of panting breaths and thundering heart rates. Sam wasn't sure if she was alive or dead and honestly didn't care. She would be happy to pass right back into oblivion in her current position and would have if a strange voice hadn't intruded on the moment.

"Caleb, JD, if you've got the energy left, you have visitors," a man called from down the hall.

Sam's eyes popped open, her face flaming instantly with embarrassment. Above and below her, twin growls sounded, the vibrations tickling her chest and back. Their growls turned to groans the minute she startled wiggling, demanding freedom.

"Go away, Derek!" Caleb shouted back. He appeared to know that his order would be ignored. Already he was pulling away and reaching for his clothes. JD followed suit. Rolling Sam to his side before sliding his cock out, his command for her to sleep was drowned out by the newcomer's shout.

"Come on, guys! What, did your little woman wear you both out?"

"He's dead."

Chapter 24

"Derek! You shouldn't say things like that!" Claire Jacob elbowed her husband in the ribs as she hissed at him. The jab turned his grin to a wince, but only for a moment. The sound of stomping feet and muttered curses grew louder as the McBane boys obviously rushed to dress.

"It worked, didn't it?"

"Yeah, if your goal is to get your ass kicked."

"Don't sweat it, honey." Derek dropped a quick kiss on her cheek. "I know what it takes to get a wolf out of his mate and back to business. It was necessary."

Claire rolled her eyes at that and caught Lilly's snicker. The tiny investigator had made herself right at home despite the cuffs keeping her arms pinned behind her back. Claire felt more than a little guilty about the cuffs. She really hadn't expected Derek to go that far, but she couldn't apologize to Lilly in front of him.

He'd know something was up. It was hard enough getting away with anything when your husband was a werewolf with the ability to scent a lie. Her best defense was to distract him with sex.

The man was perpetually horny, would throw over anything if he thought he was about to get some. He was probably right about what it would take McBane and his twin to leave their mate's bed.

One look at the stormy faces of the twin brothers storming down the hall made her think there had to be a better way. Derek was about to get hurt.

"What the hell do you want?"

"Get the hell out of our house!"

"Can't. I got some news for you."

Derek sounded almost thrilled about that fact. It was his normal attitude when dealing with other males. He hadn't sounded thrilled about what Claire had told him just an hour ago. No, then he'd been growling and barking out questions.

Claire knew Derek considered the McBanes family, even if they weren't related. It had something to do with them all being alphas of their own packs. As far as she could tell, it was a bond that might be stronger than blood.

"Then say it and leave," JD snapped.

Claire had to stop herself from snorting. That was typical of Sheriff McBane. The man did not comprehend the concept of polite. What she had seen of him, JD was always halfway to pissed off, a short trip for a man with his temper. In contrast, his brother Caleb was a flirt.

He'd even managed to make an unexpected appearance at her baby shower a month ago. Oh, he had apologized for the interruption, explaining that he thought Derek and him were supposed to hang out.

Claire hadn't bought it for a minute. The charmer had wheedled his way into the large group of women and spent almost all afternoon selecting which one he was going to take home.

He had decided on two. When Derek had found out, he'd been none too pleased. Liking the McBanes didn't change the fact that Derek didn't want any of the Covenanters around his bitches. They were for his pack and his pack alone.

That discussion had gone about as well as this one was going, only the roles were reversed. Now it was the McBanes with their paws clenched into white-knuckled fists and Derek smirking.

"Well, Narian?"

When they used Derek's title, Claire knew blood was soon to be spilt. Derek didn't seem concerned. He turned and gave her a little nod. Claire turned to look at Lilly, who was still slouched down in one of the kitchen chairs. The other woman just closed her eyes on Claire's pointed stare.

"What the hell is she doing here?"

"She told my wife an interesting story that I thought you would like to hear."

"Like what?"

"Claire?"

Claire took a deep breath. "Lilly was telling me about her case to give me inspiration for my next book. She—"

"What about client confidentiality?" One of the brothers cut Claire off to shoot that question at Lilly.

Claire caught the woman's shrug and knew it was the reason behind the intimidating growl that echoed through the kitchen. She may be mated to a werewolf and a little furry herself at times, but those growls still made her skin prickle to attention. Except when Derek did it. Then it made something else come to life.

"Go on, Claire, tell them before we have to start digging a hole for the body."

"Lilly told me that—Samantha, right?" At one of the men's nod, she continued. "That her ex bought a curse and used it on her…"

It took Claire ten minutes to get the entire story out thanks to all the interruptions. Derek had been wrong. Knowing the details only made the twins more aggressive, though their attention turned on Lilly. Not that the investigator appeared concerned.

Even vulnerable with her hands cuffed behind her, Lilly still acted as if she could take on all three werewolves. She responded to the twins' grilling and demands for explanations with quick and glib answers that only fed their building rage.

"I think," Claire stepped in when one of the brothers made a move on Lilly, "you should focus your anger on the guy who cursed your mate. He is, after all, the one who is trying to kill her."

"She's right." Caleb didn't sound happy about that fact. "We need to have a word with Bruce."

"I think a few," Derek offered.

"I'm not done with you." That gem from JD had Lilly rolling her eyes and another growl vibrating through the kitchen. He turned toward Derek. "Can you keep an eye on Samantha for a little while?"

"Not a problem."

"Keep this one," he leveled a finger at Lilly, "away from her."

"Sure."

It took the brothers less than five minutes before they were headed out the door. They paused only long enough to remind Derek to keep Lilly away from their mate and make sure Samantha remained in bed. With that, they were gone.

Derek ambled out onto the porch to watch them leave. Claire watched him through the window as he walked around front. She knew he was going to be settling into a rocking chair, as far away from Lilly as duty allowed him.

"Well." Lilly's sigh drew Claire's eyes to her. "Want to play some cards?"

"What are you going to do? Hold them in your teeth?" Claire smirked.

Lilly didn't respond to that directly. She arched her back and leaned her head as far down as it would go. It was enough for her hands to work their way into the tresses. A moment later, she was sitting upright, and Claire caught the glint of metal before she heard first one cuff and then the next ratcheting open.

A second later Lilly dropped the cuffs on the table, and Claire watched as she slid the pick back into her hair. Claire had to shake her head. That was one of things she liked about Lilly. She was prepared for anything.

* * * *

JD and Caleb didn't speak a word to each other on the hour-plus drive into Savannah. JD drove with the precision of a laser-guided missile straight to Bruce's motel door. They knew he was in there. A quick call to Tex had told exactly where they would find their prey.

He answered on their first knock and couldn't get the door closed fast enough to keep them out. Bruce cursed and fought, but he was no match for the two of them, and in short order, they had him shoved into the truck and headed back toward their territory.

Bruce didn't have to wonder about where they were headed. He was a wolf. He knew the score. What did surprise him was that the two beasts on either side of him had figured out the game. He hadn't given them that much credit.

This had always been the risk. There wasn't much he could do about the situation but hope to fight his way out of it. With two against one, that was going to be a challenge. He could have offered up Candice for the peace offering and slunk out of town, at least until he figured out a new way into Samantha's checkbook.

The guys wouldn't take Candice. He'd studied up on their breed. They needed Samantha. The money was just a bonus to them. What really annoyed him was they didn't have to work hard to get either. He, on the other hand, had to wade through more shit than a pile left by a diarrheic elephant.

First, there had been Samantha herself. What a stupid bitch she was, believing any man would love her for that body. Bruce almost felt sorry for the two assholes he was with. They were stuck with that for the rest of their lives. No doubt she'd only get fatter as she popped out their pups.

Samantha had nothing on Candice's body. Now there was a lean, beautiful woman. Nice ass, great tits, and easily spread legs, what more could a man ask for? That woman would fuck anything for the right price. How Candice thought he could care about her was beyond Bruce.

It just went to prove that, despite the looks, Candice was just as dumb as Samantha, thinking he would have shared the money with her. She might have been a good fuck, but no woman was worth that much money. It was ironic, though, that he would have killed her right after he collected the cash, and she was likely to kill Samantha if the two pit bulls killed him.

Eventually they'd take Candice out, and that would only leave Brett, that sniveling, whiny wimp that he'd pimped Candice out to. It was a shame about that. Bruce had been most looking forward to eliminating that spoiled brat. He'd have to take comfort in knowing that Brett would gamble away his inheritance in short order.

That was just annoying to think about. There were so many better things to do with the cash, like buy a boat and a lot of pussy and go for a cruise. That was first on Bruce's list. By the time they landed, he'd have converted all the bitches into his servants. A pack full of cock-hungry bitches…Bruce sighed. That was a dream only a genius could come up with.

It looked to remain that way. Bruce scowled at the monster-sized man to his right as the truck jerked to a sudden stop. They were buried deep in the wilderness. He didn't need an explanation on where they were as the other brother dragged him out of the truck and shoved him to the ground.

The scent of the pack was all around him. This was their hunting ground. Every pack had one, some land privately owned where they could run free in their fur. Bruce had never had a place like that, but that didn't mean he hadn't invaded other packs' ground. The trick was in not getting caught.

"You have two choices." The growl drew his eyes to the brother who had been driving. "You can tell us the name of the witch who cursed our mate and only fight one of us, or you can say nothing, and we'll both rip you to pieces."

"Two against one?" Bruce scrambled up. These were alphas. They were used to making the rules, but their honor would be important to them. "Not exactly honorable, is it?"

"About as honorable as cursing a woman who has done no wrong to you. Make your choice now or we'll choose for you."

Since there was only one choice they could make for him, Bruce knew exactly what he was saying.

"And if I win the fight, the other brother will let me just walk away?"

"You have our word."

"Okay, you cocky bastards. It was Suriha, down in Beaufort." Bruce smirked. "Now, which one will it be?"

"Me."

"Caleb—"

"It's my right."

"It's mine too."

Bruce almost laughed as the brothers got into a pissing contest over which one of them would do the actual fighting. Obviously, they'd forgotten to think of that in this well-laid plan. Not his problem. Bruce moved farther away, stripping out of his clothes.

One brother he could handle. Especially if they already did some damage to each other, which, listening to the way their argument was going, just might happen. It took a few minutes, but they managed to decide without coming to blows that the one named Caleb would do the honors. The large man came forward, stripping out of his clothes with every step.

"Ready?"

"Whenever you are."

In a blink, Bruce was looking through feral eyes at the largest wolf he'd ever encountered. For the first time in his life, he knew fear. The emotion was there and gone as the massive beast sprang forward.

Chapter 25

"Gin."

Claire barely looked at the hand Lilly laid down before scooping up the cards and shuffling them. She'd played enough cards with the investigator to know that Lilly was either lucky or an excellent cheat.

"So," Claire dealt another round. "You going to tell me the rest now?"

"The rest?"

"The rest of the story, who is really after Samantha." Claire shot Lilly a quick look before lifting her cards up. They were crap.

"Bruce is really after Samantha." Lilly barely spared a glance at her cards before pulling and discarding a card in one motion. "JD and Caleb are going to kill him. You don't honestly think I would send them after an innocent man or you wouldn't have helped me."

"I'm not sure why I did help you." It took considerably longer for her to pull the three of clubs and contemplate it before discarding it. Lilly snapped it up.

"You wouldn't have had to if Samantha had done what I wanted and told her damn mates about Bruce when she was in the hospital." Lilly slapped down the five of diamonds. "That woman is beyond contrary."

"Says the most difficult woman in the state."

"I thought you were trying to wrest that title from me."

"It's just the hormones." Claire grunted as she pulled the ace of spade. That card she kept. "If you could have children, I'm sure you'd outdo every pregnant woman on the planet."

"Seven thousand years plus and the thing I'm most grateful for is that I can't have kids." Lilly grinned. "And I think the world is grateful too."

"You don't ever wish—"

"Nope."

Claire didn't press. It hadn't been easy to get Lilly to confide the truth behind her past. She didn't trust easily, and Claire understood why. She hadn't trusted Lilly when she first met her either.

Of course, that had a lot to do with the way Lilly behaved when they first met. The investigator's know-it-all attitude had irritated her, but her knowledge of Claire's past association with a demon had outraged her.

Once they had gotten over their misunderstanding, the two women had formed a bond that went thicker than blood. Both knew the guilt and alienation that took over a marked person's life. Lilly had it worse, though.

There was no hope for her. Claire had thought that there was none for her until she'd met Derek. It hadn't been easy, but she had escaped the hell that had enveloped her life.

Now she had a husband who doted on her, parents that were sometimes a little too pushy, a sister to help her cope with her new family, and a son on the way that, if he turned out like his dad, was going to keep her very busy. It was a dream she'd never dared to fantasize about before.

"So?" Lilly snapped her back to the moment. "You going to draw a card?"

"Oh, yeah." Claire pulled the jack of hearts.

"You tired? Need to take a nap?"

"No." Claire watched as Lilly snapped the jack off the discard pile.

"I was just asking because I know you breeders need your rest."

"Breeder?"

"Gin." Lilly slapped her hand down.

"Breeder?"

"That's the old term." Lilly gathered the cards Claire tossed on the table. "Back before Harak gifted the wolves with the ability to shift. When he originally built his army of beasts, he had little use for the smaller females, and most were eliminated. The remainders were called breeders."

"You are a vast wealth of information," Claire commented as she picked up each card as Lilly dealt them to her.

"Thank you."

"I wish you wouldn't share it."

"Except when you're pumping me for ideas for your books. How is the script coming anyway?"

"As good as it was when you asked me earlier today." Claire narrowed her eyes on the tiny investigator. "How is it you turned this conversation completely around?"

"What you mean?"

"I mean you sent JD and Caleb after Bruce, but I know you. You don't give up the big catch when you're fishing. So he has to be a distraction."

"I hate fish. Never eat it. You gonna pull a card?"

"Lilly." Claire slapped her cards down on the table.

"Fine. Bruce isn't a distraction. He's a serious threat."

"But?"

"There is another player."

"I knew it. You're going to keep this one for yourself, aren't you?"

"I do like my entertainment."

"Lilly."

"Sorry, Claire." Lilly met her gaze. "It's my problem. I'll take care of it."

"And Samantha?"

"I wouldn't let anything happen to her. Now, you going to pull a card or not?"

* * * *

They only played for another half hour before Claire did need that nap Lilly had kidded her about. Lilly helped the very pregnant woman settle down on the couch before returning to the kitchen to snatch a beer out of the refrigerator.

Derek's lip curled in distaste when she stepped out onto the porch, and she had to fight her own reflexive annoyance with the wolf. His eyes dropped to her wrists, and his eyes glowed with anger.

"Did Claire take the cuffs off you?"

"I picked the lock. Here." Lilly held the beer out to him.

"Like I'm going to take that from you."

"What? You think I poisoned it?"

"Did you?"

"Fine." Lilly threw back the bottle and guzzled almost half of it before presenting it to him. "There, you happy?"

"Why are you bringing me a beer anyway?" Derek reluctantly accepted the bottle.

"Because Claire asked me to." Lilly turned back to the door.

"Where is she?"

"Peeing. I was just saving her the trip."

Lilly didn't wait for a response before banging back into the house. It took nearly twenty minutes for the drug to take effect. When the bottle crashed to the ground and he slumped over, Lilly knew he was out.

He hadn't taken much of the potion in. It wasn't going to be long before he woke up mad and looking to kill. She had to work fast.

* * * *

"Hey?"

There was a familiarity to the bed being bounced beneath her and that too-cheery voice calling her. Sam blinked her eyes, fighting through the moment of déjà vu to the current reality of the moment.

It was hard with Lilly smiling down at her. The investigator was again dressed in all black, making Sam wonder if she owned any other color. It was really irritating. Black was for women who needed to look slender, not for well-shaped women like Lilly.

"You're up, good." Lilly tossed some clothes on the bed. "Get dressed. We need to get moving."

"Moving? We're going somewhere?" Sam croaked, struggling to understand the strange world she had awoken to. This wasn't her bedroom, nor JD and Caleb's room. "Where the hell am I?"

"Jesus, do they fuck that good?"

"Oh…yeah." Sam scratched her head. It was coming back to her now. "What are you—"

"You really shouldn't talk." Lilly cut her off. "That's bad for your cords."

"Not you—"

"You sounded much better earlier." Lilly shrugged. "Get dressed. We really are in somewhat of a rush here."

"I'm not going—"

"Two choices, you can go in your nightshirt or fully clothed."

Damn it! Sam really wanted to fight over that. She hated ultimatums. The problem was she was in no condition to fight and Lilly looked more than capable of enforcing her will. With jerky, annoyed motions, she snatched up her clothes and began to pull them on.

Lilly wasn't kidding about being in a rush. She put one hand on Sam's arm and all but dragged her own the hall. Sam did pull her to a stop when they passed through the living room.

"Who are they?" Sam glared at the two strangers passed out on either couch.

"That's Derek Jacob. He's the police of chief for Wilsonville. That is his lovely mate, Claire. Wonderful woman."

"Why are they asleep?"

"Because she's six months pregnant and he's lazy." Lilly tugged on her arm. "Now let's move."

"You didn't do anything to them, did you?" Sam was no match for Lilly's strength. The woman might be small, but she sure was strong. Despite Sam's resistance, she had her out the door in seconds.

"I would never hurt a pregnant woman." She sounded insulted at the idea. It was the first time Sam had heard her sound anything but obnoxiously happy, and it took her aback for a moment.

"I just…" Sam stumbled over the words, not at all sure of how to apologize or even why she was bothering. Hell, the woman was bossy, aggressive, and seemed to do whatever the hell she wanted. Was it so weird that Sam thought she had somehow put that couple to sleep?

"Forget about it." Lilly yanked open a truck door. "Get in."

"This is your truck?"

"In."

Sam took that as no, especially when Lilly climbed into the other side and had to wrench the long bench all the way forward to reach the pedals. She had the keys, probably lifted them from the guy inside.

She'd said he was a police chief. *Stealing a cop's car.* Sam shook her head. She had to give Lilly credit for having more balls than she did. Either that or the investigator suffered from serious retardation, because this was definitely something she was going to have to pay for.

Sam kept her opinions to herself. There was no point in pointing out the obvious. She remained silent for almost a half hour, but finally her curiosity got the better of her. Knowing it was probably hopeless, she pressed Lilly again for answers.

"Now do I get to know where we are going?"

"We're going to save your ass." Lilly made a sharp turn onto a Highway 21, cutting out a line of cars streaming at them.

"And that would be…"

"Madame Mae Lee's house." Lilly cut her a quick look and grinned. "She's expecting us, and you don't want to keep a Voodoo priestess waiting. Bad luck, you know?"

A chuckle almost escaped Sam, but at the last moment, she managed to make it sound like a snort. Lilly wasn't kidding about not keeping the woman waiting. They flew past a fifty-miles-per-hour sign going at least seventy to cut off another car as the lane narrowed from two to one.

Less than five minutes later, Lilly was slinging the truck around a corner and hauling down a road that looked like it was trapped in the past. If it weren't for the asphalt, Sam could have easily imagined a horse-drawn carriage clambering down the road, past the small brick buildings, and into the embrace of the welcoming oaks.

"Where are we?"

"Frogmore. This area is referred to as Penn Center." Lilly spoke without slowing down despite the posted limit having dropped now to thirty-five. "During the civil war, the plantation owners abandoned their farms. Since there was no bridge to the mainland, the former slaves built up their own society. They still speak Gullah in these parts."

"Gul…what?"

"It's an old slave language."

The history of the area boiled through the air, reaching out intangible fingers to slowly wrap any interloper in their cold embrace. She could almost feel the dead watching her through lifeless eyes as Lilly made another veering turn.

The sensation only increased when she pulled an abrupt stop in front of a small house. It looked in need of a lot of repair and a good cleaning. Shaded by a massive sweet gum tree, the yard teemed with life as flowers and herbs grew all around despite it being February.

The plants here seemed to grow all on their own, fighting for space and trying to outdo their neighbors for brilliant colors and welcoming odors. Sam slid out of the truck and into the soft sand beneath, almost afraid to take a step for fear of trampling on the vegetation.

"Ah, my beautiful flower, you have arrived," a woman called out as she stepped out onto the porch.

Sam's eyes widened slightly. She had been expecting the woman to be wearing some kind of hippie outfit with big dangling earrings and a scarf wrapped around her head. This woman, with her tight blue jeans and black T-shirt with foxy glittering on her chest, was surely not the Voodoo priestess.

"Mae!"

Lilly corrected Sam's assumptions as she grabbed Sam by the arm again. In a repeat of the scene back at the cabin, she dragged Sam through the tall flowers, toward the door.

"Thanks for making time for us." Lilly came to a halt. "This girl is in dire need of your help."

"I can sense that." Mae studied Sam with such intensity she felt like squirming. "You stink."

"Excuse me?"

"I fear letting you in my house with that stench. Bad magic, that's what it is." The woman raised her rounded chin as her eyes narrowed in on Sam's necklace. "That, though, is very pretty. Do you mind if I try it on?"

"What?" Sam's hand covered her precious jewelry. "I think not."

"Huh, well…" Mae 's chocolate brown eyes darted toward Lilly.

"Samantha's really fond of the necklace."

"I can tell. I understand why. Such beauty is rare. Very rare."

There was a hard tint to the woman's last statement that made Sam's arm hairs rise in warning. Something was amiss here. That woman wanted her necklace.

"I guess." Lilly didn't sound convinced. "But we didn't come here to talk about jewelry, Mae. Not to be pushy, but—"

"You're in a rush." Mae finished for Lilly, pushing her face right into the shorter woman's. "Always the same with you, Lillian. You must learn to slow down and enjoy life before there is no time left to savor."

"Yeah, I'll take it under advisement. Now about the curse—"

"Tea first."

Sam had no explanation for it, but she felt there was something more that was being said. As if the two other women were corresponding in a way Sam couldn't understand. The sensation prickled at her nerves, and she suddenly became concerned for her safety.

"Fine." There was no breaking Lilly's hold as she moved her forward. "Let's have a cup, and then, maybe, we can get to Samantha's problem."

Sam watched the other two women defensively as they guided her into the house. Her guard was up, and she barely noticed her surroundings other than that they were cluttered and smelled of a wild mixture of herbs. Reluctantly she took the seat that Lilly all but shoved her into.

She eyed the teapot suspiciously, relaxing only slightly when Mae Lee poured all three glasses from the same pot. At least they weren't going to poison her. The priestess caught her look and smiled.

"Do you not like tea? I could get you something else."

"No. Tea is fine." As long as they were all drinking it. Sam hesitated until she saw Lilly gulp it down in one swallow.

"Damn, that's good tea." Lilly shoved her glass at Mae. "Give me some more."

Sam watched the other two women drink and chat, pretty much ignoring her as she began to tentatively sip her tea. Damn, it was good. Despite her earlier reservations, she found herself draining the cup and two more before she began to realize something was wrong.

It was too late then. She thought that she should run right before the room went black.

* * * *

Lilly looked over at Samantha as her head hit the table with a thud.

"She was suspicious of the tea," Mae commented, sipping from her own cup.

"Not suspicious enough of the cup, though."

"I'm just glad I'm not one of your clients, Lillian."

"I wouldn't take you. You'd be too difficult."

"One day you're going to be on the receiving end of your own wit."

"Thank you."

"It wasn't a compliment." Mae breathed in deeply as she set down her cup. "You are right about the necklace. I can feel the bad coming from it."

"She seems very protective of it."

"Part of the curse." Mae rose and moved toward the sideboard. "It's a very powerful magic. Few could do this."

"Any guesses?"

"Not a human."

"That's what I thought."

Mae turned and dipped her hands in scented oil. "Now, we must remove it and destroy it."

"How long is this going to take?" Lilly frowned at her watch.

"You do not rush magic, Lillian."

"Yeah, well, I got three werewolves who are going to be looking to make a meal out of me if I don't get Samantha back into bed in time."

"That is the risk you took." Mae pushed Samantha's hair out of the way.

"Well if I'm damned anyway, I might as well hang out for a reading. See how it's going to end."

Chapter 26

Sam groaned and blinked as the world slowly came into focus. The wood-plank ceiling overhead threw her off for a moment. Then she remembered that she was at the cabin with JD and Caleb.

Their house had burned down, she'd been to the hospital, JD had cried because of her, and...had Lilly been here? Was it just a dream? She tried to remember, but the images were hazy.

The harder she tried to focus, the more her head hurt. With another groan, she rolled to her side, intending to bury her face in the pillow, but finding a hard, hot chest instead.

"Samantha?" Caleb threaded his fingers through her hair. "How are you feeling?"

"Like shit."

"It'll wear off in a little while." His hands slid down to smooth over her back and pull her more firmly into his embrace.

"Where is JD?"

"At the station."

"He got called in?"

"No, he's trying to teach Lilly a lesson by arresting her."

"Lilly?" Sam lifted her head. "So it wasn't a dream."

"Far from it." Caleb met her gaze with a look that told, despite his calm tone, he was far from relaxed. "She went too far this time."

"What is he charging her with?" Lilly tried hard to piece all the fuzzy images together into a coherent scene.

"Anything he can think of—kidnapping, drugging, theft. He would have added grand larceny, but Claire insisted that she gave Derek's truck keys to Lilly."

"Claire? Derek? They were asleep on the couch, right?"

"Claire was asleep. Derek was drugged."

"Why?" Lilly reached up to rub her aching head.

"Because he wouldn't have let you walk out of here with her otherwise."

"No." Lilly dropped her hand to glare at Caleb. "Why did she take me...God, I can't even remember where we went."

"That's a shame. Lilly wouldn't tell JD."

"Why did she do this? What did she do to me?"

"Oh, she broke the curse, or so she claims."

"The curse. She helped me?"

"You could look at it that way." Caleb begrudgingly nodded.

"And JD arrested her for that?"

"He arrested her for the way she went about it."

"Caleb!"

"What?"

"You can't let JD arrest her for helping me," Sam snapped.

"Oh, don't get all pissy now. He's not really going to arrest her. He's just annoying her and venting some anger that is, I might add, wholly justified."

"You're sure?"

"Yeah. Don't worry. Lilly can handle herself." Caleb sighed and ran his hand back up to her neck, forcing her head back down. "JD just doesn't like her."

"Hell, I don't like her either, but you don't see me arresting her," Sam muttered.

"I'm glad," Caleb stated after a few minutes, "that you don't like her. I really don't want her around you."

"I don't think you have to worry about that if the curse is broken. I imagine her job is done now."

"Yeah, it's over." Caleb sighed. "We can finally go on with our lives."

Sam thought about that. On with their lives, but in which direction? Now that the whole curse thing was over…

"What about Bruce?" Sam's head popped back up.

"What about him?" Caleb opened one eye at that question.

"He's not going to just give up."

"Don't worry." Caleb closed his eye. "Bruce is gone for good."

"What does that mean? Gone for good?"

"It means what it means."

"Caleb."

"Let it go, Samantha." Caleb pulled her back down. "You don't really want to know anyways."

No, she probably didn't if he was saying what she thought he was saying. Sam trusted Caleb. If he said Bruce was no longer an issue, then she would no longer be concerned about him.

That left her back where she had started, trying to figure out what to do with the rest of her life. There was no escaping Caleb and JD. She didn't really want to, but neither did she want to become a stay-at-home plaything for them.

She needed to work, needed some independent direction in her life. She just didn't know what that was. Sam closed her eyes and sighed. That problem was going to take time and some work to figure out.

Where the hell was her necklace?

* * * *

Monday

Sam watched Tex move around the kitchen from under lowered lashes. It was wrong, and she knew it, but couldn't stop herself from admiring his perfect body. She excused her shameless behavior by rationalizing that any healthy woman would stare.

Tex was built like JD and Caleb, big, hard, and tanned. That he liked to walk around the small cabin wearing nothing but a pair of faded jeans wasn't her fault. JD and Caleb had certainly told him often enough to put a shirt on, but Tex just seemed to love to go around half naked.

Sam had a feeling that was because he knew she was looking. If Caleb had thought he was a charmer, than he'd failed to spend any real time around his cousin. Tex was shameless when it came to flirting.

Even if he hadn't had a body made for sin or deep chocolate bedroom eyes, he'd have still gotten more lucky than half the men on the planet. With his quick grin and easygoing charm, Tex had a way of getting under a woman's defenses.

Even though he had player written all over him, Sam had still found herself telling Tex her entire life story before she could think better of it. In five minutes of knowing him, he had felt like an old friend.

It was all good until he'd turned that charm on Vicky when she'd shown up to check on Sam the other day. When she saw her younger sister giggling and blushing, Sam knew she had to put a stop to that before it got out of hand.

Tex might be a great guy with no intention of hurting a single woman, but Caleb had made it quite clear that Tex fell in love at the drop of a hat. Ten minutes later, when he met the next woman, he was in love all over again.

JD had echoed Caleb's comments, but with a much harsher tone. He thought his cousin was as stupid as a wolf could be when it came to women. If it weren't for Tex's twin, Cal, half the female population would have been mated by now.

Apparently, Tex and Cal didn't suffer from a pure Covenanter bloodline. They were a mixed-breed of Covenanter and feral. Their feral nature allowed them to mate and breed indiscriminately. It was an ability that most organized packs loathed, which was why feral wolves were often eliminated.

Tex and Cal had avoided that fate, because they had agreed to adhere to the Covenanter's mating rituals. That had made her feel a little better about Tex's obvious interest in Vicky, but not good enough to approve.

JD had personally handled the matter for her. He had reminded Tex of some redheaded love who he was supposed to be meeting in two weeks when he headed out west. When that had failed to impress Tex, JD had resorted to threats and violence.

That had worked at getting Tex's eye off of Vicky, but then it had locked back down on Sam. She knew he was just flirting with her to drive Caleb and JD crazy, but it was working to her benefit.

The more jealous they got of Tex, the louder they made her scream in pleasure at night. Sam knew that they were just showing off for Tex, proving to him that their mate was well satisfied by them. It didn't bother her in the least, because she was so well satiated.

"You thinking about JD and Caleb again, aren't you, darlin'?" Tex slid into the chair next to her at the kitchen table.

"Uh-huh." Sam blushed slightly.

"Yeah, you got that smile on. They're some lucky cusses to get a woman like you."

"They're not here to appreciate the flirting, Tex," Sam pointed out even as she felt her face heat up even more.

"Who says I do it for them?" Tex popped open his soda can with a wink in her direction.

"You're too much."

"I do try." Tex paused and then gave her a sly grin. "So, you going to be inviting that sweet little sister of yours over again?"

"You stay away from Vicky, Tex." This time Sam didn't have to fake the hard tone.

"Ah, I wouldn't do nothing to her she wouldn't enjoy."

"That's what I'm afraid of."

"You'd enjoy it too, and I'd enjoy it better with the both of you."
Tex wiggled her brows.

"Pervert."

"That I am, but I'm just trying to make you smile, sweet thing."
Tex reached out to run a quick finger across her lips, and Sam
couldn't help but smile at the too-friendly touch. "You got that
worried look on your face again, and it sure does bother me to see a
woman worrying."

"I'm just thinking…"

"About what to do with your life?"

"Yeah."

"Bakery."

"What?" Sam looked over at him.

"You should open a bakery." Tex expanded his answer. "You
bake like nobody's business, and there ain't no sweet spot in town.
You could do like a Samanthabucks, coffee and sweets."

"Samanthabucks." Sam laughed.

"Yeah, you got the money. What the hell? Give it a try."

"I only know how to bake certain things."

"They got schools."

"You think JD and Caleb are going to let me go away to school?"

"It doesn't have to be a four-year degree. I'm sure you could go
somewhere and just take a class here and there. Besides, you can't let
those boys rule your life." Tex put down his soda. "You don't want to
be bitter at the end of it, thinking you gave everything up for them."

"You're just saying that because you'd love to see them squirm
while I'm away."

"That's true." Tex grinned. "But you really should think about it."

"Hmm."

Sam had to admit the idea held appeal. So, she'd think about it.
Why not? Her attention diverted when Tex scratched his chest and
stood up. He headed for the door.

"Where you going?" Sam called out.

"I think I left my cell in the truck, and I got a pretty little brunette that might be giving me a call." Tex grinned lecherously. "Don't want to disappoint the sexy lady."

"Don't you think you should put some shoes on? Or a shirt?"

"Honey, I was born naked, and, God willing, I'm going to die that way too."

* * * *

The screen door banging closed drew Lilly's gaze back to the porch. She narrowed her scope as she watched some half-naked sex god walk toward the oversized pickup parked in the yard.

This one had been the sentry the alpha assholes had put on watching Bruce. Lilly wouldn't have admitted it out loud, but she didn't mind watching him. He liked to go around half naked, and a woman would have to be dead not to appreciate what he was showing off.

Despite the fact that she had never met him, and partly because he was so good looking, Lilly didn't like the man. She didn't need to meet him to know his type. From the tricked-out truck to the hard body, he was definitely a playboy.

There wasn't a woman who had gotten within five feet of him who he wasn't grinning and drooling all over. It was a mutual reaction. Most of the women drooled at first sight of him.

Lilly might have drooled a little herself, but that just added to her anger. He was a werewolf, and she hated werewolves. They were arrogant jackasses who thought, just because they could grow fangs, everybody should defer to them.

Her silent tirade was cut short when a big-breasted brunette came around the side of the building. There she was. Candice. It had eaten Lilly alive with annoyance when she'd lost track of the bitch.

Lilly was the best damn tracker in the whole fucking state, possibly the Southeast, but somehow Bimbo Barbie had managed to give her the slip. That fact had made Lilly even more determined to catch the woman, and she'd known just where Candice would eventually show up.

Candice hadn't let her down. Neither was the sex god who was doing his best to con the clothes right off of Candice. He had his arm around her already and that shit-eating grin in place.

It didn't surprise Lilly a lick when he suddenly fell face-first into the ground. She caught the flash of a black Taser when Candice leaned down to give him a second hearty dose of electric shock treatment. Good for her. Lilly hoped the shock was strong enough to make him go in his jeans.

Lilly wasn't going to interfere with that noble goal, but when Candice turned her attention toward the house, Lilly readied her crossbow. It had been a long debate on whether to bring the rifle and just kill the bitch or go with the crossbow and dart her.

She needed the brunette alive. There were questions that needed answers. With only two people to get them from, the woman was the weaker link. That didn't mean she couldn't hurt the other woman. Actually, pain was a necessary negotiating tool when dealing with her type.

The arrow whooshed out of the bow with speed that made the hairs around her ears waver. A second dart followed before the first had even embedded itself in Candice's thigh. Anticipating the direction the bitch would fall, Lilly's second shot hit her other leg.

Candice went down and, after a moment of twitching, fell still. By the time Lilly made it out of the tree and across the yard, the woman was out cold thanks to the poison she'd dipped the bow tips in. She'd also have problems ever walking normal again.

Not that Lilly cared. Nor did she bother to glance at the werewolf who was laid out across the grass. She intended to head straight into the house to tell Samantha what needed to be done, but as she stepped over the blood that was already leaking out of Candice's leg, her eyes diverted to the black box in her hand.

It was smaller than the Taser, and it had a set of digital numbers that was counting down. That could only mean one thing, and she had little more than a minute to handle the matter. That didn't leave her much time.

* * * *

Sam was just putting the milk back in the refrigerator when the back door flew open. Lillian Masterson was there, her eyes zeroing in on Sam. Strangely enough, the investigator didn't step into the room. Not so unusual, she immediately began issuing orders.

"Anybody else here?"

"No. What are you doing here?"

"Any living things in the house, cats, dogs?"

"No. Why do you care?"

"Let's go." Lilly jerked her head and began to turn around, but Sam's response stopped her cold.

"I'm not going anywhere with you."

"Why do you always have to make things difficult?" Lilly stormed at her.

"Stay away from me!" Sam shrieked and turned to run. She didn't make it a single step before Lilly's hand clamped down on her arm and began dragging her backward. "Damn it! Let me go!"

No amount of thrashing or fighting managed to break Lilly's hold. It didn't even slow her down. Lilly pulled a cussing Sam right out the back door. Sam threatened her with everything she could think of, especially JD and what he was going to do to Lilly once he found out about this.

The words died in her throat when she saw the blood staining the back steps and the familiar brunette strewn across them. Her mind went blank for a moment as Lilly pulled her over the woman's body and she took in the two large arrows sticking out of each leg.

"Did you do that?"

"Yes." Lilly shoved Sam away and toward Tex, who was laid out facedown in the grass. "But I didn't do that. Grab his legs."

"What's wrong with him?" Sam knelt down and pulled his head up, brushing the dark strands of hair away from his forehead. "Tex."

"There is going to be a lot more wrong with him if you don't grab his legs," Lilly snapped, shoving Sam back and looping her arms under his armpits. "Now help me."

"I don't know why I'm listening to you," Sam muttered to herself as she grabbed one of Tex's ankles in each hand.

He was a lot heavier than she had imagined. Lilly was a good deal stronger than she had thought. Carrying most of the weight, she dragged Tex backward away from the house.

"I don't even like you."

"I don't care."

"All you do is get me into trouble."

"I'm the one who got slapped into cuffs and hauled down to the station trying to help you."

"You stole a cop's car."

"Truck."

"Truck," Sam corrected, rolling her eyes. "What did you think was going to happen?"

"I thought maybe somebody would appreciate the fact that I saved your ass," Lilly snapped. "Obviously I overestimated the importance of your well-being. I guess your mates don't really care if you live or die."

"Now that's just rude."

"You know, Samantha. Normally I pity the women who have to suffer through a Covenanter's final mating act, but not you."

"What do you—"

Sam's sentence ended in a scream as the cabin behind went *boom*. The loud explosion echoed out through the forest and vibrated back in ominous waves. The sudden sound startled her so bad she tripped and fell over Tex.

He groaned slightly under her, but Sam's attention was fixated on the cabin blossoming into flames. Moving with amazing speed, tongues of orange and yellow devoured the wood structure from the ground up. It was unnatural.

"It's a good thing you're rich considering the way you go through houses," Lilly commented from overhead. Her dry tone drew Sam's eyes up to the tiny investigator. She was watching the cabin burn without an inch of remorse on her features.

"You did this," Sam accused.

"Nope. The brunette bitch did." Lilly's eyebrow raised as the porch roof collapsed on top of the woman she'd just referred to. "I guess she won't be doing it again."

"Hey!" Sam scrambled up to her feet to chase after Lilly as she turned and strutted off. "Where the hell are you going?"

"Anywhere your mates are not likely to show up." Lilly threw the words over her shoulder.

"Damn it, Lilly! Get back here." Sam managed to catch Lilly by the arm, but despite her extra weight, she couldn't slow the pint-sized woman down.

"No can do." Lilly shook her off. "Got places to go and people to help."

"Damn it!" This time when Sam grabbed Lilly, she came to a stop, even turned around to face Sam. "I'm not going to be the one to explain a dead a body and another burnt-down house to JD!"

"I'm sure as hell not going to do it." Lilly grunted. "He'll just blame me."

"If you leave now, I'll blame it on you too."

"So what? You're going to anyway."

"I don't like you."

"So you keep saying." Lilly sighed. "Look, the bill is in the mail. Pay it, and you never have to see me again."

"I'm not paying you."

"I'll sue. Don't think your mates will be to happy to hear what I have to say on the witness stand."

"You're blackmailing me?"

"Whatever works." Lilly's eyes focused on something over Sam's shoulders. "I think you have a puppy to tend to. See you around, Samantha Hark."

With that, Lilly turned and sauntered off. Sam would have chased after the other woman, but Tex's groan made her waver. Duty finally won out over anger, and she turned back to JD and Caleb's cousin.

Tex was struggling to sit up, one hand gripping his head while the other held his side. Sam got down on her knees to lend him some support.

"What the hell happened?" Tex moaned before his eyes widened on the flames consuming the cabin. "Ah, shit. JD's going to blame this on me."

Chapter 27

One Week Later

Sam's gaze shifted to Caleb, then back to JD. They were up to something, and it was pissing her off. She didn't feel well and wasn't enjoying the mystery of their surprise trip out into the wilderness.

Her current bad mood was a first in the past week. Despite the fact that she'd blown up her future mother-in-law's house, she'd been lost in a euphoric haze for the past several days. It wasn't just because JD and Caleb had kept her well loved, but they had also said it.

Well, Caleb had said it. Right after he arrived on the scene to find her healthy as his mother's house crumbled into the ground. He'd pulled her into his arms and thanked God she was all right. Then he'd kissed her senseless and told her he'd loved her.

JD had copped out with a "me too." Sam hadn't let that stop her from enjoying the moment. She knew that much was hard enough for him to say. Eventually, JD'd get around to actually forming the words.

He'd better do it soon, Sam grumped silently. If he didn't, he'd find his ass cuffed to the bed, and then she'd torment the hell out of him until he told her what she wanted to hear. The image made her smile.

The enjoyment was temporary as a painful cramp curled her over. Dropping her head between her legs, Sam groaned and cursed. This shit hurt, and she knew exactly who to blame. It wasn't lost on her that there was a full moon tonight. She was certain she knew what that meant.

"You'll feel better soon, sweetheart." Caleb rubbed her back.

"I'm going to turn into a dog soon, aren't I?" Sam snarled, tossing her hair out of her face so she could add a narrow-eyed glare to sharp words.

"A wolf." JD corrected her with a good deal of annoyance.

"I hope I bite you."

It felt like her bones were bending, near to breaking. Her muscles burned, contracting harshly. This went beyond sucking and straight into pure hell. She really did hope she remembered to bite both their asses for doing this to her.

God, she had spent all her life trying to get rid of chin hairs, shaving her legs, pits, and even occasionally her belly. Now she was going to have a full body beard. Why that seemed to arouse JD and Caleb, she had no idea.

There was no denying the twin erections flanking her. Then again, it wasn't so surprising. They walked around that way. Sam was beginning to think it was a werewolf thing, because Tex walked around that way too.

Or he had before JD had booted him out of their rental and sent him out west to chase after some redhead. Whoever the woman was, she didn't stand a chance. Tex could charm the habit off a nun. He could probably charm the obnoxiousness right out of Lilly.

Thank God she'd disappeared. Lilly had sent a bill. A very large bill that was sitting on Sam's desk waiting to be paid. Sam would pay her, but she wasn't planning on being timely about it.

Another powerful contraction seized her body, and for what felt like an eternity she drowned in a blinding wave of pain. She barely felt Caleb's hand soothing her back or his assurance that the first time was always the hardest. She did feel the gearshift when JD hit the brakes and she lurched forward, banging her head into the hard knob.

"I hate you," Sam growled.

"We're here," JD declared in a tone that sounded suspiciously satisfied.

"Here" was in the middle of a pine forest, which was really nowhere. Nowhere was apparently a popular spot. There were trucks, SUV's, and cars parked all around. It was eerie because there wasn't a single person to be seen.

JD and Caleb weren't perturbed by the situation. Caleb kicked open his door, latched a hand around her wrist, and dragged her out into the cold winter night. The biting wind made her tug on her wrist, trying to get back into the truck.

"Uh-uh." Caleb forced her out of the way and slammed the door.

A second later the lights lit up, and the security alarm beeped. Wild howls and excited yapping sliced through the air, making Sam realize they were not as alone as she thought.

She stood there looking around, feeling anxious. It was no more pleasant of a sensation than the cramps and pains that had plagued her on the ride over here. Those had at least eased. It was probably just the adrenaline.

"Strip."

"What?" JD's command drew her eyes away from the shadows of the forest and back to where Caleb and he were already in the process of doing just that. "I will not!"

"Why?" Caleb paused with his hands at the edge of his jeans. His shirt was already discarded in a puddle on the leaves.

"We're outside!"

"Strip." JD's glare disappeared behind a waterfall of cotton as he ripped his shirt up and off.

"We're in the middle of nowhere." Caleb popped his jeans open.

"I know there are people around," Sam snarled. "I can see the vehicles."

"They're all naked too." Caleb shrugged and shucked off his jeans.

"I don't care!"

Sam stared in amazement as the two brothers finished stripping off the remainder of their clothes. She bundled her jacket tighter around herself.

"It's freezing out here."

She added another point to her list of reasons she was not going to participate in this insanity. It didn't look as if they cared. JD stalked toward her with a hardened expression that she knew too well now.

"I told you to strip." He growled in that tone that told her he was planning punishment and then a mauling.

"Might as well obey him, Samantha," Caleb called out cheerily. "If you don't, then you'll just rip your clothes when you transform and we'll have to drive you home naked."

"I don't want to transform." Sam knew she was pouting like a little kid, but damn it, she didn't want to become a dog.

"Now, Samantha."

"Fine!" Sam began jerking at her clothes. "Whatever you say, *master*. It's not like it matters what I think."

Sam flung her jacket at JD. It slid down his chest as her sweater hit him in the face. She tugged her shirt up, still bitching at him through the cotton.

"One day you're going to push too far and I'm going to give you yours." She threw the long-sleeved turtleneck in JD's direction and reached for the button on her jeans. "Then we'll see whose ass is cuffed to the bed."

Sam continued her tirade about unbending assholes who had turned her into some damn dog girl, dragged her out into the middle of the forest in the middle of a cold winter night, and then ordered her to strip.

By the time she flung her shoes up and off, the heat of her anger had warmed her through. It was a temporary relief. The curses pouring out of her mouth stilled when she finally looked up and realized she was standing there alone.

No way...Those assholes left me here!

Sam's head jerked around in every direction, but JD and Caleb were gone. She wanted to yell for them, but the fear of attracting anybody else or anything else's attention kept her lips closed.

Screw this.

She reached for her clothes. She'd walk the hell home. As she reached for her underwear, a massive cramp rolled through her entire body, and she fell over, in too much pain to scream. It felt like her bones were trying to force their way through her skin, and her muscles were being shredded. Then things went peacefully black.

* * * *

JD watched as Samantha writhed on the ground. The first time any werewolf transformed, it was always painful, even for those born into the pack. He remembered his first time when he was sixteen.

It wasn't a pleasant memory. It wasn't abnormal for the person to scream while going through the process, especially women. JD took the same pride in watching Samantha bear the agony in silence as he did in the fact that neither Caleb nor he had let his pain vocalize itself. It was fitting of the alphas' mate.

No doubt Samantha would think he was sick for it, but he couldn't deny that it aroused him watching her smooth skin and generous curves twist into the trim, fur-covered lines of a small dark-haired wolf.

The sight excited the wolf inside him. That was his bitch, and the wolf wanted her now. JD could feel the beast trying to shift and fought to control the impulse. It wasn't time yet. It would be soon, very soon, but first there was the chase, followed by the fight. Then they could get to the final mating.

They weren't going to get anywhere if Samantha didn't immediately get up. *Stubborn woman, even more obstinate wolf,* JD growled to himself. He wanted to go give her a nudge, but it was a dangerous thing to approach a new wolf in human form.

If he did it in wolf form, he'd give her more than a nudge and to hell with the rules. Violating the traditions of mating could cost him more than he was willing to pay, so he stayed still and tried to will her to get up.

It took several minutes, but finally Samantha stirred. She rolled over onto her stomach and began to rub her head with her two front paws. The gesture was so cute, JD had to smile.

She woke up that way as a human too. Every morning he had to dodge her elbows as she rubbed her eyes and pushed her fingers through the tangled mass her hair had become during the night.

Finally, she gained her feet, looking around and sniffing the air. JD knew she was smelling all the other wolves in the area. Even in his human form he could smell them. His pack was all around, ready for the festivities to begin.

Samantha didn't appear to be concerned. Instead of the traditional response of new wolves, she didn't take off to find a hiding place from the dangers lurking in the night. With her normal disinterest in tradition, Samantha dropped her head and began sniffing the ground.

With movements so slow JD ground his teeth together, she followed a scent trail straight to where Caleb had left the tailgate down. If she got into that bed and went back to sleep, JD was going to lose it.

She didn't. Instead she pulled down pieces of their clothing until she had made a big mess on the ground. Then, with an insight that surprised JD, she began to roll around in the pile. It was a common thing for a wolf to do, to try to cover itself with the scent of another animal to disguise its own.

Something inside him warmed at the idea that, even in her wolf form, Samantha trusted them. JD assumed that she wanted to smell like Caleb and him for protection, but a moment later, when she began ripping and shredding the fabric with her teeth and paws, he readjusted his opinion.

Hell, she probably really is going to bite us.

Samantha didn't stop until the ground was covered in confetti of cotton and denim pieces. Apparently, she was not done venting her anger, and her attention turned to the tires of his truck.

Not until all four tires were shredded and the truck had sunk almost a foot into the soft sand did she stop. There was going to be hell to pay for that. JD didn't care if she had done it in wolf form or not.

At least she was trotting toward the edge of the neutral zone. She was going in the wrong direction, back toward the main road, but Caleb and he would turn her toward the mating grounds. That was their first task in this ritual, to run her right to where they her needed to be.

It was time for the game to begin.

* * * *

She wasn't sure where she was going. All she knew was that she was feeling aggressive, and if any of the other wolves out there got in her way, they'd get hurt. With that mindset, she held her head high and trotted in the direction some internal sense told her to go.

She didn't make it far down the dirt road before she smelled them. They were near, and her lips drew back to bare fangs ready to taste blood. They were the ones who deserved to be hurt. Why? She wasn't sure, but she knew it to be the truth.

Her determination wavered slightly when the first appeared. He was huge. Snarling and growling, he effectively blocked her path, and she wasn't dumb enough to think she could take him on.

That didn't mean she was going to back down. She bristled and did her best to look as intimidating as possible. Apparently her attempt lacked in effect, and the second wolf prowled out of the woods, coming closer than she liked.

Their growls intensified, their eyes narrowing on her. In an instant they sprung, and she caved. Turning tail, she ran for all she was worth, putting as much distance in between them as her legs could muster.

Fear blinded her thinking, and she plunged into the forest with no sense of direction. Her lungs were burning as they were forced to expand too rapidly. So were her muscles. There was no choice but to suffer and push harder. She could not go back the way she came. Going forward was the only option.

Just when it felt like her legs were going to break from the stress, she was hit hard from the right. The impact threw her several feet into a tumble that had her yelping with distress.

The high-pitched sound of distress increased in intensity as the unfamiliar male tried to force her to turn over into the mating position. She fought him, but he outweighed her.

The scales shifted in her favor when another wolf suddenly blasted the strange wolf off her. It was a temporary victory, as a third male charged in to knock her down again. She had barely finished rolling when a fourth wolf joined the fight.

This one had a familiar scent. So did the fifth that waded into the middle of the brawl. The sounds of yelps and growls filled the still night as more and more wolves appeared to join the battle.

She gained her feet, looking for an avenue of escape. There was none. Wolves of all sizes and scents formed an impenetrable circle around the chaos. She looked for an easy target and charged. Before she could barrel over the tiny female, a much larger male stepped forward to block her path.

This one didn't attempt to force her into a mating position, but chased her back toward the writhing mass of fur in the center with sharp nips and dangerous growls. The fight was winding down as the injured limped toward the sidelines. The exodus continued till there were only two wolves remaining.

She recognized more than their scents. The odor of their arousal was thick in the cold air. This time there was nothing standing in their way and no direction she could escape in.

They pranced around her, growling and snapping at her, but she didn't lie down for either of them. Instead, she returned their aggressive postures with her own. The difference was they weren't actually trying to hurt her.

It was a futile fight, only succeeding in forestalling the inevitable and rallying up their arousal even more. She thought that might be why they were indulging her ill attempts to ward them off. They were playing with their food before they ate it.

That suspicion was confirmed a second later when one came in low, knocking her feet right out from under her. This time she took the roll with ease, but didn't make it back onto her feet before the other had his teeth sunk into her neck, his weight pinning her down as he lay across her.

She expected to be mounted immediately by the other and was startled when she felt a cold snout pushing her tail out of his way. She swooshed her tail, swatting at him as she struggled to be released. All she got for her efforts was more of the first wolf's weight.

It was sick and disgusting, and she growled out her annoyance until his tongue licked over her. Oh, that felt good, even better when he did it again. In seconds he had her growls turning to whimpers, her tail lifting as she arched her back for more of the pleasure.

She wasn't aware of the second wolf lifting off her or her own head lowering to the ground. When the arousing caresses stopped, she whined, not ready for it to end. A moment later she was back to whimpering as the heavy wolf mounted her.

The large knob of his cock pressed against her opening, and she shifted, allowing him better access, craving what minutes ago had seemed so objectionable. He bit hard into her shoulder drawing blood as he slammed his full length into her.

The momentary pain of the bite was lost in a sea of pleasure that had her howling. The sound was echoed back to her by the pack as the others gave in to their own needs now that the mating had begun.

* * * *

Sam struggled through the foggy shroud of her dreams. They had been pleasant when she was unconscious, but as the biting cold cleared her mind, she realized now they had been a nightmare.

Pieces were crystal clear, while other snippets were hazy, fading into nothing more than emotion. Fear and annoyance had rimmed the edge of the most devastating pleasure she'd ever felt as she had rutted with…

Sam blocked that thought from its conclusion. It was disgusting, reprehensible, and she was not ever going to think about it again. Instead she focused on the fact that her right arm was freezing, and so was the top of her leg.

The rest of her was near to sweating trapped in the sauna blanket known as JD and Caleb. One of them must have left the window open. The two barbarians generated enough heat to make the sun jealous on even the clearest of summer days.

Even though they normally kept her quite warm, any part or limb not tucked safely between them was left to freeze. The cold was annoying her, stopping her from escaping back into sleep. Sam would be damned if she was getting up to close the window. She wasn't the one who opened it.

She was draped over one twin, JD from the smell of him, and she wasn't going to give up her position. Caleb could close the window. All she had to do was wake him up.

A hard jab in the gut did the trick. He groaned and muttered a curse, trying to adjust his position without getting up. Sam wasn't going to let him escape his destiny.

"Window, Caleb," Sam muttered, jabbing him again.

"What window?" Caleb didn't sound any more awake than she did.

"The one that's open," Sam snarled. "I'm cold."

"There is no window." JD yawned. She could hear it in his tone and felt his jaw bumping into the top of her head.

"What do you mean there is no...window?" The end of her demand came out as a whisper as she jerked her head up and opened her eyes.

Ah, damn! Damn, damn, damn, double damn. It hadn't been a stupid dream.

The jackasses really had put her through her paces last night. If doing so in wolf form wasn't perverted enough, they'd done it in front of an audience. That was unforgivable, even more so than turning her into a damn dog girl.

Before she could get the words clogging her throat out of her open mouth, JD sealed her lips with his own. Sam forgot how mad she was at him as he ravished her mouth. Callused fingertips bit into her sides as he lifted her, positioning her over him. Her legs straddled his, and she could feel the heat of his erection pushing against her swollen pussy lips.

JD broke the kiss to nibble his way down her jaw. Sam's eyes closed as she tried to catch her breath. He was so good at making her forget everything else, like how she was supposed to be mad at him.

"I love you, baby," he whispered into her ear.

"Damn it, JD!" Sam jerked her head back, would have shoved off him, but his arms around her back held her securely.

"What did—"

"Don't give me that innocent look," Sam snapped, wiggling to demand freedom. "You're trying to bribe me out of my rightful anger."

"I'm not—"

"It's not going to work." Sam cut him off again. "What you did last night was disgusting and unforgive—"

JD cut her off again. When she felt Caleb's lips kissing their way down her spine, Sam gave up.

There would be time to be mad later, a whole lifetime.

Epilogue

Lilly looked up through the web of barren tree limbs to the gray sky above. The monotony of the shades of brown and black that flowed out like a morbid sea around her was only broken by the occasional palm frond trying vainly to interject color into the lifeless world of the winter forest.

The man tied to the pine tree across from where she was sitting groaned and shifted slightly. Lilly watched him carefully, but he made no more motions. Her eyes wandered again, her hand tightening around the gun. She wanted to believe that this was the end of the case, but something inside her warned that it was only the beginning.

Her concerns had been confirmed when the McBane cabin had gone down in flames. Those hadn't been normal flames. They'd been hellfire. In all of the worlds, there was only one type of creature that could command hellfire. Even among the ranks of the demons, there were few who could command that fire into living flame outside of hell.

The few that could were powerful and motivated beyond the simple gratification of the lower demons. They were the planners, generals of Lucifer's army, and it could be no accident that they had shown up twice this past year in the laid-back coastal waters of South Carolina.

The last one had been Agakiar, and his focus had been on Claire, or so it had seemed. He'd failed to capture her soul and then failed to return, not a good sign in the larger scheme of things. Worse was Lilly's conviction that the events of the past weeks were not contrived by Agakiar's hand.

Agakiar was a high-level general, but there were those who were more powerful. Their missions were a great deal more deadly in intent. They had the power to keep Agakiar from continuing his supposed obsession with Claire.

Patiently she waited, contemplating all the possibilities for almost an hour before the man finally, groggily, began to come around. As his glazed eyes began to search over the ground, he realized he was bound.

"There is no point. You're not getting free." That stilled his twisting motions as he searched for freedom.

"What the—"

"I'm not interested in talking to you, Brett."

"Who are—"

"I want to speak to he who lies beneath."

"I don't—"

"I want to speak to he who lies beneath, now!"

That shut him up. In perceptible degrees the man in front of her changed, his body going lax, his head rolling back slightly, and his eyes darkening from pale blue to a perfect black. Lilly felt the shivers race over her as she felt his presence come fully into her dimension.

"Lillian. It has been too long."

"Why?"

"You never call," the man whined. "It breaks a—"

"Please! I'm not interested in your theatrics. I want to know why you wanted to kill Samantha Hark."

"Who?" His eyes rounded innocently.

"Don't." Lilly rose up. "You know exactly what I'm talking about. Bruce Crane may have bought a curse to kill Samantha Hark, but he was too late. Brett Morison had already cursed her. Why?"

"What makes you think I had anything to do with that?"

"No human cursed that necklace. You cursed it."

"Are you sure?"

"Do you think I wouldn't recognize your power?"

"Why would I curse this Samantha's necklace?"

"Why did you?"

"Money?"

"Try again."

"Perhaps it wasn't her I wanted to die," he teased.

Lilly stared at him, her mind whirling around that comment. Most of the pieces were there, but they weren't fitting together.

"You're going to try again." Lilly spoke more to herself than him.

"Bit by bit, Lillian, it all comes together."

"Something is coming. I have felt it getting stronger."

"Questioning your loyalties?" He smiled, showing too much teeth. "Always want to be on the winning side of a war."

"You've mistaken me for somebody else."

"Hmm." He shrugged at that, taking it for what it was worth. "Then pray to The One for absolution. He wouldn't welcome you into His house when this life runs out. You don't belong there with the holy ones."

Lilly knew she was not going to get any more from him. Without a word, she raised the gun. At the sight of the blackened barrel pointing at him, he smiled.

"The Fates always condemn or reward for a reason, and we all try to get around them."

The shot rang out through the forest, shattering the illusion of peace, but only for a second.

THE END

WWW.JENNYPENN.COM

ABOUT THE AUTHOR

I live near Charleston, SC with my two biggies (my dogs). I have had a slightly unconventional life. Moving almost every three years, I've had a range of day jobs that included everything from working for one of the worlds largest banks as an auditor to turning wrenches as an outboard repair mechanic. I've always regretted that we only get one life and have tried to cram as much as I can into this one.

Throughout it all, I've always read books, feeding my need to dream and fantasize about what could be. An avid reader since childhood, as a latchkey kid I'd spend hours at the library earning those shiny stars the librarian would paste up on the board after my name.

I credit my grandmother's yearly visits as the beginning of my obsession with romances. When she'd come, she'd bring stacks of romance books, the old fashion kind that didn't have sex in them. Imagine my shock when I went to the used bookstore and found out what really could be in a romance novel.

I've working on my own stories for years and have found a particular love of erotic romances. In this genre, women are no longer confined to a stereotype and plots are no longer constrained to the rational. I love the anything goes mentality and letting my imagination run wild.

I hope you enjoyed running with me and will consider picking up another book and coming along for another adventure.

Jenny

Siren Publishing, Inc.
www.SirenPublishing.com

Printed in the United States
210879BV00005B/17/P